EYES ON THE STREET

ALSO BY RONIN PARKER

The Fake Museum

EYES
ON THE
STREET

RONIN PARKER

187TH Street Books
a division of Toyns Publishing
New York, NY

187th Street Books, a TOYNS Publishing imprint | New York, NY

Copyright © 2023 Ronin Parker

First Paperback Edition: April 2024

To purchase copies of this book in bulk, please contact us by email at toynsbooks@gmail.com

All rights reserved. No part of this book may be reproduced or transmitted in any form or by any means, electronic or mechanical, including photocopying, recording, or by an information storage and retrieval system—except by a reviewer who may quote brief passages in a review to be printed in a magazine or newspaper—without written permission from the publisher, except where permitted by law.

This is a work of fiction. Names, characters, businesses, places, businesses, events, incidents, and accidents depicted are either the products of the author's imagination or used in a fictitious manner. Any resemblance to actual persons, living or dead, or actual events is purely coincidental.

Book designed by Tony Golde

An earlier version of this book, with significant differences, was published serially as "The Whole World After Us," "Surviving the Days" and "Run the Heights."

ISBN: 978-0-9970678-5-9

10 9 8 7 6 5 4 3 2 1

FOR MY PARENTS

THEN

THE MAN WITH THE GUN

HE HAD BEEN PERCHED THERE *with the rifle for almost nine hours. His whole body was stiff, and he was worried whether that would affect his aim when the target finally showed up. Stretching was out of the question. It might draw attention to him and ruin the hit. The men who had hired him would not be happy with that result. Nor would the other assassins that he assumed were hiding somewhere in the sea of people on the floor below. This was too big a job to rely on just one man.*

But something seemed off. The target should have arrived by now. That alone was not alarming, as city traffic could slow down even the promptest and most conscientious people. No, it was something in the air, something in the way people below were acting. Not all of them, but the security guards for sure. He knew crowds—he had looked down on them from his gunman's perch many times before. Eastern Europe, South America, Africa. The people couldn't have been more different, but crowds still behaved the same throughout the world. The buzz, the conversations, the movement. In his line of work, he had to take these things into account, to know when to shoot and how to escape undetected.

Now he wished he'd brought a radio. He eschewed them for a couple of reasons. It was too easy for someone to get cold feet and call off a hit at the last minute, which was bad for business. The men who hired him might try to get out of paying. And even if they paid, they were still a liability because they knew his identity and how to contact him, but were not implicated in an assassination the way they would be if he went through with it. On top of that, radios were technology, and you could not always rely on them. A random squawk or piercing high note from the device would cause everyone to look in his direction, and then he'd be trapped, stuck up on the ledge near the windows he had climbed through the night before.

So: no radio this time.

Which also meant no way to find out what was going on below.

He would just have to wait it out and hope the target showed up soon.

He had been hired to kill someone, and that was what he planned to do.

NOW

CHAPTER 1
THE WOMAN FROM THE FOURTH FLOOR

I'M NOT the tallest kid in school, but I can reach the top shelf at the grocery store, which I guess makes me useful, in a way.

It all starts when my mom tells me to help the old lady who lives on the fourth floor with her chores. I don't even know the woman's name at first, but she's small in the way that some elderly people are, like they've started to shrivel or shrink and their posture isn't great.

My friend D'Argyle says that grandparents don't shrink as they get older, that they were just always tiny, but I don't listen to half the stuff he says, because it's usually nonsense he reads on the internet.

Anyway, this old woman is too short to reach some of the upper shelves at the grocery store, so she needs me to help with shopping. Her name, it turns out, is Willa Marrillion.

"Call me Willa," she says when I meet her at the Key Food on Broadway.

"That's alright, Ms. Marrillion," I say.

Mom would throw a fit if she caught me calling this lady by her first name.

"There's no need to be so formal," she says. "If you call me Ms. Marrillion, it will feel like you're my chauffeur."

I shake my head and laugh.

"If anyone in the store hears me call you Willa and tells my mom about it, I'd be in *real* trouble."

She looks up and down the bread aisle where we're standing.

"There's nobody else here," she says. "But it's good to be a bit paranoid." She leans closer and says quietly, "That's what's kept me alive all these years."

Before I can ask what she means by that, she's pointing at a loaf of multigrain bread on the second shelf from the top.

"They always put the stuff I want on the high shelf," she says. Then she flicks a bag of Wonder Bread with disdain. "They put this stuff here in the middle where it's easiest to grab. You know the company pays the store to put their cheap products on the best shelf? So you have to go out of your way to be healthy."

Now she sounds like one of the conspiracy theorists who yell at people on the A train between 125th and 59th streets.

"It's true! I'll show you a magazine article about it," she says.

Meanwhile, I've put the bread she wants in the basket.

"Let me see that," she says, picking it up. "You need to check the expiration date. Sometimes they put the old bread up front and the good stuff in the back."

But this bread must meet her standards, because she puts it back in the basket and we keep shopping.

I won't tell you about the whole trip, which seems to take *forever*, but is only about 20 minutes by the time we check out. Actually, it isn't all that bad. While she is particular about the food she wants, she does tell me a lot of tips about the grocery store, which I wouldn't know otherwise. I make a note to look some of this stuff up on YouTube when I get home and see if it's true.

A lot of times, we trust old people because they seem wise, but I figure they can be liars like the rest of us. Or just be plain wrong sometimes. As it turns out, I never get to check out what she says on YouTube because of what happens next.

I've brought my backpack, and put a lot of her stuff inside it after she pays for her groceries. Plus we fill up two reusable bags that we all have to use now since they charge for the plastic ones. I mention this because it explains why I have to wait in her apartment while she unloads the stuff from the store — I can't leave my backpack here, and she is a little slow putting things on shelves. She's very organized and puts everything exactly where it belongs. I would help her, but I don't know where anything goes. The top shelves of all her cabinets are empty.

"Why put stuff up there, when I can't reach it?" she says.

"I guess that makes sense. Maybe you could put things you hardly use on those shelves."

"Then I'd use it even less," she laughs. "Out of sight, out of mind, like they say."

It feels like it takes forever, but it's probably only like 10 minutes until she takes the last item, a case of Ensure protein drinks, out of my backpack.

"Thank you very much," she says.

"Don't mention it. I can come back next week, or if you need something before then, just give me a call." She doesn't use text messages, so she can only get in touch with me over the actual phone.

And then, just as we're talking about it, her landline rings.

She picks it up and says, "Hello."

Then she listens for a little while.

"Are you sure? … Ok, thank you."

She hangs up and looks at me.

"Oh dear. You better get back home as soon as you can. Some people are on their way here to kill me."

CHAPTER 2
LOCK THE DOORS

I LAUGH when she tells me people are trying to kill her.

"No, I'm afraid I'm serious," she says.

"But who'd want to kill…" I let the sentence trail off.

"An old lady like me?"

She got me! That *is* what I was going to say. But I realize it's not nice to call her old, so instead I say: "No, I meant who'd want to kill a *nice* lady like you?"

"Nearly everybody, dear."

She hands me my backpack and tries to guide me towards the door.

"You didn't sign up for all this, though. Thank you for your help with the groceries."

I can't just leave and let her get killed, assuming this isn't some elaborate joke. (Do old people even make jokes like this? I start to wonder if I'm part of some prank show like that *Bad Grandpa* movie. I look Ms. Marrillion up and down to make sure she's not an actor in elaborate make-up. No, she's definitely a real-life old lady.)

"I have to help you," I say. "I can't tell my mom that I got you groceries and then left you to die."

"But they're only after me. It seems a shame to get you

involved. You're so young, you have the rest of your life to look forward to."

"Do you want to die?" I ask her.

She thinks for a moment.

"No, I can't say that I do."

"Then let's get out of here," I say. "These people who are coming, they wouldn't have any way to connect you to me, would they?"

"Not for the moment. I suppose if they asked around or checked the surveillance footage at Key Food, they might see us together."

The way she casually mentions that the killers could get access to security cameras at the grocery store should make me run away as fast as I can, but I told my mom I would help her, so I don't have a lot of options.

"Well, come to my apartment for now. We can figure out our next step from there. I guess call the cops."

"No," she says. "We can't do that. We can't trust the police."

I laugh because I don't really like the cops, but I don't expect an old woman to feel the same way. "Okay, we won't call the po-po," I say.

"You haven't even asked *why* they're trying to kill me."

"I figured it was because they're bad guys," I say. "Isn't that how it works in movies?"

"I suppose they *are* the bad guys. Anyway, just so you know, it's not because of anything I did. It's because of something I saw that I shouldn't have. But I can't tell you what it is or it might put you in danger."

"Please, can we talk about this in my apartment?"

"Oh, yes, I suppose that's a good idea. It seems a shame to leave all these groceries behind."

"You can come back and eat all your soup when it's safe."

"That might not be for a long time," she says. And that turns out to be the understatement of the year.

So next we leave her apartment, and she locks the door behind her. Despite the fact that someone is apparently coming to kill her, she moves kind of slowly. I guess that's just another thing that happens when you get old. You forget how to be fast.

"Should we take the stairs or the elevator?" I ask.

"Probably the stairs. The super has a hard drive with all the footage from the elevator cameras. They might look at it and see us leaving together. We wouldn't want that, would we?"

This sounds like a good plan, except that she takes the stairs *really* slowly, holding onto the rails, putting one foot down, then another on the same stair, and all the time I'm worried about these killers. Will they have guns? Knives? Lasers? I'm not even sure lasers are real outside of *Star Wars*, but D'Argyle swears that the army has them and uses them to blow up tanks and stuff. I'll believe it when I see it, which I hope is not today. I'd hate for my last thought on Earth to be: "Whoa, I guess lasers are real!" just as I'm zapped to death. Anyway, I'm pretty sure nobody with lasers is out to get this woman.

Finally, we get down to the third floor, where I live, and we dawdle down the hall to my door. I get my key out and open it. Once she's inside, I follow behind her and lock all three locks on the door, even the security chain we *never* use. Mom claims she used to latch the chain back in the 1990s when it was a dangerous neighborhood, but I can't believe it was ever as bad as she says.

"Now what?" I ask. This is my first time running away from killers, but she seems to have been doing it her whole life.

"Do you have the app on your phone that lets you look at the vestibule?"

"The lobby cam? I can get it."

Our super set up a camera above the building's front door so we can check and see who's there if someone we don't know buzzes. To be honest, I always just buzz them in without checking, because why not? The app is a little slow and not worth the effort. But now that I have a reason, I reload it onto my phone so we can see everyone who comes to the front door.

We sit next to each other on the couch and watch the black and white video.

It's mostly kids coming home from school with their parents, families I recognize from the building. Then a police officer shows up. At least, I think it's a police officer, until he starts pressing all the buzzers, the way you do when you don't know anyone in the building and are hoping to just get lucky.

"I don't think that's a real cop, Ms. Marrillion."

"No, it probably isn't. But the gun seems very real."

There's no sound on the video feed, but somebody must buzz him in because pretty soon he pushes open the door and enters the building.

Less than a minute later, we hear the gunshot.

CHAPTER 3
OUT ON THE STREETS

IN MOVIES, people are always shooting through closed doors. It's like a hitman will show up, ring the doorbell, then fire right through the door, killing whoever's behind it. Or sometimes it's the other way around and a person inside is shooting out through the door at the bad guy with the gun or the cop or the bad guy with a gun who is a cop. Then little shafts of light shine through the bullet holes.

I never quite understood it, because the doors in my apartment building are *way* too thick for that sort of thing. I mean, unless you have a bazooka, I don't think you could shoot someone *through* a door here. But that's because it's an old building, pre-war they call it, built way back in the 1930s before America learned how to make cheap buildings.

So when the guy dressed as a cop shoots into Ms. Marrillion's door, it can't kill anyone inside, and not just because her apartment is empty. But when he fires again and again, like he does, eventually the locks give way and he is able to kick the door in. We can tell all this from just listening, since we're just one floor below.

A few seconds pass. I guess he's looking through her apartment to see if she's in there. Ms. Marrillion and I just stare at each other. We've sort of both agreed to remain silent without actually talking about it.

Next thing we know, the guy is in the hallway yelling.

"If I find out any of you are hiding that woman, I'm gonna kill you!"

We can hear him trying the other doors in the hallway, not knocking, just turning the knobs, then kicking and pounding, like he's angry.

In the distance, we can hear sirens. Someone must have called the police, the *real* police, and they're on their way.

We look down at my phone and see him exit quickly through the front lobby. He must be in a hurry to get away before the actual police show up and ask him who he is and what he's doing.

"Well, that was certainly an adventure!" Ms. Marrillion says.

I laugh a little, but I'm still scared, and I have no idea what to do next.

"Should we try to talk to the police when they show up?" I ask.

"No. In fact, I'd like to get out of the building now, before they show up and start asking questions, trying to talk to everyone in the building."

"Aren't you afraid that guy will still be somewhere around here?"

"I hope not. But I've put you through enough trouble. I can just take the elevator down and go out the back way."

The basement of our building has an exit that leads to a paved area, where there's a gate to the side street. It's kind of like an alley, but closed off unless you have a key.

"Let's at least get you a disguise," I say, heading for the closet. I hope she doesn't mind looking silly.

We're in a hurry, so I don't have time to figure out a *good* costume. I just go all in, pulling out a Yankees hat, a rainbow scarf, some cheap sunglasses we got at Coney Island, and a big hoodie that says DEEZ on it. I won it in a contest, but my mom says I'm not allowed to wear it. Hopefully Ms. Marrillion won't ask what it means.

"I don't look like me anymore," she says.

"That's good. If I walk next to you, we can pass for some other people."

"It's too dangerous for you."

"You said that guy wouldn't stick around, right?"

"I'm not sure. To be honest, it's the first time anyone's ever tried to kill me."

"Let's talk about it later. I'll get you somewhere else and then we'll figure it out."

I check the hallway and there's no one there, so she comes out and I lock the door, then we walk to the elevator. I want to run, but she can't move that fast. The worst part is waiting for the elevator because we just have to stand there, waiting for it. We're wearing disguises and will avoid looking directly at the camera in its corner.

It finally comes and for a second I wonder if someone with a gun will be inside, but it's empty, so we take it down to the basement, then walk out the back door. The sirens are much louder by this point, as a few police cars have parked in front of the building. None of them are paying attention to the side gate, though, so we're able to walk out onto the sidewalk.

"Maybe we can hide out at Cafe Buunni," I say.

"For a little while, at least. But do you mind if we take the elevator at the subway station? I don't know if I can do the stairs."

The cafe is up a big hill from where we live. There's an enormous staircase there with 130 steps (I counted!) that leads up to the shops near Pinehurst. It is a bit of a workout, especially for someone her age, so we walk to the subway station on 184th that has an elevator. We take it up to the top of the hill. Then we walk through Bennett Park to Pinehurst, and turn towards the cafe. The whole time, I'm looking over my shoulder for that fake cop or anyone else who might be trying to kill her. This takes up so much of my attention that I forget to ask her all my questions about what exactly is going on.

On top of that, I start to see the city differently. It's strange since I spent all my life here so far, but now I'm checking every block for a place we can hide if we need to, or looking at how difficult the terrain will be for Ms. Marrillion.

We somehow make it to the coffee shop without any trouble. She says she's going to pay for my drink and snack and she's not taking no for an answer. I've been trying all different kinds of coffee lately, because I don't like the taste of it but most grown-ups drink it so I feel like there must be some trick to it.

She gets herself a plain coffee and croissant. I order an iced Americano, which is something I haven't had yet, and the jalapeño cornbread. While she's putting cream in her coffee at the little station near the bar, a guy comes in, sweaty, obnoxious, a kind of guy I've never seen in here before.

"Don't look up," Ms. Marrillion whispers. I stir my drink for way too long.

"I'm looking for my grandma," the guy says. "She's old, and she wandered off."

They display local art in the cafe all the time. Luckily, this month it's a series of framed paintings, and I can see the guy's reflection in the glass in front of me.

He's holding up a photograph of Ms. Marrillion.

"Anybody in here seen this old lady? She goes by the name of Willa. She's probably confused or whatever." He pulls out a wad of cash. "I'll give $500 to anyone who can find her for me."

Everyone who has been minding their own business looks up from their coffee now.

I think we're in trouble.

CHAPTER 4

THE MISSING PERSON

THIS GUY IS OFFERING $500 for the woman standing next to me, and now he's looking at everyone in the coffee shop. I don't know if anyone has recognized Ms. Marrillion as the woman in the photo yet, but it's only a matter of time. The guy certainly has everyone's attention.

Then the barista steps out from behind the counter. She smoothly hands Ms. Marrillion a cup of water and says, "Here's your agua, Ms. Malinche."

Ms. Marrillion quickly takes the drink and says, "Oh … uh … gracias" without looking up.

Then the barista gets between us and the big man.

"That woman you're looking for was here about ten minutes ago. She got in a red BMW that went up Pinehurst." She points in the direction the fictional car had gone.

"Thank you," the man says, turning to go.

"Hey. What about my $500?" the barista asks.

"If I get the woman, I'll come back and give it to you," he says, laughing. Then he pulls out his cell phone and runs up the block away from the cafe.

"I could tell that man wasn't looking for his grandmother," the barista says. "He was so disrespectful. And a cheapskate! I knew he couldn't be related to you, Willa."

"That was quick thinking with the water and fake name," Ms. Marrillion says.

"I saw it in a movie once. I could tell you were incognito, since you wouldn't normally dress this way. Do you need me to call the police?"

"Oh no," Ms. Marrillion says. "We don't have to get them involved. Besides, I've got Lee here to look out for me."

"Then you're in good hands," the barista says. "Did Lee pick out these clothes for you?"

"I needed a little disguise. I'm not sure what 'Deez' means, though."

"We should get going, Ms. Marrillion," I say, before the barista can explain.

"Be careful, and come back anytime," the barista says. "We've always got your back."

Outside, we keep moving, walking towards Cabrini.

"I've been thinking we can stop at my friend D'Argyle's place," I say. "I'm a little worried about heading back to our building."

"Will that be alright? I wouldn't want to intrude."

"It should be fine," I say. "We might have to watch D'Argyle play video games for an hour or so. It's all he likes to do."

I take out my phone and text him to see if he's home.

"So you think someone in the police is after you?" I ask Ms. Marrillion while I wait for him to reply.

"Not exactly," she says. "It's hard to explain. People with access to the police, or people who have infiltrated the police— they may be trying to find me. So as soon as an officer or detective reports me to their precinct, it's only a matter of time before someone will come for me."

"But you ain't been running your whole life?"

"No. I guess I've known since childhood that something like this *could* happen. After a while, though, I figured I was safe and kind of forgot about the danger. I thought I was out of the woods."

D'Argyle texts me back to say he's on his couch playing RDR2. I almost text him "OK if I bring a woman over?" but I realize he may get the wrong impression. And I worry that someone could be monitoring my phone, so I don't mention Ms. Marrillion. That'll be a surprise for him.

We can still hear sirens down the hill.

I realize my mom might hear there was a shooting in our building and freak out, so I need to text her. But I don't want to explain everything that's happened, so I just tell her I'm on my way to D'Argyle's to hang out.

She texts: "Did everything go OK with Ms. Marrillion?"

I hate to lie to my mom, so I just reply: "Helped her with shopping and got groceries back to her place. She was nice. I was very polite."

Eventually, I'll have to explain what's *really* going on, but that can wait.

Mom texts: "How'd I end up with such a good kid? =) Pizza OK 4 dinner?"

This usually means she has to work late at the hospital.

I reply: "Yeah, extra mushrooms?"

She gives this a thumbs down because she hates mushrooms.

"D'Argyle lives down on Bennett," I tell Ms. Marrillion. "I figured we can take the elevator at 190th."

"Thank you. The stairs in the park are too rough for me. I can usually make it down Overlook, but if we have to run, I'm afraid I might take a tumble."

I try to imagine her running, but it's not pretty.

We walk around Cabrini behind the church and up towards the playground they just rebuilt.

A lot of people are out playing hoops and working out. I feel like we're safe here. If that guy from the coffee shop turned up, I could yell that he's a perv, and everyone would come running to chase him away.

We stop at the corner to throw away our trash from the coffee shop.

"I haven't been up north in a long time," Ms. Marrillion says. "Maybe I could take a train up to New Hampshire and hide there for a while."

"Wouldn't they be able to find you by tracking your credit cards or something?"

"Hmm, I suppose they could."

"It might be easier to stay in the city. There's a thousand places you can get lost here."

Just then, my phone makes a squawking noise. Hers does too. I can hear it from inside her purse.

To our right, half the phones on the playground make the same sound. It's usually an amber alert or a weather emergency. I've gotten used to ignoring them. This one, though, shouts:

! SILVER ALERT / MISSING PERSON !

There's a physical description of Ms. Marrillion, but it claims she's an elderly woman with dementia and people should call the police if they see her in the neighborhood. I notice the people in the park reading the message and it's only a matter of time before someone recognizes her.

Just a second ago, I was thinking how nice it was to have a concerned community that could help protect us from that sweaty guy. Now I'm worried the concerned community will lead him right to us.

I hear somebody shout, "Hey, I think that's the old lady!" and suddenly everyone is coming in our direction.

CHAPTER 5
GOING DOWN

"HOLD THIS FOR A SECOND, PLEASE," Ms. Marrillion says, handing me a small pair of scissors from her purse. I worry that she wants me to fight off the crowd with this little knitting tool. If the guys were made of yarn, I might have a chance, but they're mostly big swole dudes who use the playground instead of a gym to work out. They do pull-ups and push-ups and stuff like that.

Then I see Ms. Marrillion has gotten her phone out of her purse and is looking at the Silver Alert on it as the people get closer to us.

"Thank you for your concern," she says to them. "I assure you I'm not suffering from dementia, and, I'll have you know, I don't consider myself elderly!"

This calms everyone down a bit, although they still seem a bit suspicious.

"If we see this Silver Alert woman, we'll be sure to call the police," she says. "We wouldn't want her to get in any trouble."

Many of them turn back towards the playground like they're ready to go. But one big guy holding a basketball is still looking at her.

"Maybe we get a reward if we help your family find you," he says.

"There's no reward for me, dear. Anyway, you should get back to playing basketball," she says, smiling now. "From what I saw, you could use the practice."

All the other guys break up laughing and hollering at this. I think if Ms. Marrillion wasn't such a sweet old lady, it's the kind of insult that could start a fight, but the guy eventually starts laughing along with everyone else.

"Aww, she too sharp to be senile," he says.

"She's not wrong, Lou," one of his friends says. "You having a bad day."

"I'm just getting warmed up is all," Lou says. He starts dribbling and turns back toward the court. Soon they're all heading back to the playground, muttering to each other about the old Deez lady.

"Phew," Ms. Marrillion says. "That was a close call."

"Was I supposed to stab someone with the scissors?" I ask her.

"Heavens, no! My goodness, Lee, what sort of woman do you think I am?"

"I wasn't sure why you gave them to me..."

"I didn't want to poke myself while I was getting my phone out of my purse, so I handed them to you. You can put them back in now." She holds her bag open. I drop the scissors into it, and then she closes it quickly. "One thing I've noticed is that confidently using a smartphone makes people take me seriously. If a teller at the bank is being rude, or someone at a store is ignoring me, they start behaving better once they see I have a phone and know how to use it. Maybe they're worried I'll film them being rude to an elderly person and it will go viral."

"You just told those people you weren't elderly," I remind her.

"That was just to get them away from us. I'm certainly not young! Anyhow, I think using a smartphone makes me look about 10 years younger."

"To be honest, Ms. Marrillion, I wasn't sure you had a cell phone, because you still have a landline at home."

"I'm glad I still have a few surprises in me. We'll need them all if we're going to get out of this mess."

I notice she's saying "we" now, as if we're both in this together. That's good, because I was getting a little worried she'd try to ditch me and face whatever it is by herself. She may be a tough old lady, but everybody needs help sometimes.

We're walking towards the 190th Street station at this point, and we have to go down a set of stairs to get to the elevator entrance, which slows our speed a little.

"I never noticed this," I say. "The elevator doesn't go all the way to street level, so it wouldn't help if you're in a wheelchair. Or you have a stroller."

"Yes, it's not terribly accessible. On the bright side, if someone was chasing us on a motorcycle, they'd have trouble following us down here."

"Do you think that will happen?" I ask her.

"I hope not," she says. "Motorcycles are very loud and unpleasant."

It sounds both cool *and* scary to me, until I remember the *Bourne* movie where Matt Damon rides a motorcycle down some stairs in Africa, and then I just hope that nobody who's coming after Ms. Marrillion is as good at killing people as Jason Bourne was.

We make it into the little building and press the elevator button.

"I always feel a little bit safer here," Ms. Marrillion says. "Have you learned about the Cold War in school?"

"Sort of," I say. We did learn about it, but I don't remember it very well.

"In the 1950s, they considered building fallout shelters down below. This station is so deep and surrounded by thick rock that they thought people could survive a nuclear blast if they were down in the tunnel."

"Whoa, that's crazy," I say.

The elevator arrives. We get in and press the button, and it begins its descent.

"They would have had to build water facilities and more bathrooms, but they never got around to it," she says. "Still, I've always told myself I'd head this way if I heard bombs were coming."

"You had a plan for if we got nuked?"

"We all had plans like that back then."

"So you were worried about getting bombed *and* some pack of randos coming to kill you one day?"

"I have lived in interesting times," she says.

"No doubt."

"Have you heard that expression? *May you live in interesting times.* It's supposed to be a Chinese curse, although I think it was actually invented by the British."

"Never heard it before."

The elevator opens and we step out. A few feet away, a large white man in a tracksuit sees us. His eyes are bugged out and he has thick sideburns.

"Where do you think you're going?" he says to her. "Get back in the car. And your friend, too."

He grabs Ms. Marrillion by the arm and forces her back into the elevator. I have no choice. I step in alongside them.

The man reaches into his pocket and pulls out a can of something, which he sprays on the triangle mirror in the corner of the elevator where the security camera is hidden.

"Now we got some privacy," he says. Then he pushes the up button with his elbow and the door closes.

We are trapped.

CHAPTER 6
SELF DEFENSE

"SO GLAD I RAN INTO YOU," the guy says, as the elevator slowly makes its way back up towards Fort Washington Avenue. "I guess I must be lucky. Of all the fellows in the neighborhood, I'm gonna get the reward."

He puts the spray can back into his pocket and pulls out a pocket knife, which he flicks open to expose the blade.

"I don't know what you did, lady, but a lot of people want you dead."

He turns his back to me and pushes her into the corner.

"Now, Lee!" she shouts.

And I think: *What?*

Clearly, she wants me to do something at this exact moment, but I have no idea what it is.

"Go ahead, do it, now, Lee!" she says again.

At this point, the guy turns around to see what I'm doing.

He looks me up and down, still holding that knife in his hand.

"Don't be a hero, kid," he says. "This ain't about you."

Then I hear a clicking sound and his eyes roll up in his head. He falls toward me, and I jump out of the way. He hits his head on the floor, and that seems to knock him unconscious.

I look up and see Ms. Marrillion is holding some sort of Taser.

"Well, that was effective!" she says.

"I wasn't sure what you wanted me to do when you said 'Now.'"

"Oh, I didn't have anything specific in mind. I just needed to distract him, and figured he would turn around if I implied you were about to do something."

The elevator reaches the top and the doors open. We're in luck —nobody is standing there.

"Let's go back down again," I say, and push the down button.

The man is still out cold.

"Check his pockets," she says.

I find the spray can and some black plastic zip ties.

"I don't like the look of that," she says.

"Maybe we can slow him down a bit," I say.

Then I use a zip tie to connect both his wrists tightly.

"That should stop him from attacking people in the subway," I say.

"It *was* quite rude of him," she says.

"What about the knife?"

"Don't touch it, you don't want your fingerprints on it," she says.

Then she pulls a napkin out of her bag and uses it to pick up the knife gingerly.

"All the same, we can't leave it here where he can get at it."

The elevator has reached the bottom once again. This time, we get out safely and nobody is around. I press the up button and send the man back to the top of the hill. Ms. Marrillion drops the knife in a trash can as we walk towards the long tunnel that goes to Bennett Avenue.

"Things are heating up a bit," she says. "Does your friend live far?"

"No, D'Argyle lives pretty close to the station."

It feels strange to hear nothing but our footsteps echoing in the tunnel, so I talk to make noise.

"Have you used that Taser thing before?"

"No. But I watched an instructional video so I would be prepared. I just stuffed it in my purse afterward, without reloading it, so we can't use it again if we run into any more goons. All I have left now is pepper spray."

"And those scissors you gave me before," I say.

"If it comes to that, I think we should just surrender, Lee. I don't think we can beat these guys with one pair of scissors."

When we finally get to the end of the tunnel and out onto the street, we can hear sirens again, and a police car races by us, probably heading towards our building. It's only been about an hour since that fake cop came looking for her and shot up the place. My mom is going to hear about it soon, so I'm hoping we can stay with D'Argyle long enough for me to call her and tell her what's *really* going on.

Eventually, the coast is clear, and we cross Bennett to get to the red brick apartment complex where D'Argyle lives. It's got a little lawn in front of it that we have to cross. After that, I text him to let him know we're downstairs, and he buzzes us in.

"Don't worry, Ms. Marrillion," I say. "There's an elevator."

"Hopefully it's less exciting than our last elevator trip!" she replies.

It is, and we get to the fifth floor with no problems.

I can hear him playing all the way out in the hall, because he's got a subwoofer turned on. My mom says we can't get one of those because it will bother the neighbors. I guess the people in D'Argyle's building don't mind. Or maybe they all hate him? It *does* seem kind of loud outside when you're not playing the game and can only feel the vibrations through the floor.

We get to his unit and Ms. Marrillion holds up a hand to stop me.

Then she puts a finger in front of her mouth, telling me to be quiet. We hold our heads close to the door and listen carefully.

Inside, we can hear things breaking and someone is yelling, "You're going to go to jail! The law can deal with this!"

It sounds like trouble. We start to back away, and I try to figure out where we can go next. Where would we be safe?

At that moment, D'Argyle's door swings open.

CHAPTER 7
UNKNOWN CALLER

I JUMP BACK A BIT, and Ms. Marrillion reaches into her purse. I don't know if she's planning to grab the pepper spray or the scissors.

But I only see D'Argyle in the doorway.

"Took you long enough, Lee," he says. "You take the stairs?"

"We took the elevator, but I'm afraid I walk slowly," Ms. Marrillion says.

"Are you alone?" I ask him.

"No, I've got all of the Yankees in here. Plus an ATV gang on my couch." He shakes his head. "Nah, it's just me."

"I thought I heard people yelling in there."

"Ah, that was just Pearson in *Red Dead Redemption*. I was robbing his store, and he got mad, started screaming at me." He looks over at Ms. Marrillion, who has taken her hand out of her purse without a weapon. "This isn't your granny, is it?"

"No," I say, laughing. "But we'd better get inside."

He moves back into his apartment and we follow. I close the door and latch all the locks behind me.

"This is my neighbor, Ms. Marrillion."

"It's a pleasure to meet you, D'Argyle," she says.

"Any friend of Lee's is a friend of mine," he tells her.

"Do you mind if I sit on your couch?" she asks. "We've been walking a bit, and I'm afraid I've gotten tired."

"Make yourself at home."

Ms. Marrillion sits down and seems to relax a little.

"If you want to play some Mario Kart, we can switch to that," D'Argyle says. "Just grab the second controller. You can't be worse at it than Lee." On the screen a man in a cowboy hat is standing in a field.

"I'm afraid I didn't quite understand what you said in the hallway before," Ms. Marrillion says, "about who was screaming at you."

"Oh, yeah. I was playing *Red Dead Redemption* 2. It's like a Western, you know from old movies? Anyway, after you finish the main game, one of the guys from your crew, Pearson, he opens a small store. Just for fun, I wanted to see what happened if I tried to rob him when I found him. He didn't like it."

"We're in a bit of a situation," I say. "I couldn't explain it over the phone."

"Whoa, you're not the cause of all those sirens I heard earlier, are you?"

"Not exactly, but the police are looking for a guy who's looking for her."

D'Argyle sits next to her on the couch.

"Don't worry, lady. You're safe here."

"Thank you, young man. Hopefully we won't stay too long. I wouldn't want to get you tied up in all this."

And what exactly *is* all this? I'm still not even sure myself. So far, I only know that a lot of people are trying to find her and kill her. She seems to have known it might happen, but wasn't actively on the run before now. I'm guessing something happened recently that set this all in motion, but I can't imagine what.

"Ms. Marrillion, I know you don't want to get us involved, but we may be able to help you more if we know what's going on," I say.

She sighs and thinks this over.

"I suppose you're right. But I don't want to tell you too much, as that could put you in danger."

"Hold up," D'Argyle says. "How much danger are we talking about?"

"Someone with a gun tried to shoot her," I say.

He nods his head and pumps his fist. "I knew it! That's what I'm talking about!" Then he makes gun sounds like Kendrick Lamar: "*Doo! Doo! Doo! Doo!*"

Ms. Marrillion looks uncomfortable for a moment.

"It didn't sound quite like that," she says. "But it was very loud and scary."

"I'm ready for it," D'Argyle says. "I've been practicing on *RDR2*. I'm a good shot with sidearms *and* long arms."

"But you don't actually have a gun," I say.

His smile disappears.

"Oh yeah. I guess let's try to avoid the gun guy for now." He uses the remote control to turn off the TV. "But you go ahead and tell us what you can, Miss Marleen."

"Let's see," she says, not correcting him about her name. "Where to start?"

It gets quiet for a second and then we hear more sirens outside.

"It goes back to my childhood," she says softly. "I saw something. I was a witness."

This kind of makes sense. I've seen a bunch of movies where criminals try to kill someone before they can testify in court. Except she is saying she saw something when she was a child, and she's *super old* now. (I wouldn't say that to her face, obviously.) I can't imagine her being called into court to testify about a mob hit or whatever she saw when she was young.

"For a long time afterwards, I lived in fear," she says. She's careful with her words, I think like she doesn't want to say too much. "I was always worried someone would break into my room at night and take me from whatever home I lived in. Or just kill me in bed."

It's weird to hear her talk this way. A few hours ago, she was just the quiet old lady upstairs who needed help with her groceries.

My phone vibrates and we all jump a little, startled. I see it's my mom calling, but I click on decline. I *never* do that, but I'm not sure how to explain to her what's going on just yet.

"Over time, I guess I was able to put it behind me," Ms. Marrillion says. "It seemed like the danger passed. The people involved in what I saw were older than me. I thought they must all be dead by now. Maybe I was wrong. Or maybe their children or grandchildren are trying to take care of whatever unfinished business they left behind."

"What kind of people are we talking about?" I ask. "You said earlier they may have somebody inside the police?"

"That's the tricky part," she says. "It's everyone you can imagine. Every disreputable character they talk about in your history books at school: they're all after me."

"We don't really use books in school that much anymore, Mrs. Marinelli," D'Argyle says. "My teacher, Mr. Allison, says they leave out too much important information, so he brings in his own stuff for us to read. I understand what you mean, though. It's still got bad guys in it. Seems like you can't really get famous history without *being* mad evil or *helping get rid of* mad evil."

D'Argyle's phone rings, and again we're all scared for a moment.

He picks it up and looks at it. "Unknown caller," he says. "It might be my guy." He doesn't want to say *which* guy in front of Ms. Marrillion, but it's a guy who uses a burner phone.

He answers it and I hear an icy cold voice say something to him. His eyes bug out like he's terrified. He looks out the window as if someone might be watching us. "Hold on," he says. Then he hands me the phone.

"It's for you," he says.

CHAPTER 8
TELL ME YOU'RE SAFE

A VOICE in my ear scares me more than anything that's happened so far today.

"Kid, you are in such a huge amount of trouble," it says.

"Hi, Mom," I answer.

"You are always — ALWAYS — going to answer me when I call if you want to keep that phone. Understand?"

"Yes."

"I thought something had happened to you! Somebody said there was a shooting at our building."

"Oh, uh, yeah."

"And you didn't call me right away to let me know you were safe?"

"I was a little busy."

"You can never be too busy to talk to me, got it?"

"I got it."

"Now, what's going on?"

I don't know exactly what to tell her. But I guess she was loud enough that D'Argyle and Ms. Marrillion could hear her. Ms. Marrillion gestures for me to hand her the phone. Who knows, maybe she can talk me out of this situation? I give it to her.

"Hello, is this Lee's mother?"

My mom finally starts speaking at a normal volume so we can only hear Ms. Marrillion's half of the conversation at this point.

"I'm afraid I'm responsible for this. You see, after Lee helped me with the groceries, I received some troubling news that … well … some people were coming to kill me."

My mom says something here.

"Yes, very inconsiderate of them," Ms. Marrillion says. "I would be happy to live a few more years and take my secrets to the grave. But, in any case, Lee refused to leave me alone to face them. We went to your unit, and then a man came into the building looking for me. He was dressed like a police officer. It didn't seem safe to stay, so we snuck out, and Lee helped me make it to D'Argyle's home, where we are now."

Again my mom speaks, but we can't hear her.

"I don't know if we have a long-term plan," Ms. Marrillion says. "I'd like to stay here and rest for a little while, but then I hope to get out of your hair. Unfortunately, I can't trust any of the authorities at this time. But I hate to think I'm endangering anyone else. Maybe I will try to head up to Vermont. I think it's nice there this time of year."

Ms. Marrillion nods her head and gives me back my phone.

"Hey, Mom," I say.

"OK, Lee. I'm very proud of you for insisting on helping Ms. Marrillion. But once we get through this, we're still going to have a long talk about you declining my call."

"So, am I in trouble, or did I do good?"

"I can be proud of you and mad at you at the same time," she answers. "That's called motherhood."

I roll my eyes and Ms. Marrillion smiles at me. D'Argyle has turned the TV back on and is playing *RDR2* on mute.

"Stay where you are, and I'll come get you."

"You still bringing pizza?"

"We may have to skip dinner until we make sure everyone's safe. Just sit tight. D'Argyle's probably got a lot of snacks in his place. I assume his mom is working, but if she gets home, have her call me." D'Argyle's mother is a counselor in the Bronx and we're not supposed to bother her when she's on shift.

"I love you, Lee."

I'm silent for a moment.

"Me, too," I say and hang up, then toss the phone toward D'Argyle on the couch. He pauses his game.

"Ms. Marrillion, you think it was safe to say that much on the phone?"

"Oh, yes. I doubt the people who are after me could have been listening. They might have been able to tap my phone, but there's no reason they would have been listening in on D'Argyle's calls. I didn't even know he existed before this afternoon!"

"I *been* here!" D'Argyle says, laughing.

"I'm sure you have," she answers. "If I go on the run, they'd be able to track my movements through credit cards and things like that, but I'd always be a day or so ahead of them. A rogue agent in the FBI, for instance, could get access to information from databases and files, but couldn't run 24-hour surveillance on me by themselves. And besides, they don't want to follow me, they just want to kill me."

I get up and walk to the window, where I close the curtains.

"Just in case," I say. Somebody would have to stand right in the middle of the courtyard with binoculars to get a chance to see into D'Argyle's place, but why bother risking it? Hopefully, someone in the neighborhood would confront them for being a creep snooping in windows, but you'd be surprised what people can get away with sometimes around here.

"You know, Lee," Ms. Marrillion says quietly, "you shouldn't be ashamed to tell your mother you love her. I spent a lot of my early life in an orphanage, so I know. You're lucky to have her."

"Yeah, she's pretty good, as far as moms go. She's on her way here and she'll figure everything out."

Then, just as I'm feeling safe for once, the TV blinks off, the lights go out, and the apartment goes dark.

CHAPTER 9
DRUG RUNNING

BLACKOUTS ARE a fact of life up here, especially in the summer. Everyone turns on their AC and the grid shuts down. Most days it wouldn't be a big deal, and I'd go to the park or something, but now me, Ms. Marrillion, and D'Argyle are stuck inside. The streets are too dangerous for us at the moment.

The fan blades slowly stop spinning, and soon we're left sitting in the stifling apartment. On top of that, it seems like we'll need the internet to help us protect Ms. Marrillion, and that's going to drain our phone batteries quickly.

I would put mine in airplane mode, but I have to leave it on in case my mom calls again.

"I hate to make things worse," Ms. Marrillion says quietly. "But I need to get a prescription filled at the drugstore. I was going to go up after we bought my groceries, but that phone call changed my plans."

"You don't have any pills left?" D'Argyle asks.

"I think I have a week's worth," she says, "but they're in a container in my bathroom."

"The fake cop with the gun shot up her place," I say. "So I don't think we can go back there."

"I can call up to the pharmacy at the top of the hill and see if they'll deliver," Ms. Marrillion says. "Although they may be suspicious about delivering to another address than the one they have on file. And I wouldn't want to get your home possibly mixed up in this, D'Argyle. The men who are searching for me might threaten the pharmacists in order to get them to reveal my location."

"Maybe I could pick them up," I say. "They let me pick up my mom's prescriptions sometimes if she has to work past their closing time. And they know I live in the same building as you."

"It could work," she says. "But I hate for you to risk anything. That man in the subway elevator saw you, so he could be trouble."

I explain to D'Argyle: "We kind of tased a guy and tied him up at 190th Street."

"That is wild!"

"She did the tasing," I say, nodding at Ms. Marrillion.

"I knew she was a banger!" D'Argyle slaps the couch in excitement. "Way to go, Miss Lemarrion!"

We don't correct him about her name.

"I think if I change clothes again, I'll be safe," I say. "You should call now so they have time to get your prescription ready. D'Argyle, can I borrow some clothes?"

"I got the perfect outfit," he says, which scares me. I feel like he's going to dress me up real bad. He runs to his bedroom while Ms. Marrillion calls the pharmacy. Luckily, they're fine with me picking up her prescription. That's the nice thing about living in a neighborhood like this, where people know each other and look out for their neighbors.

D'Argyle comes back with what looks like a pile of garbage.

"Yo, Lee, you want to dress up as the Trash Monster?"

"You still have that?"

"My mom was so proud of me, she wouldn't let me throw it away."

In fifth grade, D'Argyle dressed up as a Trash Monster for a presentation about the environment in science. I played Solar

Panel Person and covered myself in aluminum foil. The Trash Monster was much more popular.

"I can't show up to the pharmacy dressed as garbage."

"I know, I know. Just kidding." He goes back into his bedroom and returns with a shirt that is straight-up fugly. It's got a hideous pattern on it that looks like vines growing on a computer chip.

"Is that from Jimmy Jazz?"

"Naw, it's from that knockoff store, Frankie Flash. You know the one up near 238th? I was at that Buffalo Wild Wings for some family thing and I spilled sauce all over my shirt. I had to get a new shirt to wear on the way home, and this was the cheapest one they had."

"I don't think that guy from the elevator would recognize me in it, but I might get killed just for wearing something so ugly."

"Oh wait," he says. "I also have a wig from when I got into TikTok."

A few minutes later, I head out, hoping the disguise keeps me safe. Since we left the guy at 190th Street station, I want to stay away from there. If possible, I want to avoid my building, because I figure they might have it staked out looking for Ms. Marrillion. I take the back door out of D'Argyle's building onto Broadway, then go into Fort Tryon Park. After that, I take the trail up the hill to the other park entrance. This is a little close to the subway station, so I just have to hope I'm unrecognizable.

It seems like I must be. I make it all the way back to 187th Street without anyone stopping me, take off the wig, and head into the pharmacy. The drug counter is in back, and they're expecting me. They don't even recognize me at first, which makes me feel good. But once I say who I am, they give me the prescription and let me charge it to Ms. Marrillion's card.

I'm feeling good now, because I wouldn't want her to die of plain old sickness while people are out there trying to murder her. I've got the white paper bag in my hand and I walk back to the front of the store.

While I'm deciding the safest way to get back to D'Argyle's, a big black SUV rolls up and screeches to a halt, parking sloppily with the front tires on the curb at the corner of 187th and Fort Washington. Two dudes in business suits and sunglasses jump out, with earpieces like the Secret Service wears, and what look like guns under their jackets. One plants himself on the corner and scans the sidewalk, while the other bursts into the pharmacy.

He's blocking my exit.

CHAPTER 10

AFRAID FOR REAL

MAYBE HE SHOULD HAVE TAKEN off his sunglasses when he came inside, though. Then he might have seen the pharmacy desk in the back. Instead, he shoves me out of the way and stomps toward the normal checkout at the front.

"I'm looking for an old lady named Willa Marrillion. She just used a credit card here."

The clerk shrugs, and I go outside as fast as I can. I don't know if the guy in the suit will figure out I used Ms. Marrillion's card in the back of the store, but I don't want to wait around to see.

I casually try to blow past the other guy standing watch on the corner, but he sees me.

"Hey, you," he growls at me.

"Yeah?"

"You seen an old lady here a minute ago?"

I consider lying to send them looking in the wrong direction, but I just want to get away from here as fast as I can.

"Nah, man," I say. "But there's lots of old people around."

"Your shirt's got a real complicated pattern," he says. "It's nice." That's messed up, because like I said, the shirt is mad ugly. Also, it means he may remember me later, so I keep walking.

I note the license number on their SUV as I go by, and as soon as I get to the big staircase going down to the bottom of the hill on Overlook Terrace, I take out my phone and write it down. I'm not sure what I can do with it, but I figure it can't hurt.

On the way down, I clock everyone I pass, hoping nobody seems suspicious. There's the usual people doing exercise, running up one side, and some construction workers about halfway down, eating sandwiches and smoking. Nobody takes any interest in me, which is good. I pull the wig out from the pocket I had stuffed it in and put it back on. Then I keep walking down. I get to the street in one piece.

I'm pretty close to the building where Ms. Marrillion and I live, so this could be dangerous. But I have to get the prescription to her. I didn't ask what kind of drugs they are, so I'm not sure if it's something she needs urgently or not. Anyway, I don't want to leave her alone with D'Argyle too long. There's nothing wrong with D'Argyle, it's just that she might get scared, since she's not in her home and she's with some stranger she just met a few minutes ago.

There are sirens and cops all over 187th at the corner where I live, but nobody seems to be looking for me yet. I go past the synagogue and turn left on Broadway. I figure this street is safer since there's more people that could help me if I get in trouble. They had electricity at the top of the hill, but down here people have come outside to get some fresh air and cool off. Old men are playing dominos, and kids are running around while their mothers fan themselves.

There's a crowd outside the good barbershop, and I can see inside that they're just using scissors since their clippers don't work. Not much is happening outside the funeral home, but the fancy restaurants on the next block are busy serving drinks. My mom says they're a sign of gentrification, but sometimes I think she just uses that as a word for anything new in the neighbor-hood. Like if there's a new Dominican restaurant she thinks is too fancy, she'll say that it's more gentrification ruining the neighborhood. Honestly, I'm surprised she didn't blame the hitmen trying to kill us on gentrification.

It's strange being afraid in the city. Before I was born, my mom says, there were times when it *was* dangerous in this neighborhood. Sometimes in old movies or TV shows, I'll see a little bit of that past. They always start by showing a subway train covered in graffiti, and then there's two or three old drunk dudes standing heating their hands over a fire in a metal trash can.

The thing is, I've never even seen a metal trash can like that in real life. These days, all the garbage goes in plastic cans, or recycling bins. They even started collecting compost in brown plastic tubs. Compost is just dirt and old food. (Mom calls *that* gentrification, too.)

This is the first time I've actually been *afraid*. I'm not afraid of my neighbors, I'm afraid of the people descending on my block: the guy in the cop uniform who can't be trusted and just starts shooting. The guy from some sort of crime family intimidating people in a local business. The guy threatening an old woman in the elevator. Where do people like that come from? Not from around here, that's for sure.

At 192nd Street, I turn left again and cut back to Bennett Ave. Once I get back to D'Argyle's with the prescription, I think we'll finally be able to rest for a bit, as long as it doesn't get too hot for Ms. Marrillion with no fans or AC. If we're lucky, the power will come back on.

Of course, just as I start thinking about being safe, that's when I see a guy in tracksuit running down the sidewalk in my direction.

His hands are still zip-tied together.

But that's not stopping him.

CHAPTER 11
RIGHT BEHIND ME

HE RECOGNIZES ME RIGHT AWAY, I can tell. The ugly shirt and wig don't help. I guess I was the last face he saw before he got electrocuted and knocked out, so I made an impression on him.

I turn and start running back towards Broadway, figuring there are more places to hide and disappear there.

I can hear him shouting at me, swearing and cursing. He's in beast mode.

His hands are still tied together, but I bet he could hit me or kick me, and that might slow me down enough to cause problems. I don't know if he's working alone. And if the police come, I'd have to explain everything that's going on, and Ms. Marrillion said that isn't safe.

I'm running uphill, back the way I came, looking behind me to see where he is.

He hasn't slowed down. He's pretty fast for a big guy, especially one who was unconscious a little bit ago. I'm just barely slowing down going through intersections, but he is running through them blindly at full speed.

Maybe he's forgotten about Ms. Marrillion and now he just

wants revenge on me for what happened to him in the elevator. He's shoving dudes out of the way like a pro wrestler.

Normally in this part of town, people would try to do something when they see a guy chasing a child, but I think the blood on his face and his hands being tied together is scaring everyone away. He seems too crazy to try to calm down. Maybe someone already *has* called the police, but they're all busy investigating the gunfire in my building and can't respond.

At 184th Street, I get an idea that might help me.

His hands are still tied together, which will make it hard for him to grab things and climb.

So I turn just past the Staples and run up towards Wadsworth Avenue.

Halfway up the block, there's a construction site. The whole area is sealed off with big sheets of wood to keep people out. Further downtown, this sort of thing is usually covered with posters for music and DJs. Up here I guess they don't think we're worth selling stuff to.

I toss the prescription bag over the fence, then jump and grab the edge of a board that says POST NO BILLS on it. It hurts my hands a bit, there must be something rough at the top. But I pull myself up and throw one leg over, then the other. Now I'm hanging down on the other side. It's not too far to drop, but instead of smooth pavement, there's a bunch of broken bricks and rocks.

I'm worried I'm going to twist my ankle. But I'm even more worried that this guy is going to catch me, so I let go and fall. I land pretty badly, and fall to my side. I get a bit scraped up, and my hands are cut, but I don't have time to stop. I find the prescription bag and run across the empty lot.

There used to be an old church here, but they tore it down about five years ago and haven't started building anything new yet. I guess it's more of an abandoned lot than a construction site.

Big weeds have overgrown a lot of it, which helps me because pretty soon I'm out of sight of the wall or even the little square windows they put up every so often so people can monitor what's going on at this construction site, or in this case, what isn't going on at this construction site.

I turn around and see a pair of hands appear at the top of the fence I just climbed over. At first, he can't get a grip because his hands are tied together palm-to-palm. On the second try, he gets one hand around the board at the top and the other is curled up in a ball under it. It disappears again, though. I think he couldn't get enough leverage to pull himself up with one hand.

Eventually he's going to figure out a way to use one of the windows for support, or just tear down the boards in a rage to find another way in, and I don't want to wait for that.

Now it's just a matter of outguessing him. I could come out on Wadsworth, or cut through the back of one of the buildings onto 183rd Street, or go back down to Broadway through a connecting alley. Hopefully he's still trying to get over the wall and not running around the block trying to find me on one of those streets.

At first, I rule out going back to Broadway, because if I can't find an open back door, I'd have to climb over a roof and that block is where all the cops from the 34th Precinct park their cars.

Then I get lucky, though, because I hear someone coming out of the back of the big building on the corner of 183rd and Broadway. I forgot about it because it's been empty for so long. It used to be a party store, but that got evicted to make way for a new food hall. *More gentrification,* as my mom would say. It finally opened a few weeks ago. If they're using the kitchen, I know the back door will open at some point when it gets too hot, or the chef takes a break to vape.

I cram the wig and prescription into pockets, then climb the fence. Two busboys look up at me. I shrug and they just kind of laugh to themselves as I go past them into the back of the food hall, stumbling out from the kitchen into the seating area. The lights are off from the blackout, and I can see Broadway through the window, but people outside can't see in because of the darkness.

I'm looking to see if the coast is clear when someone grabs me from behind.

CHAPTER 12
BAR FIGHT

"YOU CAN'T BE in here, kid. You gotta be 21, since we serve booze."

It's a bouncer, and he shoves me towards the door.

"Can't I just say for a minute? I'm hiding out from a dude," I say, but the bouncer isn't having any of it.

Just then, two things happen.

First, the power comes back on, and there's a humming noise as the AC kicks in. The lights all flicker on, and we're no longer standing in the dark.

The second thing that happens is the dude who's chasing me runs by the front of this food hall. Since the lights are on, he can clearly see me, and he stops and pounds on the door.

"That's him!" I say to the bouncer, who's dragging me towards the door by my ugly shirt.

The guy presses his face up against the glass to make sure it's me, getting his blood on the door as he does so.

"Whoa!" yells the bouncer, letting go of me. I back up and see a second security guard at the bar.

"Do something, this guy's out of control!" I tell him.

"I don't work here," he says. "You think every big tall guy in a black t-shirt is a security guard? I run a tech startup, I'm just here for margaritas."

The guy from the subway elevator is wrestling with the bouncer, who's trying to throw him out of the food hall. I was right to be afraid, because even with his hands tied together, he beats up the bouncer, kicking him in the knee, and then shoving him sideways. The bouncer's knee must be really damaged, because he falls over, screaming. I back up towards the kitchen as the guy comes toward me.

He reaches out to grab me, but he misses and his hands only pluck the wig from my pocket. Suddenly, he stops and then gets yanked backwards.

Margarita Guy, who said he wasn't a security guard, has a hold of Tracksuit and throws him across the room. He knocks into some tables and chairs, making a loud crash as he falls to the ground.

"Stay down," says Margarita Guy, but Tracksuit doesn't listen and tries to swing a chair as he gets up.

It's clumsy and doesn't hit anybody. Margarita Man kicks him hard in the head. He flops back onto the floor, unconscious for the *second* time today. I mean, unless he got knocked unconscious even earlier in the day before he ran into me and Ms. Marrillion in the elevator. Then this could be the *third* time he was knocked unconscious. Who knows? He seems to get knocked out a lot in the short time I've known him, so maybe it's a thing with him.

"Thanks, Big Rick," the bartender says to Margarita Guy. "Your drink's on the house."

"Do me a favor," Big Rick says. "Tell the police your bouncer beat that guy up." He points to the tracksuit guy lying on the ground. "I don't want to get messed up in this."

The bouncer has pulled himself up by this point.

"You got it," he says. Then he turns to me. "And you gotta get out of here, kid. We could lose our license if the cops find someone underage on the premises."

I head to the door, thinking it's relatively safe now that the tracksuit guy is out of the picture.

"But hey, if you have any older friends who like to drink, send them our way," the bartender calls to me as I'm leaving. I guess Ms. Marrillion is an older friend, but I don't think she'd like it very much here.

I head out onto Broadway, then turn right again, heading back towards D'Argyle's place. The mood of the street has changed now that the power's back on. Broadway always feels alive. In school, we learned it's the oldest street running up and down the city, so no wonder it's always popping off. Broadway was even here before the white people came, although it wasn't called Broadway back then. I've never been to a Broadway show, but it's nice to know the street near my apartment is the same one where all the fancy people sing and dance and stuff downtown.

I start running, even though nobody's chasing me. Nobody I know about, anyway. Still, I'll feel better after I get these pills to Ms. Marrillion.

On the way, I start thinking about places we could stay other than D'Argyle's if we need to. Mom probably knows more people with apartments, and they're adults, so they could just give her permission. All my friends would have to ask their parents before they could take us in.

There are the kids from school, but I also start thinking about less obvious choices. If some thug like the tracksuit guy or the police start asking around, it won't take them long to find out who my friends are, and then they'd know where to look.

The trouble is, when you're in danger, it's your friends you want to turn to, not people you only *kind of* know. Two brothers work at the deli nearby, and the younger brother seems pretty cool, for instance. Would he help us? His older brother is probably nice too, but he's at the grill all the time, so it's the younger brother at the cash register that I talk to most of the time. I don't even know his name, though. He's just been "that guy at the deli" to me my whole life. Hard to ask for a life-or-death favor from someone whose name I don't know.

All the people who volunteer at the Word Up Bookstore seem like they're helpful and want to do what they can for the community. Would one of them take in Ms. Marrillion for the night? For all of mom's complaints about gentrification, I wonder if Ms. Marrillion would be more comfortable in a rich newcomer's home. I mean, they probably have the kind of comfortable mattresses that an older lady would need to go to sleep.

And it's not just that I'm asking a big favor. I'm also putting anyone who helps at risk. That's something I need to worry about. Have you ever sat down and made a list of people who would be willing to die for you? It's probably a pretty short list. Or a list of people you'd be willing to die for? It'd probably be short, too.

I bet a lot of times when someone dies to save another person, they don't really think it through ahead of time. They just act ... and end up dead.

CHAPTER 13
IF ALL ELSE FAILS

I MEAN, think about how I ended up in this situation: I was with Ms. Marrillion when she got that phone call, and I knew I had to help.

But if it had been some other way? If you woke me up one day and said, *some people are going to try to kill an old woman in your building, do you want to risk your life to stop them?* To be honest, I don't know if I would have said *yes*. I didn't even know her this morning!

The thing is, we're just acting on impulse, trying to stay alive. And so far we've been lucky. I know we can't keep at it this way, though. We need to start planning ahead a bit more, so we don't end up in situations where split-second decisions could get us killed.

For instance, my mom's always trying to get me to think about college. It's hard to worry about something that won't even happen for a few years, when I've got so much going on in my life right now, you know? Even before the stuff that happened today. *You have to think long-term,* she tells me. *Look at the big picture.* And maybe I finally understand that now. I don't want to spend the rest of my life running up and down these streets looking over my shoulder. I need a plan. *We* need a plan. We just need some breathing room to figure it all out.

I get back to D'Argyle's building and nobody suspicious is hanging around, so I buzz up and he lets me in. I take the stairs again and knock on his door. We should have arranged some sort of secret knock, I guess. Instead, I just say "It's me," and he lets me in.

"Any trouble?" he asks.

"I lost your wig," I tell him.

He locks the door, and we head over to the couch, where I hand Ms. Marrillion the prescription.

"Did something happen to your hands?" She says.

"I had to jump a fence. I ran into our friend from the elevator."

"Oh dear, I'm sorry."

"Not as sorry as he is!"

"Ahhhh! Did you kick his a**?" D'Argyle says. Then he mimes kicking someone and makes sound effects for his kick.

"Nah," I say. "But the bouncer at that new food hall did." I guess, technically, Big Rick isn't the bouncer there, but I remember that he didn't want to be involved, so I'll let the bouncer take credit, even though he didn't want to help me.

"Oh, is that place open?" Ms. Marillion asks, surprising me.

"Yeah, are you interested? They're looking for customers."

"I might stop in for a lemonade. I'm just glad it's finally open. I hated to see the space vacant for so long. D'Argyle, might I trouble you for a glass of water so I can take my pill?"

"Of course, Ms. Larrymellon."

She smiles at me. I guess he didn't learn to say her name while I was gone.

"I think we need a plan," I tell her, "for what we should do if stuff goes wrong."

"A contingency plan! That is excellent thinking, Lee."

"When we're on vacation, my mom sets up a meeting place as a backup in case one of our phones dies and we lose touch. Like she'll say, 'If all else fails, we'll meet at 8 at the restaurant,' or something like that."

"In case we get separated, you mean. Or if it becomes too dangerous to communicate over the phone?"

"Yeah," I say. "I was thinking we can set up a morning and night meet-up that we can use if we need to."

"I like the sound of that. It should probably be somewhere public, where it's easy to fit in with a crowd, I guess. That way, if one of us needs to stay there for a while waiting for the other person, it won't be conspicuous."

"That makes sense. Maybe it should be two different locations, too, so that you don't get noticed hanging out all day at the same spot."

We think for a while, and D'Argyle comes back with the water. Ms. Marrillion takes her pill.

"What about a church?" I say. "Aren't they always open?"

"They're supposed to be," Ms. Marrillion says. "But I may not be safe in a church. Also, they aren't always crowded, so I think somewhere else might work better."

"What about that McDonald's at 181st?" D'Argyle asks. "The one across from the *Real Steel* movie theater."

"That's the old Coliseum," Ms. Marrillion says.

"Yeah, we always called it the *Real Steel* theater, because that was the last movie they played before they went out of business. So the marquee just said *Real Steel* and *Contagion* for most of our lives."

"It's a shame," Ms. Marillion says. "That used to be a grand movie palace, but they chopped up the interior so many times it didn't have any of its character left by the time they started tearing it down. Originally, it was one big theater, like the United Palace. Have either of you been there?"

"My mom took me to see *The Sound of Music* there," I say.

"My cousin's graduation was at United Palace," D'Argyle adds. "And it's where John Wick went to the ballet in *John Wick 3*. Did you see that one, Miss Mellymaron?"

"No, I'm afraid I missed it," she says.

"Let's say McDonald's from 8:30 to 9:00 AM," I say, trying to get us back on track. "I think there's a lot of morning traffic we could hide in."

"Man, that's crazy early," D'Argyle says.

"I was just thinking it's a little late," Ms. Marrillion laughs. "Of course, I'm at the age where I go to bed early. But it's good to have that settled. What about an evening meeting?"

"Maybe the corner of Dyckman and Broadway?" I suggest. "There's a Starbucks and a lot of foot traffic from the subway. Plus, it's close to the park if you need to sneak in and out. Unless that's too far."

"This is only for emergencies, so the distance should be fine," Ms. Marillion says. "How about 5:30 to 6:00 PM?" She looks at D'Argyle when she says this, since he thought the other time was too early.

"That seems about right," he says.

"Very good!" she says, clapping her hands together. "Now, what about weapons?"

This isn't what I expected her to say, so I laugh.

"We need to be prepared, Lee. There's a war coming our way."

CHAPTER 14
A FISTFUL OF ENEMIES

"LET me tell you who is coming after me," Ms. Marrillion says.

"You mean coming after *us*," I correct her.

"I suppose so. But remember that you can get out whenever you want. They're not after you, and you have your whole life ahead of you. If the you-know-what hits the fan, you don't have to see this all the way to the end. Promise me you'll keep that in mind."

"I promise."

"First of all, there is a part of the government that would be happier if I was dead," she says. "Not the whole government, thankfully, but some high-ranking officials."

"Whoa," D'Argyle says. "Like you mean the President? He knows who you are?"

"I hope not, but one never knows. It's possible some of these men don't even know my name, or anything about me. They have abstract reasons for wanting me dead. It might be easier for them not to ask anything about me. That way, I'm just an anonymous target, and they sleep better at night."

"You mean the government would kill people without knowing who they are?"

She laughs. "That's the main way they kill people. Through

wars or neglect, they kill people who are just statistics to them. It's very rare for them to kill a specific person."

"Man, our government is messed up!" D'Argyle says.

"That's one way of putting it," she replies. "Although ours is relatively functional compared to Russia's, and they probably want me dead, too. That's quite alarming, because they have even fewer qualms about murdering civilians."

"None of the guys we've seen so far seemed like Russians to me," I say.

"That's true. It's possible they haven't entered the picture yet. At the same time, they might have hired someone local to try to get rid of me." She takes another sip of the water D'Argyle brought her for her pills. "It would be nice if we could determine who initiated all of this. You know, that phone call I received was to let me know that an old, dear friend had been murdered. If we could figure out who killed her, then that might clear things up."

"And it's our government or the Russians?" I ask.

"Unfortunately, no, there are several other groups involved. On the bright side, we may be able to pit them against each other."

"Aww yeah, just like *Last Man Standing*!" D'Argyle says.

"Hold up," I say, "that's what that sitcom's about? The one with the Buzz Lightyear guy?"

"Not the TV show, Lee, the Bruce Willis movie. He's this shooter caught between two gangs in the old days, but then he tricks them into fighting each other instead of trying to kill him."

"I haven't seen that," I say.

"Neither have I," Ms. Marrillion adds.

"Yeah, it was on cable one day. Although I heard it's a remake of an old Japanese movie."

"It does sound a bit like *Yojimbo*," Ms. Marrillion says. "Have you ever seen that?"

"Naw, but I'll put it on my list," D'Argyle says. "I keep track of all the movies people recommend to me, so I don't forget." He takes out his phone and then has her spell the title so he can write it down.

"You said there were some other groups besides the government and the Russians coming after you?" I ask, hoping we can figure out a plan.

"Ah, yes. Let's see. There's also the mob, or what's left of them. Documentaries make it sound like a lot of them were arrested and shut down, but I suspect some of them are still out there, doing what they do."

"You mean like in *Scarface* or *Goodfellas*?"

"Yes, D'Argyle," she says. "The mafia."

"Anyone else?"

"I hate to say it, but I believe some members of the Catholic Church are also involved. Not the current Pope, he seems very nice. But possibly some other high-ranking officials."

"I knew the government and the Russians and the mob all had hitmen," I say, "but I didn't think the church had any."

"I don't believe they have any sort of full-time soldiers," she says. "They are powerful, though, and have a lot of adherents all over the world. They could persuade someone to do almost anything."

"And that's everyone?" I ask.

"Everyone that I know of. It's possible that some other sort of group has gotten involved in the intervening decades, but I have no way of knowing."

"So we just need to figure out where we can go, where we'll be safe from the government, the Russians, the mob, and the Church."

"Maybe outer space," D'Argyle says. "Can you buy a ticket on one of those new rockets like the guy from Amazon?"

"I'm not quite that rich," she says.

"Yeah, they're only letting billionaires up there anymore, it seems like."

"This neighborhood might be pretty safe," I say. "There's hardly any Russians around, at least not the kind who would do their government's bidding, and it feels like *our* government forgot about us a long time ago. We have a few gangs, but I don't think they're part of the mafia. And that just leaves the Church. As long as we stay away from Cabrini Boulevard, I think we'd be good."

"Perhaps for now, but someone's already started snooping around," she says. "Pretty soon they'll all be here, swarming all over the place."

"I'm not letting any of them in here," D'Argyle says.

And he means it. We could probably hole up here for a long time.

Except that the building's fire alarm starts wailing.

It's a really loud siren from out in the hall.

"Sometimes it goes off after a few seconds," D'Argyle says.

We wait, but it doesn't stop.

A minute passes.

We hear people in the hallway, evacuating the building.

"I guess we gotta go," he says.

"Can you do me a favor first?" Ms. Marrillion asks him.

"Of course."

"Bring me the sharpest knife in your kitchen," she says. "I want to be prepared for whatever's out there."

CHAPTER 15
MOVE THE CROWD

WE EACH TAKE A KNIFE: Ms. Marrillion's is in her purse, D'Argyle's is in his pocket, wrapped in paper towels so he won't cut himself. That's probably not the smartest way to carry a blade, but we were pressed for time. Mine is wrapped in the white paper bag from the pharmacy, because I believe in recycling.

We cluster in the hallway outside D'Argyle's door. He locks it behind him and hands me the extra set of keys that was on top of his refrigerator.

"In case you need to get in and I'm not around," he says.

We walk single file towards the stairs, alarms wailing.

"You think there's really a fire?" I ask.

"I doubt there is," Ms. Marrillion says. "It's too much of a coincidence. They're probably trying to flush us out of the building. Still, we can't take the chance. Based on what we've seen so far, I wouldn't be surprised if they actually set some buildings on fire."

"What worries me," I say, "is how did they know which building we were in?"

That question is answered when we get down to the street. It looks like the whole entire block is out on the sidewalk.

"They must have pulled fire alarms up and down the street," Ms. Marrillion says.

"Most of these places don't have the kind of alarm with a handle you pull like we do in school," D'Argyle says. "So somebody must have stood beneath the smoke detector with a lighter or something like that."

The faces of our neighbors are all pretty annoyed. They assume some misbehaving teenagers have pulled a horrible prank.

"Line up for inspection," Ms. Marrillion mutters.

"What's that?"

"I think they got us all out here so they can take a look and try to find me. We're in danger."

"D'Argyle," I say. "Get away from us. Right now, they have no way to connect you to us, and you'll be more useful to us if it stays that way."

"Where should I go?"

"Stay in the area, somewhere you can keep an eye on us. Just don't look like you're part of our group."

"Got it," he says, and walks off a bit.

"We'll have to hope that my costume keeps me unrecognizable," Ms. Marrillion says. "Is there any chance the man in the tracksuit who chased you before will spot you? He's seen you in your new outfit now."

I'd forgotten I was wearing this ugly shirt D'Argyle gave me.

"I'm pretty sure he's out of it. He got kicked in the head really hard." Still, he's been knocked out once before and woke back up to come after me.

We're standing in the middle of the crowd of tenants in the building's lawn near the 190th Street subway station.

"All these people will make it hard for them to pick us out," Ms. Marrillion says. "But if they do see us, it will be difficult to get away."

This whole time, we're scanning the sidewalk, looking for anyone suspicious, anyone trying to get a good look at everyone here.

Then I see them, a group of three men making their way up

Bennett Avenue from the south. They look like off-duty cops, men who yell if you get too close to their cars, or anyone else who takes too many steroids. Big shoulders, bad skin, ugly sunglasses, nearly shaved heads. The kind of guys who are always shoving protestors or hitting them with shields in Facebook live videos.

I don't want to point, so I quietly tell Ms. Marrillion about them, and she takes a look.

"That's troubling," she says.

"We could make a break for it," I say. "Head up Bennett to the park, or maybe turn onto Nagle and get lost in a different crowd."

She shakes her head back and forth.

"I suspect they're kettling us," she says. "Those three get us to move, but there's probably another gang of them at the end of Bennett, waiting to catch us on the other side."

"Then we're trapped?"

"We could go back inside the building. It seems pretty clear there's no fire."

"Wouldn't they see us? Everyone is out here, it would be noticeable if we head back inside."

"Can your friend D'Argyle create a distraction?"

"Are you serious? In fourth grade, Ms. Jacob said he was a 'natural distraction' and tried to get him switched to another homeroom."

I edge a little closer to where D'Argyle is standing and tell him our plan to get back inside the building.

"We need you to get their attention away from the door while we do that."

"I got just the thing," he says, then heads over closer to the street.

"Be ready," I tell Ms. Marrillion.

The three guys are at the building next door, mixing themselves into the crowd, trying to get a look at all the abuelas and grandmothers. They'll be here soon, and they're sure to recognize Ms. Marrillion, even in her *Deez* sweatshirt.

"WHAT TIME IS IT?!"

D'Argyle is yelling now, near the entrance to the subway.

"I SAID, WHAT TIME IS IT?!"

"It's showtime," a few people laugh.

This is what dancers on the subway always yell before they start their act. As far as I know, though, D'Argyle is not a showtime dancer. I'm not sure what he's planning to do, but he is getting people to look his way.

"When I say 'What time is it?' you say 'It's showtime!' You all got that?"

"Shut up!" someone yells, but that only encourages him.

"Here we go: WHAT TIME IS IT?!"

"It's showtime!" enough of the crowd responds.

Then he starts dancing.

He's not very good, to be honest, but people start whooping and laughing at him, and it's enough of a distraction for us. The three guys turn towards the spectacle, and we walk as fast as Ms. Marrillion can back towards the building. I try not to turn around, hoping if I don't look, they won't see me. Only when I've got my key in the door and have it open, do I risk a backwards glance.

The men have busted their way through D'Argyle's crowd and turned up empty-handed. I see one of them yelling angrily. Then a different one swings his head around and sees us at the door.

I pull it shut, so they can't get in without a key, but they're running in our direction.

"Go down the stairs, not up," I tell Ms. Marillion.

The fastest of the three guys gets to the door, and he's pulled out some sort of metal baton. He's going to smash the glass.

CHAPTER 16
FIRE ESCAPE

I'M PRETTY worried at this point, obviously.

Ms. Marrillion has gone down the stairs toward the building's lower level, which opens out on to Broadway from the back door.

What I'm thinking is that I can lead these three guys up the stairs away from her. There's a loud crashing sound as the guy bashes on the glass in the door. It cracks, but then he has to hit it a few more times to clear out enough room for him to reach in and open the door. As he's doing this, I go into the stairwell and start running up, making as much noise as I can.

My theory is that they might try to hurt me, but they don't have any reason to kill me. Right now, I'm just someone who might be able to lead them to Ms. Marrillion. I've done so much running already today that I'm getting tired. I pound on the railings and walls every so often as I go to make sure they can hear me.

It's six flights up to the top floor of the building, one story past where D'Argyle's apartment is located. When we were a bit younger, we snuck out onto the roof once just to see what was up there. It turned out to be pretty boring, just some old TV antennas and wires. But we didn't know to prop the door open behind us, and we got trapped out there for half an hour. This was before either of us had our own phones. We had to wait until we saw George D., who we knew from the building, outside on the sidewalk, and then he came up and let us back in.

I think I can hear the three guys running up behind me, but it's loud and echoing, so that might just be the sound I'm making. I can't risk stopping to listen closely. I get to the top, finally, and push open the door. There's a brick out there that people use to prop open the door, and an old paint bucket full of sand and cigarette butts from the people who sneak up here to smoke.

Grabbing them both, I hustle to where the fire escape runs down the side of the building. Then I put the brick into the can and toss it sideways over the edge. It starts clanging and rolling down the metal stairs. I run back and hide on the other side of the brick bulkhead that the doorway is in.

Luckily, the can is still banging and smashing its way down when the three guys bust out onto the roof. They head for the edge, hearing the noise and thinking Ms. Marrillion and I must be trying to climb down the fire escape.

I slip inside the big metal door as it closes. Now the men are trapped up there just like D'Argyle and I were that time when we were kids. Anyone can open it from the inside, but it's locked from the outside.

Eventually, they might be able to climb down the fire escape, but everyone out on the sidewalk will see them, so they might not want to risk it. And even if they get down to the ground, they won't know where me and Ms. Marrillion are.

I run all the way back down the stairs. Luckily it's easier going down than coming up because I'm running out of energy.

Down in the basement, I call out to her.

"Ms. Marrillion, it's me, Lee. It's safe to come out now."

She appears from behind one of the building's laundry machines. I'm not sure how she fit back there! I guess she's kind of tiny.

"What happened?"

"I trapped them on the roof. We don't have a lot of time, though. We should get away from here."

Then we head out the back door to Broadway. I guess technically this is considered the front door of the building, but I always used the door on the other side because that's where D'Argyle's apartment was, so I considered that the front. It doesn't really matter, except that this way out of the building is easy enough for Ms. Marrillion. It's not like sneaking out into an alley through a small window or anything.

"Do you know Inwood, Ms. Marrillion? It might be safer to head up there, put some space between us and those guys, but I don't know the neighborhood, so that could put us at a disadvantage."

"We can go north a few blocks. I have a friend who lives next to the old Packard Dealer, at Broadway and Dongan."

I've never heard of the Packard Dealer, but I know the intersection she's talking about.

"That's where the free fridge is, right?"

"Yes, I believe so."

"My mom and I dropped some stuff off there a few times."

It's this refrigerator on the sidewalk where people in the community can donate food and then anyone who's hungry can come and get food for themselves or their family.

I remember that I'm signed up to help clean it in a few weeks, part of the effort to keep my mom happy with things I can put on my college application some day, if I end up going. Of course, the way this day is turning out, I'm not sure I'll still be around at the end of August to clean up the refrigerator, much less do all that college application stuff.

We start walking up Broadway.

"Um, your knife is showing," Ms. Marrillion says quietly.

I look down and see that, with all the action, it's somehow cut through the pharmacy bag and my pants and now the blade is poking out the front of my pocket.

"Oops," I laugh. I take it out to try to adjust it so it's not showing.

That's why it's right there in my hand when the cop car pulls up next to us with its siren flashing.

CHAPTER 17
RICH PEOPLE DIE TOO

THE COPS GET out of their car slowly.

The driver stands near his door while his partner approaches Ms. Marrillion and me.

"What're you doing with that knife, kid?"

"Don't worry, officer," Ms. Marrillion says. "I was just teaching my friend here how to julienne carrots. We're on the way to make some stir fry."

She lies pretty convincingly, and it's hard for the cop to make a big deal out of the situation since this nice old lady is involved. He doesn't even question her ridiculous outfit.

Then the radio in their car squawks.

I don't understand everything their dispatcher says, but I hear the words "suspected burglars" and "multiple fire alarms."

The driver grabs his radio and says he and his partner are going to provide support.

"Don't walk around with that knife out," the cop says to us as he walks back to his car. "There's a lot of nutcases out on the street today for some reason. You don't want to get mistaken for one of them."

They pull a big U turn across Broadway, nearly hitting several cars, and drive off.

We walk the rest of the way to Ms. Marrillion's friend's apartment, but unfortunately, she's not home. We buzz a few times; nobody answers.

"Maybe we should go into the park for some shade," I say. It's pretty sunny out, and I'm starting to get hot. Must be all that running I did earlier.

"A short break might be what we need," Ms. Marrillion says, "but we shouldn't rest too long. I think it's safer to keep moving or find somewhere safe."

We enter the green section of the park, trying to blend in and get lost among all the dog walkers and exercisers. It's a little difficult because we're not running and neither of us has a dog. Still, there are some other people just walking, either for light exercise or to get from one place to the other, and we don't stand out that much.

"Have you ever been to the Cloisters, Lee?" she asks me.

"Not since I was a little kid. Sometimes mom and I will have a picnic on their lawn, though."

"I think it might be a safe place for us. They're open until 5, and it's free to get in since we live in New York. They try to trick you into making a donation, but don't let them fool you. Your taxes help fund them, so you shouldn't have to pay to get in."

"I don't pay taxes yet, I'm just a kid," I say.

"Well, I assume your mother pays taxes for you. Let the tourists buy tickets. Plus, we're not going to be there very long."

We walk up the hill towards the museum.

To be honest, I've never been that interested in it. I think The Cloister is mostly filled with old tombs and stuff some rich dude stole from churches in Europe. But it's possible that Ms. Marrillion knows all about it and can tell me interesting stories. Plus, as long as we're safe, I don't care *how* boring it is.

"Have you heard of the Rockefellers?"

"They're that rich family," I say. "They built Rockefeller Center, right?"

"Correct! Their fortune goes back to John D. Rockefeller. He made his money in oil. You're probably too young to remember Standard Oil or Esso gas stations, but they were everywhere when I was a child. Most of them became Exxons in the 1970s."

"I've seen Exxons."

"There's lots of money in oil, too much, if you ask me. In any case, the original Rockefeller's son John Rockefeller Jr. is the one who built Rockefeller Center. He also bought this land and built this museum. It's nice, but I'm not sure it makes up for all the damage he did to the world. Then his son, Nelson, was the governor of New York for a long time, and the Vice President in the 1970s. One of Nelson's sons, Michael, disappeared in Indonesia and may have been eaten by cannibals."

This gets my attention!

"What? Things like that happen in real life?"

"We don't know for sure, of course. He was trying to collect things for a museum, as rich people often do, and his boat got overturned in the ocean. He swam for shore, but nobody saw him again. It's more likely he drowned or was eaten by a shark."

"And I thought *we* were in danger!"

"Yes, I suppose we at least can take comfort in knowing we won't be attacked by sharks or eaten by cannibals."

"So he didn't finish collecting things for his museum, I guess."

"Not on that last trip, I'm afraid. However, he had collected numerous artifacts on earlier expeditions. They're in the collection at The Met in Central Park. It's run by the same people who manage The Cloisters."

By this time, we were near the entrance to the building. It looks a little like a castle, but a peaceful one. It doesn't have big turrets or a moat like they do in the movies.

There's a winding path to get to the door, past a few buses and more tourists mixed in with joggers and even somebody doing some kind of yoga. We keep an eye out, but nobody seems to be looking for us.

When we get to the door, she turns to me.

"Are you ready to escape into the past?"

CHAPTER 18
IN THE DEAD OF NIGHT

WE ENTER the stone building and make our way towards the ticket desk.

"Will we need to show our ID? Is that dangerous?"

"They'll just confirm that we are New York residents. I don't think they'll enter our information into any sort of database," Ms. Marrillion says. "And even if they do, I can't imagine anyone would see it and be able to respond within an hour. There's so much data out in the world today that it's easy to get lost."

"They showed up at the pharmacy pretty quickly," I say.

"Yes, they did. Credit cards and banking are probably the easiest thing for nefariously minded men to get their hands into. I'm pretty sure we should be safe here. But you'd better give me your knife, Lee. They're less likely to check me thoroughly."

I hand her my knife, which she buries at the bottom of her bag.

She's right, too. The security guard barely even glances inside her purse when she holds it open on the way past him, but he looks me up and down a few times.

At the front desk, like Ms. Marrillion said they would, the clerks try to trick us into making the "suggested" donation.

"No thank you," she says firmly. "We both live nearby."

After we show our ID to prove we're NYC residents, they give us stickers to put on our clothes, proving we have a right to be here, and we go past the gift shop into the Cloisters.

It looks a little like a set from *Game of Thrones* or something like that. All the walls are made of big stones, and it's dark, like before they invented lightbulbs. It's a little scary, to be honest. I keep thinking some dude wearing armor is going to jump out with a sword and attack us.

I don't *really* think that will happen, but this place does take you into the past, so you feel like you're living back when there were knights and dragons.

"Let's go to the Bonnefont Cloister," Ms. Marrillion says.

I nod as if I know all the cloisters and agree that Bonnefont is the best one, even though I'm really not even sure what a cloister is.

She leads the way, as I think she's been here a lot of times before. Eventually we come to a door that leads to an outdoor space with lots of plants. There's a whole bunch of columns holding up a small roof around the edges.

"A cloister is just a covered walk," she says. "See how we could walk around here even if it was raining?"

"It's like standing under an awning when you're waiting for a bus," I say.

"It is! There's also shade in case it gets too hot. Come over here, to the edge," she says.

There's a little wall that overlooks the Hudson River and we can see across to New Jersey.

"These are all different herbs," she says, pointing to the plants in the middle of the courtyard. "I wish our building had a space like this for gardening." We just have a paved space in the back where little kids ride their tricycles.

"Alright," she says, sitting on the edge of the low wall. "I think we should have some privacy here, and we can see anyone approaching."

"It's peaceful here," I say. "Or it would be if a bunch of people weren't chasing us."

"You know," she says, "I grew up in a place sort of like this. Not nearly as nice, I mean, but the same idea. It was an orphanage run out of an old convent. That's the place where nuns live."

"Like in *Sister Act*?"

"I suppose so, but without all the music and fun. It was pretty dreary. Back then, they looked down on us girls, because most of us came from unwed mothers. Do you know what I mean?"

"Not really," I say. My mom isn't married.

"Of course, there's nothing wrong with it, but people in the church used to think it was shameful if women became pregnant before they were married. So they convinced a lot of young women to give their babies up for adoption, then put the kids in orphanages. In theory, they would find homes for us with loving parents who could not conceive children of their own. Except that the numbers didn't work out. There were a lot more young girls having babies than there were families who wanted to raise them.

"On top of that, they also managed to shame the couples who could not have their own children, as if they were somehow to blame. So they often convinced themselves they did not want children rather than reach out to the church to try to adopt kids like us."

"That sounds rough, Ms. Marrillion."

"I suppose it was. I didn't realize it at the time, because it was all I knew. I mean, I understood that other children had parents and homes, we saw things like that in movies. But it wasn't like I lived in a nice home and then moved into the orphanage. There were a few girls like that, whose parents had died, and they didn't have any relatives to take them in, so they ended up with us. They were a lot sadder, I guess because they knew what they had lost."

"Did you ever get adopted?"

"I did. But before that is when all my troubles started."

She sighs before continuing her story.

"One night, when I was about 15, Sister Irene woke me up in the middle of the night. 'I'm sorry, dear,' she said. There was a man with her, a priest I think, but he wasn't dressed like one. They put me in the back of a car and the man drove away with me."

"Did you think they were taking you to meet your new parents?"

"No. I knew it was nothing good, because of how serious they both were, and because Sister Irene had apologized. I hadn't ever really traveled very far that I remembered. We went into town, but not too often, to see movies or to get groceries that couldn't be delivered, but that was about it. This trip took several hours. The driver didn't say anything the whole time. That was the scariest part. He just kept driving and looking at his watch."

I'm looking around while she's talking, making sure nobody suspicious is watching us here in the Cloisters.

"I must have fallen asleep," she says. "And then I woke up when the car stopped. It was still the middle of the night. We were in a field, and we just sat there. I started counting at first, to see how long we'd be there. When I got to 6,000, I gave up. Finally, after at least an hour, sitting there silently in the dark, I heard another car approaching. It pulled up right next to us, another man driving with a girl like me in the back. He said something to her and she got out and walked over to our car, then opened the door and sat in back with me.

"She said 'My name is Carol,' and then my driver told her to shut up. The other car pulled away. 'Don't talk to each other,' he said. We drove for another hour or so until we were in a small town. He pulled up in the back of a VFW hall and told us to get out. Imagine that: two teenage girls who don't know each other, abandoned in an alley in a city where they've never been before. The car pulled away, and we were left standing there. While we were alone, I told her my name was Willa.

"If we hadn't exchanged names, I doubt we would have ever found each other later in life. But we did, and we stayed in touch over the decades, once a week, until today. Remember the telephone call I got after we went grocery shopping? That was Carol's daughter telling me that Carol had been found dead in her room at the nursing home. They weren't sure what had happened, but I knew immediately that she had been murdered, and that whoever did it would be coming for me next.

"Lee, it seems as if the past has finally caught up with me."

CHAPTER 19
THE BATTLE OF FORT WASHINGTON

I'M NOT sure how much of her story Ms. Marrillion plans to tell me. Earlier, she had said I was safer if I didn't know why people were trying to kill her. Maybe she had just started talking about the past because this place reminded her of where she grew up.

"We were just standing there," she continues. "Carol and I, in an alley in a strange town in the middle of the night. Two girls who had only known the lives of orphans. 'Do you live somewhere?' she asked me, and I knew what she meant. 'No,' I told her. 'Just an orphanage.' I did live *somewhere*, obviously, but she wanted to know if I had a home, or if I was like her. 'Me too,' she said.

"Then a man came running up to us. He was sweaty and unshaven and he smelled like bourbon. One of the groundskeepers at the orphanage drank, so I recognized the smell right away. 'Come on, girls. Come inside with me.' Now, you know, even back then it was dangerous to follow strangers. Still, it seemed safer than standing out in the alley, and there were two of us to look out for each other, so we walked behind him as he opened the back door of the VFW and went in."

"What's a VFW?" I ask. "You mentioned it earlier, and I didn't know."

"Oh dear. You've never seen one, have you? VFW stands for Veterans of Foreign Wars. When I was younger, every town had one, a sort of clubhouse where veterans could go to be with other men like them. This was back before we understood what PTSD was. You've heard of that, right?"

"Yeah, Post-Traumatic Stress Disorder. There's a lot of movies about guys who come back from the war with it."

"In my childhood, it was called 'shell shock,' but it was really the same thing. It helped these men to talk to other men who'd been through what they went through. Fighting in the trenches, landing at Normandy, liberating the concentration camps ... they went through a lot. Anyway, it was a meeting hall of sorts. We don't really have things like them in New York, at least not as prominently. In small towns, it's a sort of meeting place with a bar in it. These gentlemen were using it as a neutral ground."

Ms. Marrillion stops talking for a moment.

"Sorry I interrupted," I say.

"Not a problem at all! Where was I?"

"You and Carol were walking into the VFW."

"Ah, yes. We were right behind the drunk man. When we got through the hallway into the main space, we saw five long tables set up with folding chairs, as if somebody were going to host a bingo night. Instead of letting us sit down, though, the man hustled us to a wall on one side of the room. 'Stand here, girls,' he said. 'Don't say nothing. Just watch and listen.'"

"Did you have any idea what it was all about?"

"None whatsoever. I think a small part of me wanted to believe that this was some strange way of getting adopted. Usually the prospective parents came to the orphanage during the day to visit with the children, but maybe sometimes they had to do it more privately at night, I thought, and Carol and I had been selected for something like that. It's silly, I know. Still, strange things go through your head and you do your best to imagine a happy ending, even when it's not likely."

"I'm hoping our little adventure has a happy ending, Ms. Marrillion."

"Me, too," she says.

One of the people who works at the Cloisters comes into the courtyard where we are and says they're closing in 15 minutes, so we should make our way to the exits.

"This was a pleasant rest, Lee," she says. "I'm afraid I was more run down than I let on. Do you think your mother has arrived at D'Argyle's apartment yet?"

"I doubt it. One of them would text or call. It's probably not safe to go back there, though, is it?"

"I'm afraid not. Since those men saw us in the building, they'll know we had a friend inside and probably keep a watch on the place. Hopefully, they won't be able to link us to D'Argyle and he'll be safe."

"So, where should we go next?"

"We could try my friend's place again," she says. "I'm a little scared to call her in advance. I think it might be useful to have some friends who they can't trace back to me through scouring my phone calls, at least not right away."

"Do you think we can risk a subway ride? We could catch the A at Dyckman Street, then take it downtown somewhere."

"I think we should be fine doing that. While we walk down the hill, we can figure out our next destination."

When we make our way through the stone walls of the Cloisters to the exit, we are up at the top of a big hill, where the museum is, so we have to take the winding trail down to street level. There's also a set of stone stairs, but they're pretty steep and I doubt Ms. Marrillion could get down them without trouble.

"Lee, do you know about Margaret Corbin?" she asks me.

"No, not really."

"This road is named after her," she says, pointing to the section of pavement that loops around the museum and heads back towards 190th Street.

"Is she some rich woman who used to live here?"

"No. She fought in the Revolutionary War."

"Hold up! They had women fighting back then?"

"Not really. She was special. She was a nurse. Her husband was manning a cannon here. They were both part of a small contingent left behind when George Washington retreated north to White Plains. The British conquered White Plains and then attacked the garrison here."

"They beat George Washington?"

"Several times. We barely won the war and became a country. But that's a story for another time. Anyway, during the fighting at Fort Washington, Margaret's husband was killed, and she took over firing his cannon, fighting off the Germans who were working with the British until she, too, was wounded. Can you imagine?"

"She was a warrior."

"Yes, indeed."

"These people coming after you must not know women can fight just like men."

"Perhaps not," she says. "But it's worth remembering that we lost the Battle of Fort Washington. Margaret Corbin was a hero, but they were outnumbered and outgunned."

"Did she survive?"

"Yes. The fort surrendered, and the British released her because she was wounded. She later received a pension like the other soldiers and moved up the Hudson River to a more peaceful place."

"We're not going to surrender, though, are we?"

"I sure don't intend to, Lee," she says. Then she reaches into her bag and hands me the knife I had been carrying earlier. "And just like John Paul Jones, I have not yet begun to fight."

CHAPTER 20

DOWN IN THE PARK

I TUCK the knife back inside my pocket, and we walk down the hill, the trail winding through the park. Somehow it feels safer here because there's no grid. I imagine the people chasing after us trying to search the park effectively, and I know it would be difficult for them.

Out in the streets, it would be easy to divide up the space they want to search. *You check the even numbered streets,* I can hear their boss saying. *Tony will check the odd ones. I'll head up and down Broadway.*

It would be a pretty good plan, especially because there aren't many places we can go to get off the streets. We can go into a store or restaurant, but it's not hard for someone to stick their head in the door and do a quick scan. They'd find us. Or if we have the keys, we could go inside buildings, but we only have keys to the places we live. They'd know to look for us there. We could use the trick that package thieves use: hitting a bunch of buzzers from the sidewalk and assuming someone will let us into the building.

But then we'd be stuck inside an unfamiliar building, possibly with only one or two ways out. We've been lucky so far that we only had to get out of our own building and D'Argyle's, which I know pretty well. If we had to escape from a strange apartment complex, we might end up heading the wrong way, finding ourselves at a dead end, cornered by the people coming after us.

The park feels a little safer. If we had camping gear, we'd be even better off. We might be able to spend a few nights in Inwood Hill Park, in a tent somewhere. I don't know if Ms. Marrillion could take roughing it like that, though. So we'd need a sleeping bag and some sort of mattress for her. I guess we'd be pretty exposed at night, but what are the odds somebody would stumble across us?

It's something to think about for later, although, like I said, we don't have the gear for it now. And it's not an option here at Fort Tryon Park, which is all rocky cliffs, trails, and trees. There isn't really anywhere to hide out and spend the night where you wouldn't be seen and easily disturbed.

Still, in a jam, we could jump off the trail here, and try to hide in the brush and small trees. If I was on the run by myself, I might just stay here for a while, knowing I'd be hard to find. That's not an option for Ms. Marrillion, though. We need to get back to the city and find somewhere inside to spend the night.

We are quiet as we walk. Partly so we can keep our ears open, but also I think we're both trying to figure out our next move. As we get down to the bottom of the hill, near the playground where Broadway runs into Riverside Drive, we come across a couple making out on a rock on the side of the trail.

To be honest, I think they're doing *a lot more* than making out. There are some hands inside of clothes and stuff. We politely avert our eyes as we pass. That sort of thing happens in the city sometimes. In this neighborhood, a lot of us still share bedrooms with siblings or other relatives, or sleep on fold-out couches in the living room. I'm an only child, so I won't have to worry about that. I have the bedroom in our apartment, and mom sleeps on the sofa. But she's at work all day, so if I had someone I wanted to be alone with, I could bring them to my apartment.

Anyway, most kids my age are always looking for places where they can be alone with each other. I know some kids at my school who started hooking up with people just because they had their own rooms, and for no other reason.

This makes me think of something.

"Ms. Marrillion, do you have much cash left?"

"I have a fair amount, Lee. And I could get more from an ATM, I think. It should be safe as long as we don't hang around too long afterward. Unless they've frozen my accounts. But I doubt they'd be able to do that so quickly. It's one thing for someone at an agency to monitor my spending and get alerts, but it takes specific warrants to lock things up so that I can't access my money. What do you have in mind?"

"Uh, it might be a little weird, but I was trying to think where we could stay tonight. There's supposedly this cheap hotel over at the end of 181st Street, near the Harlem River."

"I wonder if we'd be safe. Most hotels require you to give them a credit card in advance, and then someone could track us down."

"That's just it, Ms. Marrillion. This place isn't like that. I know because some kids at my school go there for, uh, you know, private time. When they want to … party."

"Ah! I know what you mean. The kind of place that charges by the hour, perhaps?"

"I don't know about that. But I know that they let you pay in cash and you don't need a credit card or ID showing you're 18, which is one of the reasons people my age go there."

"Hmm. If it's anything like I imagine, it's probably pretty dingy."

"No doubt. But I bet we'd be safe there, and we'd be able to get a good night's sleep. I don't know if we can keep running like this, without rest. My mom always says I shouldn't stay up late studying too hard before a test because my brain can't function properly if I don't get my eight hours of sleep."

"She's right about that. I suppose we can go check it out, at least. I *would* rest easier knowing I'm not putting anyone else at risk by staying in their home." She chuckles to herself. "If it's the kind of place I think it is, we may raise a few eyebrows showing up together."

I laugh, too. "We don't want to make an impression, though. If we walk by and it looks suitable, maybe I should get the room myself, so the clerk won't remember the two of us together."

"I think that's a good plan. I'm not sure about walking down to 181st Street on Broadway, though. I don't think I have it in me to run if someone sees us."

We're at Dyckman, which is essentially 200th Street, so we need to go 19 blocks south, still, and pretty far to the east, without running into any of the thugs coming after us.

Luckily, I know a way to get there without being seen.

CHAPTER 21
EYES ON THE STREET

IT DOESN'T MAKE sense to risk the subway for two stops to 181st Street, because then we would still have to walk across seven avenues to get to the hotel.

"If we walk a few blocks down Dyckman Street, we'll come to Harlem River Drive," I say. "I bet they're not looking for us there."

"You're probably right, Lee."

Harlem River Drive isn't like a city street, it's more of a highway. There are no buildings or businesses along it, and cars can't just pull over and stop the way they can in most of Manhattan. While the guys looking for Ms. Marrillion might have cars cruising around Washington Heights, it would be almost impossible for them to do that on a road where everybody's driving 60 miles an hour.

There are still pawn shops and dollar stores most of the way we're walking. My mom would say this portion of Dyckman Street hasn't gentrified yet. I'm not sure why that's a good thing, but she says it's better than having fancy coffee shops and juice bars.

This is still a part of town where people hang out on the street, which makes it easier to blend in. I mention this to Ms. Marrillion.

"Have you heard of Jane Jacobs, Lee?"

"No, did she also fight in the Revolutionary War?"

"Not quite. She is a bit more recent."

"You know a lot of old ladies, though."

"I suppose I do," she laughs. "Mind you, I didn't actually *know* Jane Jacobs or Margaret Corbin. I'm not *that* old."

"What was this Jacobs lady's deal?"

"She tried to prevent Robert Moses from ruining the city. Up until the 1960s, he was tearing down buildings and running highways through poor neighborhoods where people of color lived. He destroyed the Bronx, but she managed to keep him out of Washington Square Park."

"You and my mom should get together and talk about cities sometime. She has a lot of opinions."

"We have had a few good conversations on the back patio. Anyway, Jane Jacobs wrote a book called *The Death and Life of Great American Cities* where she explained all her theories about what made New York such a wonderful place to live. One of her theories was that close-knit communities have a lot of 'eyes on the street' where locals are paying attention and keeping things in order."

"You're saying we need to watch out for eyes on the street?"

"Not in this case, Lee. She meant it in a good way. The guy in the bodega, the bartender, the mom with her head out the window ... all these people kept a watch over the street to prevent trouble and crime. Old white men like Robert Moses saw kids playing in the streets and assumed they were running wild, that the city was some sort of urban blight that needed to be reigned in. Jane said that wasn't the case, it was just a matter of understanding how different people in the city helped each other out."

She stops for a moment and looked around Dyckman.

"All these people out here, they make me feel safe. If a big black car pulled up and men tried to grab us, you can bet they'd start screaming, start recording it on their phones."

"I see what you mean. The guy at the bar on Broadway helped

me when the man from the elevator came after me. And those kids playing basketball up at Cabrini were worried you might be the missing old lady."

"Yes, exactly. I suspect kids get into more trouble in the suburbs where they can be alone than they do in the city where there's hundreds of parents on every block."

We walk under the 1 Train near the bike path to Ft. George Hill and then we're on the northern edge of Highbridge Park, where there are all kinds of trees and big rocks sticking up out of the ground.

"See, now, before Jane Jacobs, people would have said this was a good street. There's nature here, a park for us poor city folk to get some fresh air."

Then she points across the street to one of the big Dyckman Houses buildings, a 14-story brick wall with little windows running up the side.

"That's the kind of thing they built back then, before Jane Jacobs. It was supposed to be a magical garden city, but it never worked. For instance, that's the back of the building, and there's no usable space on the ground, just a small strip of grass that's fenced off. So nobody's out here and the street is empty, lifeless. If one of the men trying to kill me caught up with us here, we'd be in trouble."

"I never thought about it much, but I rarely come over here."

"That's your subconscious mind. Notice we're walking faster? It's not just because people are chasing us. It's because we don't feel safe on a street like this."

We round the bend and finally reach Harlem River Drive.

After everything she's told me, though, I'm not so sure about my idea to walk along here.

"Do you think this will be safe, Ms. Marrillion? There's no 'eyes on the street' down this way."

"Well, like you said before, Lee, they probably won't be searching for us here, but we'll keep our knives handy, just in case."

"It kind of feels like we're headed out into the Wild West."

"I hope you're not going to ask me if I was friends with Calamity Jane or Annie Oakley!"

I'm not, but only because I don't know who either of those people are.

"I used to be a pretty good swimmer, Lee. So if worse comes to worst, and we have to make a break for it, you can just toss me over that barrier into the river and I'll take my chances."

I really hope she's messing with me, because I'm pretty sure that the water is toxic.

CHAPTER 22
THE OTHER KIND OF FEAR

WE WALK DOWN the pathway along the Harlem River Drive. It's not really a sidewalk, it's more like a hiking or bike trail in the grass, which is good because you wouldn't want to accidentally step onto the highway where cars are speeding by.

"This used to be called the Harlem River Speedway," Ms. Marrillion says. "Originally, it was built for horses. People used to come watch races here. That was in the 1800s."

"Whoa, that's straight-up old."

"Yes. And before you ask, I wasn't around then!"

"I know you're not *that* old," I laugh. "But how come you know so much about the past?"

"I've always been interested in history. When I retired, I had a lot of free time and started researching the neighborhood. You know, a lot of older people get into ancestry and studying their family tree. Since I grew up in an orphanage, that wasn't really an option, and I spent my time learning about Washington Heights instead."

"That night you were telling me about earlier, when they drove you to that small town. Is that when you left the orphanage?"

"No, it wasn't. I was hoping it might be, but deep down, I

knew that wasn't the case. It was too strange and scary to be any sort of adoption. Carol and I were standing there along the wall, and then other people came in. I didn't know who any of them were at the time, just older men in suits and overcoats. Every group that entered had two younger men who came to stand alongside us on the wall while the rest of them sat at tables.

"People were kind of whispering to each other. The drunk man who had brought us in was sitting at a table with some men who looked like priests. They weren't dressed that way, or wearing collars, but I'd been around enough of them at that point to recognize fathers when I saw them."

"You must have been scared."

"I was, but in a weird way. Not like today. There's the kind of fear when you're startled or you see someone in the shadows, like this afternoon. You feel it in your heart, which starts racing. Then there's a fear that's closer to long-term dread, where things are happening in slow motion and your brain is more afraid than your body. This was the second kind."

This talk of fear reminds me to look behind us to make sure nobody is following us on the trail. Thankfully, it's empty all the way back to Dyckman.

"Eventually we could tell something was wrong," Ms. Marrillion says. "Carol took my hand and squeezed it and we just stood there watching. We knew we weren't supposed to talk, that's what the drunk man had said. But what if one of the other men asked us a question?"

"I know what that's like," I said. "Sometimes in school they yell at us and tell us all to be quiet at an assembly. Then a guest comes on and asks a question and nobody answers because the principal told us not to say nothing. The principal has to tell us we won't get in trouble for answering."

"Yes, it's confusing sometimes. Especially when you're young. It's like grown-ups have all these secret rules and traditions that nobody's told you about. So Carol and I were just standing there, and we could tell everyone was talking about us. The men at the tables would turn their heads, look at us, and then turn back to each other and whisper.

"Eventually, a large man from the table near the door got up and walked over to the table where the drunk man was sitting. There was some sort of disagreement and the large man was clearly angry, gesturing and making faces and pointing towards us. The drunk man refused to budge, though. Whatever they were arguing about, eventually a man from every table got up and joined them, so there were four men arguing about us two orphan girls.

"I didn't cry, though. That was one thing I had learned growing up. The nuns said parents didn't want a child who cried, so I forced myself never to shed a tear. I thought that would help me find a home one day. I lived through a lot of bad stuff in those days, but I never cried about any of it.

"Looking back, I don't think that was terribly healthy."

"Yeah," I say. "It's good to cry sometimes, even if it's just at a movie or something. You don't want to do it too much, though, or you get a reputation. I try not to cry at school."

"That's how I felt. I didn't know *where* I was, Lee, but for some reason I knew I had to be strong, or at least pretend that I was strong. So I just stood there, willing myself not to cry. Eventually, the drunk guy seemed to win the argument, whatever it was about. In retrospect, I think they were arguing about whether to let us stay. They didn't think we belonged there on that wall with the other men."

"Because you were just girls?"

"I assume so. But the drunk guy carried the day, and although everyone else was angry, they didn't kick us out."

She stops for a moment and turns to me.

"You know something, Lee? I spent the rest of my life wishing they had."

"I'm sorry, Ms. Marrillion," I say. "Did something very bad happen to you?"

"Nothing like that," she smiles slightly. "But if we hadn't

stayed, Carol would still be alive, and I would be in my apartment, relaxing with a nice mystery novel."

"Instead of being on the run with me."

"I'm glad *you're* here, Lee. It's the people coming after me that I could do without."

Just after she says this, we hear a screeching sound as a car stops suddenly on the northbound side of the road.

CHAPTER 23

ONE FALSE MOVE

IT'S another big black SUV, about 20 or 30 feet back where we came from. There's two lanes of traffic behind it, and all those cars start honking and swerving to avoid crashing.

The SUV door opens, although there's barely enough room because of the big concrete barrier between the northbound and southbound lanes.

"Keep walking, Lee," Ms. Marrillion says. "I doubt this is a helpful friend."

I'm walking but also looking back. I wrap my hand around the knife in my pocket.

The guy is finally able to squeeze out of the SUV, and I see that he's got a gun.

"Get behind a tree, Ms. Marillion," I shout, pointing towards the woods.

Most of the trees around here are small and newly planted, but there are a few older ones that should be able to stop a bullet.

At least I hope so.

The man lifts his gun toward us, but passing cars in the south-bound lane keep getting between us, so he doesn't have a shot.

I turn around to check on Ms. Marrillion and see she's making her way into the bit of forest beside the trail. For some reason, I find myself thinking, *I hope she doesn't get poison ivy*. It's crazy what goes through your head in moments like these.

When I look back, the guy has hopped over the concrete barrier. He looks to his right and holds up his gun. A white car in the fast lane of southbound traffic brakes hard and almost hits him, but stops just in time.

The guy, a big bald dude wearing a suit, yells angrily at the car as if it's their fault they almost hit him, even though he's standing in the middle of a highway.

He turns back towards us, and I hope Ms. Marrillion is behind a tree now.

He points his gun towards me and looks like he's about to shoot as he walks in my direction. Then I hear a loud horn blaring, and he looks back to his right for a split second.

It's too late.

An old station wagon, speeding south, is swerving to the right of the stopped white car, and it plows into the man.

I think I hear a gunshot, but so much is happening so fast that I'm not sure. His legs are clipped by the front of the car, and for a moment he's on the hood, but then he's flipping over the roof, and he lands with a sickening splat on the pavement.

Another southbound car doesn't stop or swerve in time, and crashes into the stopped white car, which lurches forward and rolls over the man's body.

For a second, I consider running into the roadway to try to find his gun, but I decide it's too risky. There's now a bunch of vehicles that have crashed or stopped and people are getting out of their cars.

"Let's just go," I call to Ms. Marrillion and start walking along the trail again.

She makes her way back from the woods onto the path and we don't turn around or look back.

"I hate to leave the scene of an accident," she says, "but we weren't really involved, at least not directly."

"Yeah," I say, trying to smile, "that guy with the gun could have stopped his car for some other reason besides us."

"Did he have a gun?"

"He did. That was almost the end of our adventure."

"Luckily for us, New York is not a very pedestrian friendly city."

We're trying to make jokes to hide our fear. I'm breathing fast and I can feel my heartbeat. If I'm this worked up, I wonder if she's alright. Can old women have heart attacks? I feel like I usually only hear about men having them.

"Are you okay, Ms. Marrillion? Did you get scraped up or anything?"

"I feel like I just drank three cups of coffee, Lee. But other than that, I think I'm fine. Did you have a plan if he hadn't gotten hit by a car?"

"Not really."

"Promise me that if we're ever in a sticky spot like that, and there's no way out, you'll let them get me. Don't risk your life for me if it's hopeless."

"I promise."

"But do you truly mean it, Lee? Otherwise, I may have to try to sneak away and face this on my own. I can't bear thinking you could get hurt at your age."

"I swear, Ms. Marrillion."

And I mean it, really, I do. It's just that, in the heat of things, I'm not sure I'll remember. Sometimes I just act without thinking.

"It's a lot to ask, I know. I don't *want* to give up. But... I have lived my whole life. So had Carol. You haven't yet."

I don't say it, but I think, maybe this *is* my life. It certainly feels more important than trying to get into college or anything else.

I feel my phone vibrate in my pocket.

It's a text from D'Argyle.

Back in building. Will let u know when ur mom shows up.

I'm about to write him back, but then I start to get worried about whether someone can trace us back here. Maybe I shouldn't send a text message from so close to the accident. Or maybe it's already too late since I've read the message from D'Argyle. Is there a record of that?

Based on the TV shows I've seen, it's hard to locate somebody's phone to an exact address, since they have to do something called triangulation. I decide I'll wait to reply to D'Argyle just so there's less data for them to track us with. I also check to make sure my location settings are all turned off. Then I put the phone in airplane mode.

The road immediately to our left is empty, and then the northbound lanes beyond are starting to back up with traffic. We can hear sirens in the distance.

The path we're on starts to diverge from the roadway, up a ramp that takes us towards one of the big bridges across the Harlem River.

"Are you alright to keep walking?"

"I'm fine," Ms. Marrillion says. "I'll feel better when we're far away from that accident."

I will too.

I'm pretty sure that guy must be dead.

I knew we were in a dangerous situation, but it all feels so real now.

A single mistake and you're gone.

CHAPTER 24
WATCHING FROM THE WOODS

IT TAKES a while to get up the staircase from the Harlem River Drive to where 181st Street hits the Washington Bridge. It's confusing, because there's a *George Washington* Bridge just across Manhattan over the Hudson, and then here on the east side there's the plain old Washington Bridge with no *George* in its name.

I bet Ms. Marrillion knows the reason, but she seems really tired after the first set of steps, so I don't want to make her talk. Instead, we sit down on some benches.

The path doesn't connect directly to 181st Street here, and we'll have to loop through the park a bit to the Grand Staircase at 184th, then down Laurel Hill Terrace. It's a lot of extra walking and I should have thought about how tired Ms. Marrillion would get.

On the bright side, I can't imagine anyone is looking for us here in the woods, so we can relax for a little bit.

I've been on the run pretty much the whole day. At least Ms. Marrillion got some rest at D'Argyle's when I went out to get her pills. Little kids and old people need naps all the time. I guess one day I'll be old enough that I need to rest more, but for now, I can keep kicking it.

We can't afford to get sloppy, though. Based on how fast

everything happened, I'm assuming that guy on the Harlem River Drive didn't call anyone to tell them that he saw us. He just stopped his car and jumped out.

Eventually, someone will realize he was killed and then they might start looking for us around here. I hope that they'll think we were in a car going the opposite direction rather than figuring out we were on foot. It doesn't make that much sense — how could a guy see someone in the opposite lane and get out of his car in time to try to catch them? But so far, the people coming after us don't seem too smart, so maybe we'll be lucky.

The fact that another guy had a gun changes the whole equation, though. Before, I figured we would see anyone coming for us and that would give us a few seconds to act. If they've all got guns, though, they could shoot Ms. Marrillion before we even know what's happening.

"We'll probably need to get you a better disguise," I say. "Enough of them have seen you in that DEEZ hoodie that they might be looking for you in it."

"It's a shame that all my clothes are in my apartment."

"True. But we probably don't want you looking too much like you anyway. After we get checked into the hotel, I can go to some cheap stores along 181st and get you some more outfits."

"Maybe that Target they just opened would be a good option."

I think she probably wants *normal* clothes and not the tricked out neighborhood clothes I was going to dress her in.

"I'll get you a few different options," I say.

In the movies, guys like Jason Bourne are always dying their hair in a bus station bathroom, but I don't know how much good that will do us. I think we'll stick with hats for the time being. Maybe a big bandana.

"I think I'm ready to walk a bit more," she says, standing up.

So we take the trail around towards the Grand Staircase.

"I rarely come over here, since we have so many parks closer to our building," she says. "It's lovely, though."

It's weird how you can live somewhere so long and only really know a few blocks in any direction.

"When you were growing up, in the orphanage, were you in the city like this?"

"No," she says. "We were a bit outside of a small town, but we might as well have been in the middle of nowhere. Nobody could drive, not us kids, of course, but very few of the nuns either. Maybe once a year, they would rent a bus and take us on a trip somewhere, to the movies if we were lucky. For the most part, though, everyone and everything had to come to us. Most of the vehicles we saw belonged to delivery men. Milk, food, things like that. Then once a month, some families would come in cars to see us children.

"We'd hear stories, from the older girls, about times they snuck out at night and tried to walk into town. It was too far, and no one had ever made it that we knew about. There was a motel and a nightclub maybe a half hour away. The troublesome girls would go watch those places from the woods nearby. It was too dangerous to try to go in, because if the nightclub knew they were from the orphanage, they'd get in so much trouble. And none of us had the kinds of clothes that could pass for women going to a nightclub. Just our uniforms, our white shirts and our skirts."

"You probably didn't miss much," I say. "I think nightclubs are too loud." They're probably pretty fun, I actually think, but I don't want her to feel bad that she didn't get to go to them as a kid. "Anyway, I'll get you some nightclub clothes when I go shopping, so you'll be all set to go out next time."

She laughs.

"Oh, Lee, I think my dancing days are behind me."

"You don't have to dance at the club, you can just stand along the wall."

"That's no fun! I'd want to get out on the floor and *shake* it!"

I can't imagine what she would look like dancing, and just trying to picture it cracks me up.

Now we're on Laurel Hill Terrace, which curves around towards Amsterdam and 181st. We're almost at the hotel.

"Remember, if it looks too shady when we walk by, we don't have to stay there," I say.

"I'm sure I've stayed in worse places," she says.

I don't believe her, but I'm not going to argue.

CHAPTER 25
I NEED PROTECTION

WE WALK by the place and decide it looks decent.

I should add that we're both really tired at this point, so we might not be holding it to our usual standards. Still, it seems like we'll be safe and there's no way for anyone to connect this place to our friends or family, so we should be able to get a good night's sleep.

Ms. Marrillion gives me $200, which might be the most cash I've ever held in my life.

"Sometimes places like this will give you a discount if you pay in cash," she says.

"How do you know that?"

"Oh, I've just heard it from some friends who have stayed in these types of establishments. I myself would never."

I can't tell if she's joking or if she *has* stayed in these kinds of places. I guess she was young once, too.

"I should have a fake name, right? So they don't list my real name anywhere?"

"Ahh, this is the fun part. Since you're going in, you should get to choose your alias. Although we should try not to make it anything too memorable. We want to be forgotten."

"What about Sam Doe?"

"That might be *too* average, but you're on the right path."

"How about Alex something?"

"Alex could be good."

I decide to use Jay-Z's last name.

"Alex Carter?"

"That sounds perfectly forgettable," she says. "Which is what we want."

I say it a few times to myself so I won't forget.

"Alex Carter. Alex Carter. *I'm* Alex Carter."

"To be honest, they probably get a lot of people using fake names and won't be too suspicious."

"I guess you're right, Ms. Marrillion."

I walk inside and approach the desk.

It's weird because this is one of those things everybody seems to do in movies or television, but I realize I've never checked into a hotel before. I've only ever stayed at hotels a few times. Usually when we go somewhere, we stay with a family member or one of my mom's friends, I guess to save money. It's rare when we go to a place where we don't know anybody and mom can't find a room to rent from Airbnb or something like that. But the few times we *did* stay at hotels, mom was always the one to check in, since the room would be under her name and on her credit card.

I wonder if this is what growing up is like: a series of small events rather than some big moment. Later, I can ask Ms. Marrillion if she just suddenly felt like an adult one day or if it was a bunch of little things that added up over time.

Anyway, I get to the desk and have to get the clerk's attention. He is staring at something on his phone.

"I'd like a room, please." I try to sound as old as possible.

"For the whole night?"

"Yeah."

"One bed or two?"

"Two, definitely."

"Seventy-nine bucks. You have a credit card for incidentals?"

"I was hoping I could just pay in cash."

"Then I have to charge you $160, which includes a security deposit you can get back when you check out."

"That sounds good."

He hands me a clipboard.

"Fill out this form," he says. "It asks for I.D., but you can just leave that blank."

I write down my fake name, Alex Carter, and it asks for my address, so I put my school's, since that's the only other one I can think of off the top of my head. There's a section where I have to agree not to smoke in the room. That shouldn't be a problem unless somebody comes after us with a flamethrower or something like that.

After I complete the form, I hand it back to the clerk.

"You don't have any bags, do you?"

"Uh, not right now. I'm going shopping a little later."

"That's fine. So it's just $160."

I carefully count out the money and hand it over.

"You'll be in Room 307. Do you need an extra key?"

"Yeah," I say. "Two keys please."

He slides two key cards across the counter but keeps his hand on them. He looks at the form I filled out.

"One more thing, Alex. Be careful. Be safe. You know what I mean?"

"I'm trying to be safe," I say, and I mean it.

"Do you have protection?"

I reach down and feel the knife in my pocket.

"I have a little."

"We have these if you need them," he says. From behind the counter, he lifts up a bowl full of condoms. They say NYC on the wrapper and it looks like they have the MTA logo on them or something. "They're not the best, but they work."

I know I won't need them, but it seems like it will set his mind at ease if I take a few, so I put two in my pocket and thank him.

"Have fun," he says, and lets go of the key cards, then goes back to looking at his phone.

I grab the keys and take the elevator up to the third floor. It's kind of dirty in this place. Not filthy, but it just looks like it hasn't been cleaned for a while. There's some ceiling tiles missing, and I can see exposed wires and pipes up there.

I find 307 and use the key to get in.

I'm not sure what I expected, but it's just an average hotel room. I guess I thought it would have neon lights or red silk sheets or something, but it doesn't.

After a quick look around, I close the door behind me and make sure it locks, then take the elevator back down to the lobby.

As it descends, I realize there's probably a camera in it, and there might have been one in the lobby. I don't *think* anyone will think to look for us here, but I'm scared about leaving a trail of evidence.

When the elevator drops me off in the lobby, the clerk doesn't even look up as I exit again so quickly, and I find Ms. Marrillion on the street.

"It seems fine," I say, and hand her the second key card. "But I think we may need to do a quick costume change before you go in, because they have security cameras."

She points to a small beauty salon across the street that has all kinds of extensions hanging in the window.

"I've always wondered what I'd look like with braids," she says.

CHAPTER 26
DON'T SAY THE NAME

PRETTY SOON, Ms. Marrillion is unrecognizable again. She's got hair extensions tied into her hair, which are also held in place by a bandana wrapped across the front of her head.

There used to be a Goodwill right here, across from the hotel, but it closed a while back. So we walk a little bit west on 181st until we come to some clothing stores to get her something to replace the DEEZ hoodie she's been wearing since this afternoon. I get a change of wardrobe too, although nothing that I'll want to wear later. It's a disguise, after all. It feels like a shame that we'll probably have to throw these clothes away when this is all done, but we can't go around looking like ourselves, can we?

While we're away from the hotel, I text D'Argyle.

> My mom show up yet?

> Nah, but I'm keepin a eye out. Where should I tell her u went?

I think about this for a moment or two. I don't want to give away our hideout over text, just in case somebody is reading these messages. I'm still not sure I believe they could tap into my phone this quickly, but if somebody found D'Argyle and took his phone, they could read the texts and find Ms. Marrillion and me.

> I'm at the place Teri didnt want to go to w/ Jerah

>> ???

> I don't want to say the name. Remember Teri told Jerah HELL NO IM NOT GOIN THERE

>> Ha ha ha! Oh yeah I remember. Teri was NOT havin it.

> I think we'll be safe here

>> IDK that place is ratchet. Watch out for bed bugs yo

I don't want to think about that.

> Anyway don't put the name of the place in text and delete this exchange pls

>> Deleted. This is some real mission impossible sh*t

> Yeah

>> Stay safe Lee

> Ill try. Gonna turn off my phone for safety but u can tell my mom I'll check it regularly

I put my phone back in airplane mode, and then Ms. Marrillion and I head back to the hotel. She goes in first, and I follow her a few minutes later. The desk clerk hardly looks up at me. I think he's just there to make sure nobody is carrying a machete or bleeding or anything like that. Otherwise, they let any kind of crazy characters come in and go out all day and night. Mostly night, I bet.

I knock on the door of the room, just so I don't scare Ms. Marrillion.

"Who is it?"

"Lee."

"Don't you have a key?"

"Yes, I just didn't want you to freak out if the door started opening."

"That's alright, I was expecting you."

I unlock the door and go inside.

Because there's only a key card, the main lock is automatic. It's a little strange, since I'm used to flipping a bolt behind me. There's a second lock that takes me a while to figure out—it's a sort of metal clasp on the wall. If I turn it a certain way, the door can't open more than an inch or so. I guess it's like a chain lock, but stronger and harder to open from outside.

"I think if someone kicked really hard, they might be able to knock the door in," I say.

"Yes, it's a bit flimsy. Not like the doors in our building," she says.

"It would give us a minute or two, anyway."

"We could try to escape out the balcony, but I'm afraid we couldn't get much farther than that."

I walk over and look out. There's a tiny sliver of balcony off of our room, but the building has a strange sort of criss-cross shape on the front, so there isn't one immediately below or above us. Those floors have their balconies on the other half of the building. This means I couldn't climb down to the second floor or up to the fourth floor. My only option would be to drop straight down to the sidewalk, which would probably break a leg or kill me. And certainly Ms. Marrillion wouldn't survive.

I guess if we really got in trouble, we could shout from the balcony and try to get people on the street to help us. Maybe we could push the mattresses out onto the sidewalk and jump down? But even that seems pretty dangerous. Especially with the sad old mattresses they have in this hotel. I guess we'll just have to hope nobody finds out that we're here.

Then the phone on the nightstand starts ringing.

CHAPTER 27
BAD NEWS

"MAYBE WE SHOULDN'T ANSWER IT," I say.

Ms. Marrillion shrugs.

I decide to pick it up. Mostly because the sound is annoying and I want it to stop.

"Hello?"

"Is this Alex?"

I'm confused for a second, then remember that was the fake name I registered under.

"Uh, yeah. Alex Carter."

"This is Koto, down at the front desk." He is speaking quietly. "I don't know if I should be doing this, but I saw you on the news and figured you should know people are looking for you."

"Uh, thanks."

"Don't worry, I'm not going to call anyone. You're safe here for now. Although if the police show up, I'm not supposed to stop them, according to my boss."

"I understand."

"But listen. If I call and tell you we have clean towels down in the lobby, that means someone's coming and you should go."

"'Clean towels.' Got it. Thank you."

"The fire stairs on the east side of the building lead down to the street. They set off an internal alarm at my desk, but no loud sirens or anything."

"Thanks, Koto."

"No problem. To be honest, I've dealt with a lot worse. Amber alerts and stuff. This is a breath of fresh air."

He hangs up.

I grab the remote control from the nightstand and turn on the TV.

"The guy at the desk says we're on the news."

I put the TV on mute and flip through the channels, looking for us.

"I've never been on television before," Ms. Marrillion says. "It's kind of exciting. Although I guess I wish it was under better circumstances."

I don't find us, so I leave it on the local cable news channel, and hope that any coverage of us will cycle through again soon so we can see what we're up against.

"I can't believe you've never been on TV before," I say to Ms. Marrillion.

"Because I'm so old?"

"Well, yeah, I guess so."

"I've never been famous before now."

"Still, you've never been interviewed on the street about, like, a big thunderstorm or a bike lane or something like that?"

"I've been approached by reporters once or twice for a man-on-the-street segment, but I always said no. I didn't want to risk appearing on TV and having someone find me."

"Ah, I forgot that you were in hiding."

"I tried to live as normally as possible for most of my life, but there were a few little things I never did. Even if I wasn't afraid of the people who are after us now, I don't know that I would have been excited to appear on the news talking about some random thing just because I happened to be in the street when a reporter was there. They should be talking to experts, not your average Joe."

"Is there anything you wanted to do your whole life but avoided because of what happened to you as a kid?"

"Not one specific thing. I suppose I might have more actively pursued filmmaking. But while it's comforting to blame the powers that be for the fact that I'm not Agnès Varda or Jane Campion, I think it had more to do with choices I made on my own."

"Who are Agnès and Jane?"

"Two influential women directors. I guess they're from before your time, Lee. You've never heard of *The Piano*, I suppose."

"I've heard of pianos." I mime playing keyboards like Alicia Keys or John Legend.

"If we ever get some free time, when nobody's coming after us, maybe we can have a little miniature film festival and watch some old classics."

"As long as they're not *too* old," I say.

"Don't worry, we can find something modern. Agnès was still making documentaries until she was 90, and Jane Campion made a Western for Netflix."

"They might have some movies on demand here," I say, gesturing at the TV. "We could watch something once we finish looking for ourselves on the news."

"Perhaps if we stay here another night. But I think I'm entirely too sleepy to watch a movie tonight. I may actually lie down for a bit now, if you don't mind."

I forgot that old people go to sleep so early. Plus, we did so much walking today that Ms. Marrillion must be exhausted.

"That's fine," I tell her. "You go to sleep and I'll keep looking for us."

"Wake me up if you see us," she says.

"I will."

She doesn't get under the covers, she just lays back with her head on the pillow. I'm not sure if it's because she thinks the sheets might be a little dirty, or if it's in case we need to get up and go suddenly. Either way, it's probably a good idea.

I sit on the edge of the other bed, scanning the news.

It's strange, because I never really watch TV like this that often. I usually just check out stuff on the internet, so I'm amazed at how boring and repetitive it all is. After about 20 minutes, though, the story about us pops up.

I nudge Ms. Marrillion's foot and she sits up slowly as I un-mute the TV.

"Police say they need your help finding an elderly woman who disappeared from her home earlier today in Washington Heights," says the anchor. Then there's some footage of our building! "After a gunman opened fire inside this pre-war apartment building, one of its residents, Wilhelmina Marrillion, has been reported missing by neighbors."

A blurry old photo of Ms. Marrillion appears on screen.

"I wonder where they got that," she says.

"She may be disoriented and in the company of one or more other people. If you see her, please contact this number." A phone number appears on the screen. I don't write it down, because I'm certainly not going to call it.

"She was last seen ... wearing a sweatshirt that said DEEZ on it." The anchor barely gets through the sentence without laughing. "And now our Accu-Sonar forecast with Ed Tannery."

"I hope they find her," says the weatherman, before pointing at a map and telling us how hot it was today.

I turn off the TV and sigh.

Now everyone who watches the news will be looking for us.

CHAPTER 28
MARKED SAFE

I'M NOT sure when all the stores around here close.

"I better go out and get us some supplies before it gets too late," I say.

"And you should try to check in with your mother."

"Yeah, I'll turn on my phone when I get further away from the hotel. Do you need anything other than more disguise options?"

"Hmm. I suppose some toiletries. Toothbrush, toothpaste, that sort of thing. And I'm getting hungry. Maybe you could pick up some food? And possibly, if you can find it, a six-pack of Ensure Plus in dark chocolate or milk chocolate. Anything other than strawberry. If they don't have Plus, the regular would be the next option."

She reaches into her purse for money.

"I still have $40 left over from the $200 you gave me," I say.

"Well, take this too. Tomorrow we'll have to stop at an ATM."

She gives me another $100.

"You have your key, right? I may go to sleep."

"I think you should lock the door from the inside, just in case. I bet I can call up from the front desk so you know I'm coming."

That reminds me of the towel code. I fill her in so she knows what it means if Koto calls and says there are clean towels.

"I hope we don't have to actually request clean towels," she says. "It could get very confusing!"

"Hey, maybe we should come up with a code, too, for ourselves, in case we get split up and someone's in trouble."

"That could be a good idea. But at a certain point, I may start to forget things. We have the two rendezvous points to remember, and now a code word. It wouldn't be safe to write these things down, though."

"We don't need to figure it out just yet," I say. "I'll try to think of something while I'm out shopping."

"Be safe, Lee."

"You too, Ms. Marrillion."

She gets up and walks over to the door with me so she can lock it after I leave.

The elevator takes me down to the lobby, and I nod at Koto on my way out. Rather than walk straight towards the Target, I go east, and walk around the block and up towards 184th Street. I figure if I check my phone near the college there, Yeshiva University, it might be harder for someone to track, given how many students there are. I don't really know how cell phone towers work, though.

It's not dark yet, but it's a little scarier heading up Amsterdam Avenue than it was on the way here. Maybe that's because I'm alone this time? Or enough people have gone inside for dinner that the sidewalks are a bit less crowded. It's harder to hide and get lost, so someone might be able to see me.

At 184th, I turn my phone back on and it lights up with new messages from D'Argyle and my mom. I open the conversation with my mom first.

> Sweetie, I'm at your friend's. Please check in and let me know you're safe.

I write her back.

Im good, mom. D'Argyle can tell you where we are. I'm going shopping for dinner and things.

THANK GOD.

Then she sends a whole bunch of heart emojis.

Im going to the place u said u love but dont want on our block

???

Remember last week when we were talking to that woman near the mailboxes

Miriam?

Yeah. She mentioned a place and u said you love it but dont want it on our block

Ahhh! I know what you mean. Are you going there now?

yes

I'll meet you there.

can u make sure ur not followed?

I'll be careful.

Part of me wants to choose a place in the store for us to meet, but I'm afraid to do that without giving away our location. And I haven't been there before, so I don't really know where we could meet anyways. I'll just have to hope we can find each other.

see u soon

Love you.

I give her the thumbs up, then check the conversation with D'Argyle.

Ur mom's here

Just texted her. Does she seem mad?

Naw, more like worried I think?

Thanks for helping.

All good but was she gonna bring pizza? I'm starving dawg.

I bet she'll order u something if u ask. That way u can stay there in case we need u

cool

I'll text her and tell her.

So then I have to text my mom again.

Hey mom, can u get D'Argyle some dinner? He thought pizza was coming

Of course. I'm pretty hungry too. I'll order something to his place. What about you? Are you hungry?

Yeah, I was going to get something on the way back for me and my friend

She sends me the wink emoji.

I'll eat with you too if that's alright

Yup. Gonna turn my phone off now just to be
safe. See u at the place

It may not be cool to say, but it's comforting hearing from my mom. I see her every day, but now that I'm in trouble, it just makes me feel good to hear from her. I've been walking around the college campus aimlessly, but now I head down towards that Target on 181st Street.

I hope *I* don't become a target there.

CHAPTER 29
MOVING TARGET

I STILL FEEL a little paranoid and exposed out here. It shouldn't be too dangerous, though. Only Ms. Marrillion's face was on the news, so I don't think anybody is looking for me, except the guy in the tracksuit from the elevator, but if I'm lucky, he's still unconscious and out of the picture.

Growing up in New York, I learned how to keep my head down. Not all the time, just when I don't want trouble. Or even company. Some days you're just not in the mood to talk to people, even your friends, but you might run into them on the street, so you keep your eyes down.

Doing that now would keep people from seeing me. The problem is, it would also keep me from seeing them. I need to be alert. I can't just stare at the pavement and shuffle down to 181st Street.

So I have to look up and around pretty frequently. I think it's what they call being shifty because my attention keeps shifting around. Hopefully, it's not too suspicious.

On each block, I make a note of where I can run in an emergency. Restaurants seem like the safest option—I think they're all required to have back exits because of the possibility of fire in the kitchen. If I run into a store, I may just end up trapped, with no way out.

Cop cars always scare me, even when I'm not hiding or on the run. It's especially bad now. Not just police cruisers, either. Anything that looks like one gets my heart racing. Before now, I never realized how many white cars with writing on them there are in the city.

I think I see one out of the corner of my eye, and start to veer away from the street, then realize it's only a student driver with the name of the driving school printed on the car door.

An ambulance siren freaks me out too, because the flashing lights appear behind me before I recognize it's not the cops.

I'm heading down St. Nicholas Avenue, which is pretty wide. If I had to, I could probably dart across the traffic and hope to get away. During the day, the sidewalks are covered with vendors and clothing racks from some of the stores. It'd be like one of those chase scenes in the movies where I'm knocking down things behind me to make it harder for whoever's running after me. I wouldn't be able to turn over a fruit stand, because those things are heavy. Cars always plow through them easily in films, probably because they're props made out of styrofoam. Hollywood just likes it when fruit splatters everywhere because it looks cool.

At 181st, I turn right and make for the Target.

There's a bunch of people clustered outside it like it's a nightclub. I hope they're just enthusiastic shoppers, not people looking for me.

My mom probably isn't here yet, since she was so much further away when we texted. It will take her a while to get down here from D'Argyle's. That will give me time to shop, so I head for the door.

Until I see a cop right inside, at the base of the escalator, checking everyone's faces against something he's got on his phone.

This stops me cold.

It's probably not my photo, but there's a good chance it's Ms.

Marrillion's. It's possible that there's a description of me. Maybe the cops who pulled us over on Broadway an hour ago figured out who we were later and put out an APB.

Since I've never been inside the Target, I could easily get cornered in there. I mean, I've been in the building, because it used to be the Modell's Sporting Goods. I'm sure they've changed what it's like inside since then, though.

I walk past as quickly as I can.

This street isn't safe.

I have to keep moving.

The problem is, I need to get that stuff for Ms. Marrillion. And though I know it doesn't seem cool or tough, I want to see my mom. She probably wants to see me too.

I cut left on Broadway, trying to get away from the Target for now. I just need to think, but it's dangerous to stay in one place for too long.

In just a few blocks, I come to the back side of the George Washington Bridge Bus Station. It's got some discount clothing stores inside, so I figure I'll get some more disguises for me and Ms. Marrillion, and I think there's also a grocery store in here where I can get food and the milkshakes she needs.

The only thing to be careful of is staying away from where the buses depart. I bet that somebody's watching that area to make sure we don't sneak out of town on a bus. If we did decide to catch a ride out of town, we'd probably choose one of the worker shuttle vans that take restaurant and other low-paid staff in and out of the city to cheaper neighborhoods where they can afford to live. There's a whole network of stuff like that, off-the-radar businesses and things that serve a different community. I bet the people chasing after Ms. Marrillion don't know about them.

I get a bunch of clothing options at the Gap Outlet, making sure there are very different colors, so that if they start looking for an old woman in a red shirt, she can change into a green shirt or something like that.

Next, I head up to Marshall's, where I get a few stupid hats and cheap sunglasses. As soon as I check out, I put on a brown fedora that's way too big for me. I hope the brim covers my face a bit from any cameras overhead.

I'm about to head to the grocery store, but figure I should text my mom first so she doesn't get to Target and freak out if she can't find me.

> Change of plans. That place was too crowded.

> I'm a block away.

> Can u go to the place where they mix fries for us instead?

> Huh?

> They give us regular fries and healthy ones

> Oh yeah. Gotcha. Are you still OK?

> Im good. Headin over there now

> See you soon!

Since there was that cop outside Target, I decided to have her meet me at Burger Heights, but I didn't want to say the name of the place in the text, which is why I only mention the combo fries. They have a thing that's 1/2 regular fries and 1/2 sweet potato fries. I don't really know how much healthier sweet potatoes are compared to the regular kind, but mom says they have Vitamin A.

I'm not sure what age you start worrying about getting your vitamins, but I'm not there yet. My mom sure is, and it seems like Ms. Marrillion is, too. I guess kids don't need vitamins as badly as old folks.

At the grocery store, I get a few granola bars and things like that. Plus, I find the Ensure drinks that Ms. Marrillion wanted. They're kind of heavy, so I don't get anything else after that, just check out and start heading for Burger Heights, over on 182nd and Wadsworth Ave.

A lot of locals hang out right in front of the place, so I figure it may be a safe place to wait for mom and then to wait for food if she'll buy burgers and fries for me and Ms. Marrillion. I'm a little low on cash, so I don't think I can splurge on it myself.

As I'm walking north on Wadsworth, I notice a vehicle creeping up alongside me. It's a big white van, like the kind a small business uses, without any windows on the side. It could just be a coincidence, but I don't want to take chances, so I veer away from the road to the part of the sidewalk that's closest to the doors of the buildings.

That way, they can't just reach out and grab me and pull me inside.

There aren't really any shops open along Wadsworth, though, so there's nowhere for me to go inside and get away from them. At the intersection of 181st Street, I turn right and they turn too. The side door of the van slides open. Once they're fully out of the intersection, though, I suddenly spin around and run back up Wadsworth.

They're stuck. Because of the traffic coming west on 181st, they can't just turn around and come after me. I hear a lot of honking and look back for a second.

A guy in a suit and tie has jumped out of the van and is running after me up the street. I'm carrying all these groceries, so he's moving a lot faster than me. He'll catch up to me by the end of the block.

CHAPTER 30

YOU GET WHAT YOU DESERVE

I HAVE no choice but to keep running. I could drop the bag and I'd be a little faster, but then Ms. Marrillion might not get the things she needs to make it through the night. And if the guys chasing me looked through the bag, they'd know for sure I'm with an old lady, since kids my age don't drink Ensure.

It's uphill towards Burger Heights and I think I'm in better shape than the guy chasing after me.

"Stop that kid!" I hear him yelling behind me.

People on the sidewalk are jumping out of the way.

"Whoa, watch it," one of them says.

I'm pretty sure the guy doesn't have a gun, or at least hasn't taken it out, because nobody is screaming like they would if he was about to start shooting. It only sounds like the people behind me are being inconvenienced, not terrorized.

I can't outrun him forever, though.

The only thing I can think of is that I can lose him in front of the restaurant. If he's not from the neighborhood, he probably doesn't know the area very well.

Because my mom and I go to this restaurant a lot, I know they usually keep the door from their cellar open. It's one of those big metal doors that leads down some steep stairs to the storage area below. They're pretty common in the city.

If it's open, and he doesn't see that, I could jump over it at the last second and hope it will trip him up. Ideally, he'd fall down into the pit, a cement tunnel that would mess him up. But even if he just trips on the metal door, that would slow him down a bit.

So I keep running, pulling closer to the walls of the buildings on the right side of the sidewalk. If someone comes out of a doorway suddenly, I'll be in trouble.

"Hey kid! I just wanna talk," he says, but I don't believe him.

Then I'm approaching the place and the basement hatch is open like I'd hoped. People are standing around in front, waiting for their food, so it's faster running where I am, right alongside the buildings. This means the guy chasing me can't cut to the left, which would take him out of the path of the trap I'm setting.

"Stop him," the guy yells, and I can tell he's getting close to me.

I'm not running my fastest, since the bag is banging against my one leg, and the knife in my other pocket is slowing me down too.

As I get close, the hatch is bigger than I remember. Of course, I've never looked at it like something I'd have to jump over before. The void is about three feet long, and then there's the door, propped up three feet in the air.

"Yo, look out," someone says.

I hit my last step before it and then leap.

The bag bangs against the door a bit, but my legs clear it and I land again on the other side.

"What the f—"

Behind me, I hear the guy's shout turn into a groan at the same time as a loud crashing sound and a kind of sickening noise like a piñata being busted open.

For a split-second I'm not sure if he tripped or fell, but then I hear the other people on the sidewalk react with horror, gasping and swearing, and I know he must have stepped right into the empty gap. At the speed he was going, he must have at least broken his ankle, but it sounds like it was worse.

I can't stop, but I turn around to make sure he's not still running after me, and he's not.

After sprinting another block, I hang a right on 183rd Street and head east.

I'll need to text my mom that I'm not at Burger Heights anymore, but I want to get further away from that guy before I stop. Also, I don't know if his van followed him or maybe turned on Audubon Avenue and is heading north right towards me.

Although it's gross, I hop a fence on the sidewalk into a small protected garbage area. There's a cinder block wall up to my waist, but if I crouch down, I won't be visible from the street. I pull out one of the new shirts and put it on top of what I'm wearing. I don't have time to actually change clothes. The dumb hat I was wearing flew off during the chase, so I wrap a second shirt around my head like a bandana.

Then I take a deep breath, which is hard because it smells like garbage, and hop over the wall again, forcing myself to walk slowly now, though I really want to run. But they're looking for a kid who was running.

I have to be smarter than them.

I have to look like I belong here and there's nothing out of the ordinary.

Even though *everything's* out of the ordinary.

So I'm walking along, trying to look unobtrusive. The easiest way to do that around here is to just look at my phone while I walk. Most people avoid and ignore the idiot on the sidewalk with their face glued to their phone. But doing that makes it hard to see what's going on around me.

I settle for bobbing my head back and forth like I'm listening to music. This gives me a chance to look to my left and right periodically. And I can only hope that the people out on the streets looking for me assume I'm running, not casually walking and enjoying a new mixtape.

When I get past Audubon Avenue safely, I text my mom.

> change of plans. dont meet at last place

> I'm already on my way there, sweetie.

> i know. but something came up. will send new place in a second.

I have to think of a new place now. Not just a safe place for us to meet, but a place that I can communicate to her in some sort of code. Running away from Burger Heights has brought me back towards the college. I'm a little worried about getting too close to Harlem River Drive, where we saw that guy with the gun get hit by the car. There may be police investigating, or whoever he was working for might be there looking into what happened to him.

Then I remember a day when mom and I were walking all over town looking for a pair of sneakers for me. I'm embarrassed to say what kind. Anyhow, we kept going to all these stores and none of them had the shoes. But then we saw a kid my age wearing them across the street. I pointed him out to my mom, and she ran across six lanes of traffic to stop him and ask him where he got them.

When I finally caught up with her, she said, "Don't ever run across the street like I just did."

"Did you ask him where he got the shoes?"

"Yeah," she said. "They were a present from his uncle in Virginia."

"That's probably too far to walk, huh?"

"It is. Sorry, kid. We did our best, though."

So now I text her:

> meet me where you crossed the street to ask that kid where he got his shoes

She sends me a smiley face emoji, followed by the one that is laughing with tears coming out of its face. She usually sends me two emojis at once. I think what happens is she finds one that kind of means what she wants, and then immediately after she hits send, she finds a more relevant one.

Anyway, I'm going to meet her at Amsterdam Avenue near 179th Street, where the road runs over all the traffic from the George Washington Bridge. It's like 10 lanes of cars that disappear into a tunnel under a tall building that Ms. Marrillion's friend Jane would hate. On the other side of that building is the bus terminal and then the bridge to New Jersey.

It's a bit of an exposed location, but I think if I sit against the wall and fence at the edge of the sidewalk, I might just pass for an unhoused kid. My clothes are brand new, but hopefully nobody will look too closely.

I head down that way.

I don't know if I should feel bad about that guy who fell outside Burger Heights and probably hurt himself. It's kind of my fault, but at the same time, if he hadn't been chasing me, he would have been fine. Same with that guy who got out of his car and then got hit on Harlem River Drive.

Ms. Marrillion didn't do anything, she just wanted to be left alone. And I'm just trying to help her. Neither of us did anything wrong.

It's probably like that thing they call karma, or that saying "what goes around, comes around." Old people have all kinds of ways to say the same thing, which is that bad people get what's coming to them. Despite all those different ways of saying it, though, people keep doing bad stuff. They probably think they'll be the ones to get away with it.

Myself, I always feel guilty when I've done even the smallest bad thing, like if my friends are waiting in line somewhere and I meet up with them and join them, even though there are people behind them in line who were waiting longer.

It's not usually a huge deal. If it's a line for a movie, they would save a seat for me anyway, so it doesn't make much of a difference. If it was in a situation where there was a limited number of something for sale, then I wouldn't do it. Even though I know it doesn't really matter, I still feel bad doing things like that.

There are people out in the world who don't care. Like serial killers or politicians who just go from one bad thing to the next. I don't know how they do it. That must be the kind of people chasing after Ms. Marrillion.

After a few blocks of walking, I make it down to the meeting point. I reach into my pocket with my free hand and grab the knife handle, just to make sure it's still there.

If the time comes, will I even be able to use it? Or will I feel too guilty to stab someone?

CHAPTER 31
A PLACE THAT KEEPS SECRETS

I'M FEELING LOW.

I crouch down along the wall of the overpass, and imagine I look like a street kid.

Pretty soon I start to *feel* like one, too.

On the one hand, people ignore me, averting their eyes as they pass, just like I usually do when I walk by dudes who are passed out or begging on the sidewalk. It's tough, because I don't want to be a jerk, and I empathize with them, but there's also so many that you can't stop and try to help each one.

———

It's getting darker.

I start to wonder how much of my feelings come from what I'm doing. Like if I'm hanging out or playing basketball, my body knows I'm having fun, and I feel good. Whereas sitting on the concrete, smelling the fumes of passing cars, down near the ground, my brain subconsciously knows this is a bad spot and starts making me sad.

Or maybe I'm just crashing after all the action earlier in the day.

Either way, I can feel my eyes starting to feel puffy, like when I have allergies, or if I'm going to cry. I don't want to cry here. It will only make me sadder, and I'll look weak. If I start to lose hope, then Ms. Marrillion will be all on her own.

To distract myself, I try to think about other people who could help her. Other people who could help *us*.

Based on what she said, everyone who wears a uniform could be a threat. Police, mainly, and the FBI, who are a type of police, when you think about it.

Maybe the army? Except I don't know how you get in touch with the army. And I think the government is usually in charge of them. Ms. Marrillion said the government won't protect her, so that's probably out of the question.

I wonder if the press can help somehow. Would it be possible to get this story out there fast enough to protect her? If the whole country, or even just everyone in New York, found out the government was trying to kill a sweet old lady, maybe they would band together to help?

I doubt it.

It seems like every other day we hear the story of somebody being beaten up or killed by the police here in America or the army overseas and no amount of protesting and marching can prevent it.

Ms. Marrillion might seem safe for a day or so, but then she'd die in a fake accident, or get arrested and die in jail, or something like that.

I try to think about similar situations in the movies. I know they're not real, they're just made up stories, but I don't have much else to work with.

In *The Fast and Furious* movies, the good guys run afoul of the authorities and have to flee to Brazil. I've never been there and I'm pretty sure Ms. Marrillion hasn't either. They can't come back to America until they help prevent a world war, which is also something I don't see us being able to do. We're not action heroes —I'm already exhausted from just half a day on the run.

In every other example I can think of, the hero's only way out is to take down the conspiracy from the top. I can't picture that either, me and Ms. Marrillion repelling down the side of a building and crashing into the slick office where the bad guys are running their business. I've never climbed a rope like that, and she's probably too old.

I suppose if I had to choose, though, taking down the bad guys makes more sense than leaving the country, because if you do succeed at it, you're in the clear, whereas once you go on the run, you'll have to stay on the run for the rest of your life.

I can't figure it out. There doesn't seem to be a good solution.

I've gotten so distracted by my thoughts that I didn't notice someone creep up beside me.

"Time to move, kid."

I reach for my knife before I recognize her voice.

It's mom.

I let go of the weapon and stand up, slowly, because my knees hurt from sitting like that for so long. I hug her, which I don't always like to do, but really need to now.

"Let's get out of here," she says.

I cram the knife back into my pocket quickly, and we walk back up towards 181st Street and the hotel where Ms. Marrillion is staying.

For some reason, I feel safe now. Maybe it's because mom is beside me. She's too young to look like an old woman, so it's doubtful anyone will see us and think we're the people they're looking for.

It's too dangerous to go back to Burger Heights, so we stop at a bodega and get a bunch of sandwiches and french fries and other junk food.

"It's not the healthiest dinner we've ever had," my mom says.

"Yeah, but we earned it," I reply.

"Greasy food will make you drowsy, but maybe that's good. I can't imagine you'll get to sleep otherwise, with all the excitement."

I haven't even told her about some of the scariest parts of the day yet. I think I'll wait until we're inside to do that, though.

"Did you get D'Argyle his dinner?"

"It should have arrived by now. Plus, I texted with his mom. I didn't say too much, but let her know to get home as soon as she can. If I was in her place, I would want to know everything that happened."

When the food is ready, they pack it up in a plastic bag for us and we finish the rest of the trip.

We don't talk as we walk the last few blocks, so that we can both keep our eyes open and look out for danger. Every flashing light of a passing police car or ambulance makes me jump a little. I have to remind myself that the rest of the city is still going about its business. Not everything is about Ms. Marrillion. There are people getting sick and hurt and dying who need EMTs to come help them.

This makes me a little mad about the resources the people chasing after Ms. Marrillion are wasting. I mean, first of all, there's the cops and feds who are looking for her instead of going after real criminals. And then there's probably ambulances and police investigating the guy with the gun who got hit by a car on Harlem River Drive, and the guy who fell into the shaft near Burger Heights. None of that would have happened if they had just left the old lady alone.

"How'd you know about this place?" my mom asks as we approach the hotel.

"Uh, some kids at school talk about it as a place to go for, you know, privacy."

"*Really*," she says. She puts a lot of judgment into that one word and shakes her head afterward. Then she looks at me and I tense up.

"I hope you would know better than to bring someone here for that sort of thing," she says.

I nod. Nobody wants to talk to their mom about hooking up.

"Listen, I know you're going to take someone somewhere someday…"

"We don't gotta talk about it now, Mom." When I get upset, my grammar gets bad.

"I know, I know. I'm just saying, this place is kind of gross. If you're going to go somewhere for that sort of thing, make sure it's less dingy and *actually* romantic. This is what they used to call a *no-tell motel*. In theory, it was because they were anonymous and the desk clerks would keep things confidential, for underage kids or married men having affairs. But also, if you were in high school, and someone took you to one of these places, you would never tell your friends because it was embarrassing. You'd lie and say he took you somewhere nice, like the Waldorf-Astoria or The Four Seasons or something. So the name no-tell motel had a lot of meanings. Anyway, it was smart to come here in this situation, you little genius."

I feel like she would pinch my cheek if our hands weren't full with groceries and bodega food.

Inside the lobby, the clerk barely looks up. But at the same time, he does check us out with his eyes. He smiles slightly at me and then checks out my mom and nods slightly. I guess he's good at his job because he has to watch everyone coming in but also not make them feel like they're being watched.

I stop at the desk.

"Do you have clean towels here?"

Koto smiles.

"Not at the moment. But don't worry, I'll call you right away if we get clean towels in the lobby."

"Can I call up to the room from your phone?" I ask.

He lifts the telephone from his desk and puts it on the counter.

"Just press 4 and then your room number."

I call and Ms. Marrillion answers.

"Hello?"

"It's Lee. I'm on my way up."

"Oh good."

"My mom's coming too. We have dinner."

"Thank you, Lee. See you in a moment."

I hang up and hand the phone back to him.

Mom and I walk to the elevator. As we're riding up, she says, "Did he say they don't have clean towels? That's pretty disgusting. Especially at a place like this, where the guests need to shower when they're done with their business. I can go back out and buy us some towels at the dollar store."

"No, don't worry," I say. "It's a code he set up before. If someone shows up looking for us, he's going to call the room and tell us there are clean towels in the lobby."

"Sounds like he's used to people hiding out in his hotel."

CHAPTER 32
NIGHT OF THE JACKALS

WE GET out of the elevator, and I use my key to unlock the door.

Ms. Marrillion is standing near the television with a knife in her hand.

She smiles and puts it down on the dresser when she sees us.

Mom and I enter. I close the door, locking it behind us.

"How was it out there?"

"We survived," my mom says. "Let's eat while the food's hot."

We spend a few moments divvying up the sandwiches and then finally get dinner. I'm starving from running around all day. I hadn't really realized it before, but once I start eating, I just devour everything.

Ms. Marrillion is sitting in the one chair in the room, while mom and I sit on the edge of the beds.

"I wouldn't be alive if it weren't for Lee," Ms. Marrillion says, after eating half a grilled cheese.

I can feel my face flushing. It's embarrassing to hear people talk about you while you're in the room.

"Can you tell us what's going on? I know you didn't want to discuss it over the phone in case they're listening."

Ms. Marrillion nods her head.

"It goes back to my childhood. I apologize, Lee, because you've heard some of this before."

Then she retells the story of the orphanage and the night she and Carol were taken to that small town, and then sent into the VFW hall where everyone stared at them and argued about whether they should be there.

"I didn't really understand all of it at the time, of course," Ms. Marrillion says. "Mostly we were just afraid. I've sort of pieced a few things together over the ensuing decades. Some of it was just going out into the world and seeing more of life. Some of it was reading newspapers and history books and putting the puzzle together in my mind."

She takes a sip from a bottle of water.

"So there we were, standing against the wall, Carol and I and the other people who had been sent to stand near us. And then we just watched while the various groups seated at tables discussed things. They were serious and angry, and thinking back on it now, it reminds me of a homeowners association meeting in our building, the way one guy would get hung up on one issue that seemed irrelevant, but nobody else could get anything done until they appeased him.

"A lot of the discussion focused on dates and locations. They were trying to figure out when and where to do something. We didn't know what they were talking about, though. It felt like there had been earlier meetings that we didn't see, so a lot of what they were saying went over our heads.

"Eventually, they settled on a date. It was hard because everybody had different priorities and wanted the thing to happen before or after a certain point. They kept talking about Thanksgiving, and I wondered if they were planning a holiday party. This made me laugh, because I knew it wasn't really what was going on. There was too much secrecy and yelling. I knew it was something else. Everyone glared at me when I giggled, so I made myself stop showing any emotion.

"Then they looked over their calendars and chose a location

based on the dates they had agreed on. Each time they decided on something, they would vote by raising their hands, kind of like we did in school.

"After they had finalized the date and place, there was another argument about whether Carol and I should be there. The drunk guy at the Church table ... I realized later it was a table full of people from the Church ... he kept shaking his head and shrugging his shoulders. The men from the other tables were giving us dirty looks all throughout.

"Over time, the arguing got so loud that we could hear what they were saying. The drunk man just kept repeating, 'If you don't want them here, then we can end this thing now, and you're gonna have to kill them yourself.' I felt Carol squeeze my hand again. This went on until the angriest man stormed out of the building. Everything stopped for a while, as if they couldn't conduct their meeting without everyone else there.

"Finally, he came back in. I think maybe he had gone out and walked around the block to calm himself down. He went up to the drunk man and said, evenly, 'They can stay. Let's just get this done.'

"And then they started into the last business of the night, and that's when we realized they were planning an assassination."

CHAPTER 33
THE CONSPIRACY

MOM'S always telling me I should appreciate all the things I have, and it's never felt like I had that much to appreciate until I hear Ms. Marillion's story. Just think of all the things she had to suffer and survive before she was even my age.

I don't have a father, but she didn't have a father *or* a mother.

I live in a tiny apartment, but she lived in an orphanage dormitory.

I've been on the run from killers since this afternoon, but she's been running her whole life.

And I could get out of this if I wanted to—she's their target, not me.

Of course, I can't really leave her alone to fend for herself. That's not how mom raised me.

"Was that meeting what I think it was?" my mom asks Ms. Marrillion.

The old woman nods her head.

"What was it?" I ask. Then I turn to my mom. "How do you know what it was?"

"She knows her history," Ms. Marrillion says. "And I think she put that together with a decent guess about how old I am."

"I'm lost," I say.

"Think it through, Lee," my mom says. "She said they were planning an assassination."

In my head, I try to remember what I know from history class.

Malcolm X was killed a few blocks south of where we are now. I know because my mom always points out the place where it happened when we walk by. That might make sense if Ms. Marrillion had lived her whole life in New York, but she didn't. And based on the Spike Lee movie, the people who killed him weren't the kind of people in the conspiracy Ms. Marrillion witnessed.

And there's Martin Luther King. I've heard he was killed by just one guy, but I know some people think there was a conspiracy, especially since, after he was shot, JFK's brother was also murdered.

This train of thought just about runs me over.

Why am I thinking about JFK's brother, when JFK himself is right there?

"Are we talking about John F. Kennedy?" I ask.

My mom and Ms. Marrillion both nod their heads solemnly.

I explain how I figured it out, ruling out MLK and RFK and first Malcolm X, based on what I knew from the movie.

"You were sort of named after him, you know," my mom says.

"Lee is named for Lee Harvey Oswald?" Ms. Marrillion gasps.

"No, no," my mom laughs. "Lee is named after Spike Lee."

"I didn't know that," I say.

"Well, it seems like a night for us all to share our secrets," she says to me. She smiles in a funny way. "Your father and I saw a Spike Lee movie on the night you were conceived. But we couldn't name you *Inside Man*. We considered calling you Foster, for Jodie Foster. And even Plummer for a hot second. We didn't know if you were going to be a boy or a girl, so we were only thinking about gender neutral names. And we didn't want to burden you with the history of a family name. That way, you could have a fresh start."

We sit silently for a while.

"So these guys in the room," I finally ask Ms. Marrillion, "were planning to kill the President of the United States?"

"Yes," she says. "Although we didn't take them seriously. It just didn't seem possible. It had been over 60 years since McKinley was assassinated. And that was before the Secret Service was put in charge of protecting the President. We just thought they were a bunch of crazy old drunks talking nonsense. We knew for sure the man who was responsible for us was drunk, anyway."

She finishes her bottle of water.

"They spent the rest of the night figuring out details, who would be responsible for what. The men from the government were supposed to keep tabs on JFK and his schedule. The mob was going to recruit the gunmen, possibly bringing them over from Italy. There was some question as to whether Americans could be trusted to carry out the act. The people from the Church didn't seem to have as much to offer. Since Carol and I had been brought there by the Church, I started to worry that the other groups would decide to cut them out, and then we would be expendable."

"Why would the church want JFK killed?" my mom asks.

"I've got a few theories," Ms. Marrillion says. "It could have been a moral issue. The conservative forces in the church must have known about his infidelities. He was, as they would have seen it, a sinner."

"They killed him for having affairs?" I ask. That seems impossible to me, but I don't know what the world was like back then.

"I don't think so," Ms. Marrillion answers. "Although he certainly did more for Catholicism as a martyr than he would have otherwise." She pauses for a moment. "It's when I think about what would have happened if he had lived that I start to understand a possible motivation. Would he have stayed with Jackie throughout his old age? Or was it more likely that he would have asked for a divorce? Marilyn Monroe died in 1962, but surely someone else would have come along, someone impossibly sexy and irresistible. Then what? What if Kennedy asked for a divorce? I can't see a way that the Vatican could have granted it—everyone in America would have wanted one the next day. And what if he asked for a divorce and they said no? Henry the Eighth put them in the same position when he asked for an annulment in the 1500s, and the Catholics lost Britain when they told him no. Henry just became a Protestant and replaced them with the Church of England. John F. Kennedy was popular enough that he could have left the Catholic Church and taken most of its young people with him to some new form of Catholicism, one that granted divorces and welcomed all the baby boomers. Rather than risk that, I think, they decided he was more useful to them dead than alive. After all, if Jesus could die, why not Kennedy?"

The telephone rings, startling us all.

I answer it.

"Hello?"

"This is the front desk. We have clean towels now, if you still need them."

CHAPTER 34
THE GETAWAY

"WE GOTTA GO," I say. "Right now."

Both my mom and Ms. Marrillion leap up.

Mom moves toward the door. I see Ms. Marrillion reach out her hand and I think she needs help, but then I realize she's grabbing her knife from the dresser.

I check that I still have mine, and I can't find it at first, but then feel its handle all the way at the bottom of my pocket

"Take the fire stairs," I say to my mom, who is already out in the hallway. I keep an eye on the elevator, willing it not to open just yet.

"Does it have an alarm?" my mom asks.

"Koto said it's a silent alarm that goes off at his desk."

She scrunches up her face and pushes on the horizontal metal bar in the center of the door.

We're in luck, because it stays silent. That would be a safety issue if there was a fire, but I don't have time to worry about that now. Lights go on in the stairwell, and I can't tell if they're activated by motion sensors, or triggered by the alarm. Either way, we all hustle in and, just as the door is closing behind us, we hear the elevator chime its arrival on the floor.

Should we go up or down?

I don't know the building, but I figure it's unlikely there's a way off the top that Ms. Marillion could take advantage of. I might be able to climb or jump to another building from there, but there's no point in me getting away without her. Not to mention, my mom probably isn't ready to climb down the side of a building either.

Which means we should head downstairs.

There's no way to know for sure, but I think Koto would have said something if the street was too full of people for us to get out: "The towels are here, but I think I should send them up," or something like that.

Mom goes down first, with Ms. Marrillion behind her, and then me. Hopefully the people looking for us are in the hallway pounding on the door of the empty room. We can't hear anything, because the stairwell is fireproof, meaning it's pretty well insulated.

At the bottom, the door says:

181st Street Exit
Authorized Personnel/Emergency Use ONLY

"I guess this qualifies as an emergency," my mom says.

"When we get outside, turn left, so we don't go past the front of the hotel where they might see us," I say.

"Ready?" my mom asks.

Ms. Marrillion and I both nod.

"Let's go," she says.

She opens the door, and we brace for the sound of an alarm, but luckily Koto is right and it's quiet.

We head east on 181st Street. I look back to see if anyone's watching.

Nobody's on the sidewalk, but there's a big black SUV pulled up in front of the bus stop near the hotel. Somehow, I doubt they'll get a ticket for parking there.

We keep moving, and then I see something and get an idea.

"How much cash do we have left?" I ask.

"I've got like $200," my mom says.

"Give me a hundred," I say. "And go with Ms. Marrillion."

"What are you thinking?"

"Trust me," I say.

And then, for some reason, she does.

Mom hands me two $50s, and I jog across to the south side of the street.

There's an older woman on the sidewalk, about the same size as Ms. Marrillion. I approach her and say, "Hey, if I give you $50, will you take a short cab ride with me?"

She looks me up and down.

"No way."

"Listen, I lied to somebody and said my Aunty was in town because I didn't want to hang out with them. They're just over there." I point vaguely towards Broadway. "They saw me on the street and now they think I'm a liar because I wasn't with my Aunty."

"Sounds like you are a liar."

"True, true. But I just didn't want to hurt their feelings. Anyway, if they see me get in the cab with you and drive by, they'll think I was telling the truth."

"Fifty bucks?"

"Plus whatever change is left from the cab ride."

"If you try anything funny, I've got a Taser."

It's like every old lady in town's got a weapon in her purse these days.

"I promise I won't touch you."

"Fine," she says, and takes the $50 from me.

I flag down a cab.

Now the tricky part is making sure the guys looking for me see me with this old woman.

I look across into the lobby of the hotel and see the elevator door open again. Two men approach the desk angrily. One throws a key card at Koto. My guess is that he told them it was a key to our room, but it wasn't activated.

If I had the hotel's phone number, I could try to call him to get him to make the guys look at us, but that might take too much time. I don't know how long this lady and cab driver will put up with me stalling. So I look around, and I see an old glass Snapple bottle in the gutter.

I pick it up and throw it across the street at the SUV. It shatters across the back window, and I guess it's loud enough that they can hear it inside the lobby, because both men and Koto turn suddenly and look out. One of them runs to the door and opens it, then sees me. If it works out like I planned, he also sees the old lady in the back of the cab.

I get inside it and close the car door.

"Take a right up on Amsterdam," I say. We start moving.

I turn around and through the rear window, I see the men get in the SUV, pull a U-turn across 181st, and come after us.

Ms. Marrillion is safe for now, I guess. But what about me?

CHAPTER 35
THE WRONG WOMAN

WE DRIVE EAST, then turn south on Amsterdam.

The big SUV is right behind us. I can see the driver's face through the cab's rear window.

Suddenly I realize a flaw in my plan: They might try to kill this old lady before they find out she's not Ms. Marrillion.

I didn't mean to put her in danger. I was just trying to protect Ms. Marrillion. But I may have created a lot of trouble this way.

"Turn right again, and go west," I say.

"You gotta tell me your destination," the driver says, annoyed at me. "I'm not like a personal chauffeur."

"We're going to the police station on Broadway and 183rd Street," I say.

"You idiot, you could have walked there," the cabbie says.

Not with all the people on the street looking for me, I couldn't. But I don't tell him that.

"Why are we going to the police station?" The old lady is starting to get mad. "I thought you were just trying to trick your friends."

"Uh, yeah," I say, trying to figure out an explanation. I don't want her tasing me. "I'm just going to the new food hall across the street from the police station. But since it's new, I wasn't sure if this guy knows about it." I point at the taxi driver. "So I figured the police station was a better landmark."

"Food hall!" she laughs. "What a bunch of bougie nonsense. Might as well bring back the automats, right?"

I look at her blankly.

"You're too young," she says. Then she yells up toward the driver. "You remember automats, don't you? I miss them."

"A tuna sandwich that's been spinning around in a tube all day? No thanks!" The driver laughs as he turns onto Broadway. "I wouldn't eat that crap if you paid me."

"You're crazy," the woman says. "There was nothing like peeling back the wax paper and smelling the food. It was like eating in the future."

I don't really know what they're talking about. I could ask, but I figure I've learned enough from old people today.

Behind us, the SUV keeps inching closer. But thankfully they haven't rammed our car or started shooting. Maybe they are just keeping an eye out for now. Following us to see where we go.

"You know what I really miss?"

The woman is chatty. Perhaps she's just lonely. I guess she doesn't realize what kind of situation I'm in, anyway, since I lied. To her, this is a fine time for small talk.

"I miss the Howard Johnson's in Times Square. Do either of you remember that?"

"That place was sad," the driver says. "I used to pick up drunks there, late at night."

"Aww, you don't know," the woman says. "Back in the day, it was fabulous. I met my second husband there. We shared a plate of fried clams."

"You ate clams in Times Square?" I ask.

"They were the best," she says. "I never got sick once eating there."

Well, she sounds like a survivor, so I think she's going to be okay, even with these guys behind us thinking she's Ms. Marrillion. I'm sure they can't do anything worse than a late-night plate of clams in the Eighties could have done to her.

The driver pulls up to the police station. He can't get close to the curb because all the cops' personal vehicles are parked all over the sidewalk. My mom always complains about this.

"We should get out here," I say to the woman.

"Now I gotta walk back to 181st? What a ripoff."

She gets out of the car.

"It's safer this way. There's some people chasing us," I say.

"I knew it! I never should have trusted a kid. Your generation is nothing but a bunch of liars and scammers."

"Yeah, but your generation destroyed the planet, so I guess we're even," I say.

I hand the cabbie the $50 and he groans.

"You don't have anything smaller?"

"Sorry," I say.

"I take credit cards, you know." He points at the card reader in the back of his taxi.

"I don't have one."

He grumbles as he counts out the change.

While this is going on, the SUV stops behind us, and an angry guy gets out.

He strolls over, looking up warily at the police station, probably trying to figure out if they have cameras or he can get away with killing this woman on the sidewalk.

"Hey lady," he says to her.

"Hey yourself," she snaps back.

"Look at me."

"Why? You ain't so handsome."

"I just want to see your face first."

She reaches into her purse, maybe to grab her Taser.

He reaches into his pocket, and I think we're about to get shot.

But then he just pulls out his phone and looks at what is probably a picture of Ms. Marrillion.

"What the f—?" He turns back to the SUV and shouts, "We been following the wrong old lady!"

"Old lady?" The woman is mad now. "Your mom's an old lady! And what are you following me for anyway, you perv?!"

The guy ignores her and runs back to his SUV. Luckily for me, he doesn't think to ask why I threw a bottle at his car earlier. He's just focused on finding Ms. Marrillion. And since this woman isn't her, he assumes I must not be the kid they're looking for, either.

The SUV screeches out into traffic, pulling around the taxi, before turning on 184th, probably to go back towards the hotel.

Finally, the driver has finished counting out the change and he hands it to me.

"You said I could have that," the woman says. "And I'm pretty sure I just saved your butt from those thugs, so I believe I earned it."

I can't argue with her.

I let her take the money, and I walk uptown, wondering if my mom and Ms. Marrillion got away safely.

CHAPTER 36
WAY DOWN IN THE HOLE

SHOULD I walk back towards the hotel? Probably not. That place is off the table, as far as staying there secretly. And I bet mom and Ms. Marrillion are thinking the same thing.

Maybe my mother can come up with someplace else that's safe to go. If the guys chasing us don't know who I am yet, then they might not be able to figure out who my mom's friends are, so hiding out with some of them would be a safe bet.

Although I doubt my mom would want to get her friends involved, based on how dangerous this has seemed so far.

I figure it's worth risking a phone call at this point to find out where they are.

I reach into my pocket and there's nothing there.

No phone.

No condoms.

No knife either.

Just a hole where my pocket used to be.

I guess the blade finally cut through the bottom of the pocket. I must have pushed it in too quickly at some point. And then there was nothing to keep my phone from falling out.

It could be in the taxi, or on the street in front of the hotel. In all the confusion and noise, I might not have noticed if it clattered to the ground.

Now I'm in trouble.

Also, my mom will be worried if she tries to get in touch and nobody answers my phone.

I could go back home, since my keys are in my other pocket. But is our building safe? Unlikely, since Ms. Marrillion lived there. If I was trying to find her, and I had the resources these guys seem to have, I would stake out the building to see if she comes in or goes out. Which means there's probably someone who would notice me. Even if I'm not with her, they might grab me and try to make me tell them where she is.

I don't know where she is.

I can't imagine they'd like that answer too much.

And if they know I've seen them and can identify them in court or to the authorities—assuming we can ever find some authorities that we can trust—then they would have to kill me.

I know that from movies.

The real bad guys will never let you see their face if they kidnap you. If they do, that means they're planning to kill you.

So: no going home.

Which leaves D'Argyle.

They chased us through his building before, but they also chased me through the food hall and all around 181st, and they can't be watching everywhere, can they? I'll have to hope it's safe.

D'Argyle already knows what's going on, which is a bonus. I'd hate to have to explain everything that's happened so far to one of my other friends.

It's dark out now.

If I stay away from the storefronts, it's hard for people to see my face, so I can stay anonymous. I duck my head away from headlights of passing cars.

I'm heading downhill now, even though I'm going north. It always seems like north should be uphill since it's up. But that's not the case. And north is only up if you look at the map the way the Europeans designed it, to put themselves on top. If you flip it over, Africa, South America, and Australia are on top and north is at the bottom.

Sometimes mom looks at maps of the elevations around our building to make sure it will still be here if the oceans rise. Or if there's another big hurricane. When I was a kid, she tells me, Hurricane Sandy caused a lot of flooding that damaged low-lying buildings. Although we're at the bottom of that big staircase on 187th Street, we're still 150 feet above sea level, which seems pretty safe.

One time I asked my mom, "What if we lived at sea level? What would we do?"

She said, "If you're down at the bottom, there's nowhere to go but up."

I think that was supposed to comfort me.

As I'm walking down towards D'Argyle's, separated from my mom, targeted by thugs and hitmen, I try to convince myself that things can only get better, they can't get worse.

In the back of my brain, though, something tells me it could get a whole lot worse.

CHAPTER 37

HOW WE DIE

BROADWAY IS LOUDER AT NIGHT.

Drivers want to show off their vehicles, with rumbling bass beats, revved up engines, and even some neon underglow lights.

People around here say the original *Fast and Furious* movie was based on a magazine article about street racers in Washington Heights, and I believe it. Some nights it sounds like there's a NASCAR race happening just around the corner.

It's a different kind of traffic.

During the day, there are delivery trucks idling all over the place, and people honking as they try to get around stopped cars and backups at the intersections. It's more of a whiny sound, like cars complaining.

At night, it's like the machines are angry, yelling at each other. All the politeness is gone.

Motorized dirt bike crews run red lights in a mob, half of them up on just their back wheels, weaving in and out of stopped cars. Less noisy, but just as aggressive, are the kids on regular bicycles. I think they want to make up for the fact that they don't have engines by being ruder than the rest. They pound on car windows as they pass, circle stopped vehicles in a threatening manner, staring in at the drivers.

Usually I'm a bit afraid of them, but tonight I've got bigger concerns.

I wonder if, when all this is over, I'll go back to being scared of these guys on bikes. Or if surviving this ordeal will make me tougher. They say whatever doesn't kill you makes you stronger. I understand what they mean, but I don't know if it's true. There are some diseases you can get that make you more vulnerable in the future, even if you survive the short term. So there are a lot of things that don't kill you but make you weaker.

Down near D'Argyle's place, men are still sitting out on the sidewalk, playing dominoes and smoking cigars. It's weird, because I've only ever seen old men doing that. Do you just hit a certain age and suddenly become interested in dominoes? Or maybe the young domino players are too busy working, and it's only when you get to retirement age that you're free to sit out playing all night.

Adults are a mystery.

Just when I think I understand them, I get some new piece of information. Ms. Marrillion, for example. If you asked this morning, I'd have said she was this old woman in my building, probably a retired art teacher or something like that.

I would never have guessed she was an orphan, or was hiding out from a bunch of people trying to kill her. Do all old people have secrets like that? Maybe even my mother? I pick up bits and pieces of what mom's life was like before me from conversations, but I'm sure there's big chunks missing. Did she have her own adventures like this before? She seems to be taking it all in stride, so maybe she's dealt with this sort of thing in the past.

———

Nobody's outside the funeral home tonight.

Walking by when there's just been a memorial is always a bit depressing. You can be having a good time, enjoying yourself, then suddenly you're in the middle of a group of mourners, dressed in black, and your happiness seems insensitive.

That's unique to city living, I guess. Everywhere else, they probably put the funeral home on the edge of town, so you can avoid it unless you're intentionally going to a funeral. But here in New York, we have them right next to the beauty salon, the barbershop, and the pizza place.

I wonder if Ms. Marrillion has thought about her own funeral. Just like those men seem to have reached a certain age to play dominoes, I bet if you live long enough, you start to worry about what will happen when you die. Not what happens to your soul or whatever. I mean what happens to your actual body. Who organizes your funeral? Where will you be buried? If you have kids, I guess they're supposed to take care of that, but Ms. Marrillion doesn't have any that I know of. So I guess she'll have to plan her own funeral, if she wants it to go a certain way.

I feel like I'm too young to think about my own, but the way this day is going, maybe I should start making plans. I could make a playlist and tell D'Argyle what kind of party I want. It shouldn't be a sad memorial. I want a celebration.

If I die, let everybody's last recollection of me be a happy one.

CHAPTER 38
LET ME IN

EVERYBODY'S ALWAYS COMING and going.

I never really noticed before how busy apartment buildings are. Before, I would enter or leave pretty quickly.

Now, though, I'm watching the door at D'Argyle's to see if anyone suspicious is near the entrance, waiting for me.

And that gives me a sense of how often people walk in and out. It's non-stop. Especially just after a train or subway has dropped off passengers nearby. Because everyone walks at different paces, they don't get to the door of their building at the same time. First, young people and eager business types will show up. Then, a few minutes later, the older and slower people will show up and let themselves in. A bit after that, the people who stopped to buy something at the bodega or the Key Food will turn up, carrying bags of groceries.

That makes me think of this afternoon, how I was grocery shopping with Ms. Marrillion peacefully before all this started. She was telling me about how the companies trick you into buying what's on the middle shelves.

I was thinking, *Wow, this old lady's pretty smart*. I had no idea.

What makes me think it's ok to go into the building is when a few kids my age come in and out of the building and nobody stops them or grabs them or anything. I think the thugs would want to get a close look to make sure the kids aren't me.

I wait about 20 minutes until it seems like another train full of people has gotten off at 190th Street. I'm in the small park on the hill watching and then I make my way over and join the group of people leaving the station. Hopefully, one of them will walk to D'Argyle's building. I want to follow them in the door they've opened rather than having to buzz up to D'Argyle for him to let me in, because I'll be vulnerable in the vestibule with the building locked to me.

The timing works out, and a man with a briefcase turns from the sidewalk towards D'Argyle's. I don't follow too closely behind, which might freak him out, but once he's in, I hustle just enough to catch the door before it closes.

Then I take the stairs up, again, to D'Argyle's floor.

Nobody's chasing me—at least not that I know of—but it's still a bit scary and I'm paranoid about every noise I hear and shadow I see moving. Since I lost the knife, I'm unarmed and vulnerable.

I peek through the small window from the stairwell door to make sure nobody's hanging out in D'Argyle's hall. The coast looks clear, so I head to his door and knock.

We hadn't arranged a secret knock, but his door's got a peephole, unlike the hotel, so we don't need one.

The door swings open.

"Yo, Lee! I thought you were going to the hook-up hotel!"

"Long story," I say. "Let me in."

He steps aside and I slip into the apartment.

D'Argyle closes the door behind me and locks it.

"Where's the old lady and your mom?"

I drop onto his couch and put my head in my hands.

"I don't know," I say.

The fear and panic I'd been repressing suddenly gets to me.

"Somebody came for us and we split up. Then I lost my phone. So I don't know where they are and couldn't contact them. I need your help."

"I got you covered," he says. "Should I text your mom?"

I have to think about it for a moment.

I'm not sure how the men found us at the hotel. Did someone happen to see me and follow me there? Did someone snitch on us? I can't imagine anyone in the hood giving us up for free, but if these guys are dropping paper, someone who saw me or my mom might have passed on that information in exchange for money. I can't really blame them, since they don't know what's going on. They might assume I committed a crime or something.

But still in the back of my mind is the worry that they're able to track us through our phones. If they're onto D'Argyle's phone, they might be able to use that to locate my mom and Ms. Marrillion if we send a text.

I decide an email would be safer. I'm *pretty* sure they can't figure out where somebody sent an email from.

When I explain this to D'Argyle, he agrees, and we get on his laptop.

It's still not safe to say exactly where we are, but I want to at least let mom know I'm okay and find out if she and Ms. Marrillion got away.

```
Hey mom. I'm eating with my friend. He
says thanks for dinner. Just checking if
you're doing good. I lost my phone =( Lee
```

Now the only thing I can do is wait for her to reply.

CHAPTER 39

THE END OF THE MOVIE

"SO," D'Argyle asks, "are you just gonna spend the rest of your life on the run?"

"No," I say. "We need to figure out how to get out of this."

I explain some of what I was thinking when I sat on the sidewalk earlier, waiting for my mom. How it seems like the only options are for Ms. Marrillion to get out of the country or for us to somehow bring down the whole conspiracy of people trying to get her.

"You're forgetting one option," D'Argyle says.

I'm listening. I'm not sure if D'Argyle will come up with a solution, but at least it's a distraction from waiting to hear back from my mom and see if she's still alive.

"I'm thinking of it like it's a movie, right?" D'Argyle knows films better than anyone else I know. He even tracks down weird old foreign movies on DVD at the library so he can watch them. So maybe there's a movie that can help us.

"Usually," he says, "you're right, and the good guys have to triumph over the bad guys to take down the whole government. Except that's really hard to do, and they often skip over that part at the end of the movie. There will be some montage of news reporters revealing the secret conspiracy, but I always find myself thinking, is that it? It seems like there'd be one or two bad guys who got away, and then maybe they start killing witnesses or something. I always think the hero wouldn't be completely safe, and maybe that's intentional because they want to leave the door open to a sequel."

"I don't want a sequel of this," I say. "I just want it to be over."

"Alright, then. That means we should focus on movies with a happily ever after, no loose ends."

I smile. I'm still not sure D'Argyle can figure this all out, but it's fun to think about.

"Picture it like this. For now, we'll imagine Ms. Marrillion is an action star, because they don't make movies about old ladies fighting crime. Although now that I think of it, maybe they should. Anyway, the hero is taking on all these bad guys, corrupt cops, or the CIA, or whatever. The hero takes out the lead villain and makes a brave last stand, but then things go wrong."

"Huh?"

"Yeah, there's emotional music, and they get shot and they limp into a burning warehouse, or they fall off a rooftop into the river. You see a close-up of their eyes and it's like they're finally at peace, you know? Because they stayed true to themselves and took out the main bad guy."

"But they're dead?"

D'Argyle laughs.

"Lee, you gotta watch more movies! They trick you that way. It looks like they're dead, and then there's one of those montages where a newsperson explains how things wrapped up. Sometimes they find evidence about all the bad stuff the villain did, but sometimes they aren't exposed, and they get a fancy burial as part of a cover up. And then, just when you think the movie's over, the newscaster mentions that an unidentified body was found, in the warehouse, or floating in the river, just at the end of their broadcast."

"That's not a happy ending."

"Ah, but then they cut to a newspaper, and someone is reading the same story about the unidentified body. Except they zoom out to reveal that the person reading the newspaper is the hero."

"Still alive?"

"Of course! But now they're on the beach somewhere, with a big hat and sunglasses. Or maybe at a cafe in Italy drinking espresso. They faked their death in order to escape. Because now nobody is looking for them, and they're finally free. We probably see them smile just as the end credits start rolling."

D'Argyle is pleased with himself.

"That's pretty good," I say. "But what about the dead body? Where did that come from?"

He shrugs.

"They don't usually explain that. It could be a homeless person, or maybe one of the other bad guys. The hero just puts their watch on them or something. Ms. Marrillion is old, right? She probably has dentures, so like, she could leave them behind and the CSI people would find them and assume the body is hers."

"So we'd have to find a dead old woman and put Ms. Marrillion's fake teeth inside her mouth?" This sounds disgusting to me. Plus, I'm not sure Ms. Marrillion even wears dentures.

"Yeah, well, that's why they usually don't show that part in the movie. They just fade to black and then show the hero living happily ever after."

There's something sweet about imagining it that way. I don't picture Ms. Marrillion on the beach in the Bahamas, though. The way I see it, the last scene is set at an orphanage, probably the one where she grew up, and we see that it's a great place now. The kids are all happy and living good lives. It's all thanks to the woman in charge, and in the last shot of the movie we go into her office and see it's Ms. Marrillion. Maybe she's calling herself Carol. I guess she came into possession of a bunch of money somehow, so she's able to fund this great orphanage.

Something nags at me, though.

"D'Argyle, how does the reporter find out about the conspiracy? You know, the news anchor at the end who's describing what happened?"

"That depends. Usually there's a reporter character in the movie, and they seem annoying, but in the end they turn out to be good. Or maybe there's just a shot of a newsroom and a new character gets a mysterious envelope in the mail that turns out to be all the evidence."

"What if there is no evidence?"

He thinks about this for a minute.

"I got it," he says. "Remember when the hero killed the villain just before disappearing into the burning building?"

"Yeah."

"So what happens is: the villain explains the whole conspiracy to the hero."

"Why would they do that?"

"Because it's a movie. But also, they think the good guy is about to die, and they want them to know what happened. You know, like the way a James Bond villain always spends too much time talking about their evil plan, and then 007 is able to stop them as a result."

"If I ever become a villain, I'm never going to stop to explain my motives."

"Just don't become a villain, Lee. It's much easier! Anyway, in this kind of movie, the bad guy doesn't die, they just shoot the good guy. And as the good guy stumbles away, having been shot, we see they were wearing a wire. Then, during that last news broadcast at the end of the film, the anchor reveals that the FBI found secret recordings that incriminate the villain."

"That seems pretty complicated."

"Yeah. Another way it could go is that instead of the news broadcast, at the end of the movie, the main villain is giving a big speech, and then over the PA, we hear their speech from earlier where they explain everything they did wrong. The hero has somehow hacked into the audio system to play the recording. Then the FBI swarms in and arrests the bad guy."

This cheers me up a bit.

Maybe it *is* possible to bring down all the bad guys who are after Ms. Marrillion and *also* give her a happy new life somewhere.

"The thing about it is," D'Argyle says, "they don't make a lot of movies where the hero dies and the bad guys get away with it. It's too depressing, so people don't like it, and then the movie would be a flop. But outside of movies, tragic endings probably happen all the time."

CHAPTER 40
NO ROOM FOR MISTAKES

NOW I'M THINKING about whether it's really possible to fake Ms. Marrillion's death.

Just because they do something in the movies doesn't mean you can do it in real life.

Especially since we're only a couple of high school kids in Washington Heights.

The biggest issue would be finding a replacement dead body. It's gross and I don't even want to think about it. It's not like any of the people chasing Ms. Marrillion are also old ladies. If that was the case, then one of them could end up getting killed, and their body could be mistaken for hers. Since that's not possible, we'll have to figure out another way.

Could we fake her death without a body? I don't know.

I guess maybe if it seems like she dies in a way that her body wouldn't be recovered.

Like if she jumps off the George Washington Bridge into the Hudson and swims away.

Except there's no way she could survive something like that.

I picture D'Argyle and I throwing a mannequin dressed up like Ms. Marrillion over the side of the bridge, and it makes me laugh, but I don't think it would convince anyone. Sometimes I'll catch an old movie from the 1970s on TV and you can always tell when they threw a dummy out of a window instead of having a stuntman jump. It just doesn't look right.

I don't think it would be believable to pretend she was in a car that drove off the road and into a river. Police would eventually find the car, and then when her body wasn't in it, they'd suspect she was alive.

Maybe a shipwreck?

It seems too convoluted, though. We'd have to pretend she stole a boat, and then get the boat far enough out to sea that nobody is around, then capsize the boat so that people thought she drowned in the ocean. Except that would mean we need a second boat for her to escape onto.

What about on land?

These days, with DNA, they can identify remains of bodies under collapsed buildings and things, which makes it harder to fake a death.

Perhaps we could convince her doctor to switch out her medical records somehow? I don't know how we'd do that. And she's probably had a whole bunch of different doctors at her age, so we'd need to change out all her medical and dental records to make it work. Too complicated.

Maybe we could just trick one bad guy—make him think he killed her, and then he would report to all his superiors that she was dead. That seems like the most possible option.

I'm not sure how to go about it, but I'll keep thinking it over in my mind.

Or we figure out some way to bring down all the people involved in this conspiracy. They must be really old by now, if they were older than Ms. Marrillion way back in the 1960s. They'd have to be in their late 80s. I would think they'd be retired and in nursing homes, not plotting to kill a sweet old lady.

If mom answers my email, and I can get back in touch with Ms. Marrillion, I'll have to find out a little bit more about what she saw in that VFW, and what we'd need to do to make sure she's safe and those guys are no longer out to get her.

I probably need to get a new cell phone, since I lost mine, if I'm going to make a recording of the bad guy explaining his conspiracy and why he was trying to kill Ms. Marrillion. I doubt my mom will want to buy me a new phone in the middle of all this, though.

I figure enough time has passed that I can check my email again, to see if mom has replied.

I'm scared.

But I open D'Argyle's laptop and log back in.

There's no reply.

Nothing new in my inbox except some spam from a new shop called Instant Hoagies that opened down the block. I don't have time for their 10 percent off coupons. And I already ate. What I need is Instant Bodyguards.

Or a reply from my mom to let me know she's okay.

I try not to panic.

It hasn't been *that* long, and if she's still on the move, or worried about her phone being tracked somehow, it would make sense that she hasn't logged into her email.

Still, I worry.

I wonder if this is what it's like for her, all the time: wondering where I am and if I'm safe. Is that what parents do? As a kid, I've never really had to wonder about where my mom is. She's usually either at home or at work. And even if she's hanging out with her friends, they're probably just having dinner and wine somewhere. It's not like they'll be getting arrested or causing trouble.

Which isn't to say that me and my friends get in trouble, but I guess she might worry anyway. A lot of people my age do act up and get in trouble, especially in the neighborhoods around where we live.

I mean, it probably happens everywhere—teenagers being irresponsible. It's just that here there's so little room to make mistakes. I mean, literally there's no room. Like Ms. Marrillion said, there's always eyes on the street.

I bet kids in Texas just drive off into the fields and shoot guns and get into fights and it's just considered part of growing up. Good clean fun or letting off steam or whatever they call it.

But here in New York, you can't just go target shooting. You can't even get a gun, really. Even getting into a fight at the park could lead to getting arrested or something like that.

Anyway, I tell myself that when this is all over, I'll try to be nicer to my mom and not get upset when she worries and fusses over me. Of course, now there's actually a reason for her to be concerned. And the irony of it is that she got me into this mess by telling me to help Ms. Marrillion with her grocery shopping. Not that I blame her.

My English teacher would be proud of me for noticing the irony in the situation, but I don't think it's something I'll ever be able to tell her about.

Unless I end up famous somehow as a result of this. Like if I testify in front of Congress or something. That's another way conspiracy movies end.

I decide to keep brainstorming with D'Argyle.

"She didn't reply yet, huh?"

"No," I say. "How'd you know?"

"I figured you'd say something if she did. But don't worry. I'm sure she's fine. Your mom is tough. Even my mom thinks so."

"I know she's tough when it comes to dealing with the building's super or my teachers or telemarketers. This is different, though."

"Think of it this way: you've survived so far. And she raised you. So if you were able to figure this all out, I bet she can, too."

"Yeah, you're probably right," I say. "Thanks."

"Like Dionne Warwick says, that's what friends are for. And she's got all those psychic friends, so she knows what's going on."

I laugh. Sometimes even I don't understand what D'Argyle is talking about.

"Let's keep planning," I say. "And try to figure out how to get out of this."

"I have an idea," he says. "You have to get your phone back first, but we can do it on mine for now. There's an app called Mobile Justice that's built to record interactions with the police and other types of cops. It automatically sends the footage somewhere, so it's safe, even if your phone is confiscated. I bet we can get something that livestreams, too, in case you're not dealing with the cops but need to record it anyway. And then we set up something to record the footage."

"Great, so if I get killed, at least a video of it can go viral," I say.

"You're not gonna get killed, Lee. But we do want to be able to get audio and video of this conspiracy, so they can't deny it later. They might say you were a terrorist or something."

"I'm not!"

"I know that. But if the FBI or somebody says you are, it will be all over the news. And then a few days later, they can say, 'Oops, we were wrong, sorry,' but the news won't cover *that* part. So then you spend the rest of your life with everyone thinking you're a terrorist."

"Then I'll never be able to get into college," I say. "And my mom would kill me."

"Ha ha, she's probably more of a threat than the bad guys if it comes down to that."

"Alright, then we definitely need to figure out how to record all this stuff so they can't frame me or Ms. Marrillion."

"I'm on it," D'Argyle says. "I'll figure out all the apps we need."

Great. Now all I need is a phone.

CHAPTER 41

THE WIRE

"MAYBE YOU DON'T NEED A PHONE," D'Argyle says.

He's been rummaging around in the closet. Now he's waving something in my face that looks like a fat remote control.

"I got this back when I was thinking of starting a podcast. Remember?"

"The one about shoes or the one about movies?"

"Either. Both. It doesn't matter," he says. "Anyway, I got this microphone."

"Couldn't you just record a podcast on your phone?"

"What? No. What if somebody called me while I was recording?"

"You'd just ignore it. You can't answer the phone in the middle of a podcast!"

"I can if it's like a radio show. But who cares? I didn't actually start the podcast, so you can use this microphone."

"What do I plug it into?"

"Nothing! That's the point," he says. "At least, not when you're recording. It has its own memory so you can record the audio files on here. You'd need to plug it into a computer to get the files off of it."

"Maybe," I say. D'Argyle is notorious for pretending to do you a favor just to be nice and then, when it's been a minute, ask for something in return, like it was a transaction. Still, I can afford to pay him back somehow later if I survive this mess.

"What I was thinking was, even if you had a phone, everybody's going to be worried about it. The guys in the conspiracy, I mean. But if somehow they see your phone or even get a hold of it, they'll assume you can't record anything they say at that point. *That's* when you turn this thing on and catch them."

"It's like when somebody keeps a back-up gun in their ankle holster in the movies."

"Sure! Except it's a microphone and not a gun. And I don't know if it will fit in your sock, but I know what you mean."

"Can I try it out?" I ask.

"I think it needs batteries first. Let me go grab some."

For some reason, D'Argyle's mom likes to keep batteries in the refrigerator. He's told her that he looked it up online and it doesn't actually make them last longer, but that doesn't convince her. Plus, she says, keeping them there means she always knows where to find them. I guess she's got a point. In my apartment, we can never remember where we put the batteries. In mom's desk drawer? In the TV stand? In the kitchen? D'Argyle's mom always knows where they are.

D'Argyle brings them back and tosses them to me. I drop them on the couch by accident, because they're so cold they startle me.

"Ha ha. You better have better hands than that when you're taking on the FBI," he says.

I load the batteries into the device and try to figure out how it works.

"It's got a bunch of different settings," D'Argyle says. "But you don't really need to worry about that. Just switch this thing from *Off* to *Standby*. Then press the red circle button. The clock will start running, so you know it's working."

"How long does it record for?"

"Uh, I guess it depends what mode you're using. Maybe we do need to figure out the settings after all."

"Do you have the instruction manual?"

"Nah, I always throw those things away. It's 2021! You can find all that stuff online."

Sure enough, he searches for a bit and then finds a PDF of the original instruction manual.

"Maybe I can convince my mom to throw away that giant folder full of old warranties she keeps."

"Well, warranties are different. You need those in case something breaks. Although usually it's cheaper to just buy a new one. Because you still have to pay for postage and stuff if you want to send something back to the manufacturer."

I press *Stop* on the microphone. Then I press the little triangle button that usually means play. It sounds tinny, but I can hear what we said a few seconds before:

"Do you have the instruction manual?"

"Nah, I always throw those things away. It's 2021! You can find all that stuff online."

"See?" D'Argyle says. "It works! And it sounds better if you plug it into something. They put more effort into the microphone than the speaker, which is mostly there for you to confirm that it recorded something in the first place."

"Now I'm all set like McNutty," I say, pronouncing "McNulty" the way that the character Bubbles used to on *The Wire*. My mom let me watch it when I was younger, despite the violence and sex, because she said it was so well made and educational.

"Sheeeeeeeee…" D'Argyle begins a swear like the character Clay Davis always did, and I remember that *The Wire* also had bad words I had to promise my mom I wouldn't say in school.

She didn't want me to get in trouble.

CHAPTER 42

NIGHT COMES ON

D'ARGYLE'S MOM comes home and we convince her that I'm allowed to sleep over here. I've done it enough in the past that it doesn't seem suspicious and she doesn't try to check with my mom.

We don't tell her about any of the stuff that's going on, except for the bit we have to—that there was some sort of incident in my building, and my mom would feel safer if I wasn't there tonight, at least until the authorities figure out what's going on.

I tell her that my mom went to stay at a friend's house, and they were thinking about going out for wine time, so she won't be suspicious if she texts my mom and doesn't hear back. Maybe she's at a loud club and can't hear the phone pinging.

This doesn't take very long. D'Argyle's mom is exhausted, so she throws some sheets and a blanket on the couch for me and goes to bed herself.

D'Argyle and I stay up for a while, practicing how to use the recorder, and checking my email for messages from my mom.

I get pretty good at turning on the microphone with one hand while it's in my pocket and I can't see it.

We don't get any messages from my mom or Ms. Marrillion.

The hardest part is thinking about going to sleep.

She might be trying to call me.

If I had my phone, I could set it to the loudest setting so that it would wake me up no matter how late she called.

Relying on email, though, is tough. I'd have to just wake up every so often to see if she's written back. But then I won't get any kind of meaningful sleep.

Someone at school said my body needs sleep, and dream time, to process the day's memories and file them away. After the day I've had, my mind will be working overtime trying to figure out where to store everything.

And if you don't get enough sleep, you can just die from it. Sleep deprivation.

I guess it's like food or water that way.

Eventually I get tired enough to try to go to sleep.

I put some toothpaste on my finger and brush my teeth with it. It's weird how everyone's toothpaste tastes different. Little things like that remind me that I'm not at home.

D'Argyle finds an old digital stopwatch and sets an alarm for early in the morning.

I want to wake up, and if there's no email from my mom, go to the McDonald's on 181st Street where we said we'd meet if we ever got separated.

Hopefully Ms. Marrillion remembers that.

I hope she and my mom are there.

If not, I'll have to spend the whole day checking email and that will get tiresome.

Then we have the evening meet-up spot.

Tomorrow could be a long day of waiting.

But the sooner I go to sleep, the sooner I'll be able to move forward.

It's too late to really do anything tonight.

"Lee, if someone busts into our apartment tonight, I'll climb out the window and run for help."

"Gee, thanks," I say.

"Yeah, you know, I figure, what good can I do against a guy

with a machine gun or something? I just wanted you to know so you don't wait for me to come back you up in a fistfight."

"Don't worry. If the door breaks open, I'll just point to your room and scream 'Lee's in there!' and then, while they're torturing you, I'll go out the front door."

He laughs.

"Fair enough. But seriously, if you hear someone outside the door, come wake me up. I've got a baseball bat in my room."

"Maybe I should keep the bat out here?"

"Nah, you've got your wits to protect you."

He turns off the living room light and goes to his bedroom.

I'm alone again.

I stretch out on the couch, tuck my head under the pillow, and try to sleep.

———

I dream that I'm driving a school bus.

Which is weird, because I've never driven a car or a bus in real life. And I've only ever been on school buses a few times, for field trips. I've been able to walk to school most of my life. When I take the bus, it's usually a city bus.

So I don't know why my brain put me behind the wheel of this big yellow school bus, but that's what I'm doing, and it's out of control. The brakes don't work, and I can barely swing the steering wheel because it's so heavy, and we're just headed downhill fast. Everyone on the bus is screaming. I turn around and see that it's my mom and Ms. Marrillion and D'Argyle, plus a bunch of teenagers I don't recognize.

Next thing I know, the bus is on the George Washington Bridge heading to New Jersey. I see sirens in the rear-view mirror, but I can't stop.

Somehow, the bridge has turned into a hill. If you've ever been on the GWB, you know it's flat. I guess stuff doesn't always make sense in nightmares.

I turn around and yell: "Does anybody know how to drive a bus?"

Ms. Marrillion raises her hand.

"Then you better come do it," I tell her.

She starts walking toward the front of the bus.

When she gets next to me, she says, quietly, "If we go below 50 miles per hour, the bus will explode."

That sounds familiar to me, but my brain doesn't work quite as well in the dream as it does in real life.

"We're going fast enough," I say. "You take the wheel."

I stand up and move aside so that she can sit in the driver's seat, but as I do that, the bus suddenly veers to the right and busts through the gates.

"I can drive a bus," Ms. Marrillion says, "but I can't fly a bus."

We're soaring out into the air, and then dropping down towards the Hudson River.

I turn around and see the police cars have driven off the bridge too and are falling right behind us, like they plan to arrest us in the water.

I bet in real life, it wouldn't take very long to fall from a bridge.

In the dream, though, it takes forever.

We just keep falling.

And falling.

And falling.

Like we're never going to hit the water.

Even though we're not underwater, it feels *like we are. Everything is slow, like when you're moving around in a pool, fully submerged.*

I try to press on the brake with my foot, as if that could stop us from falling, but my muscles don't respond.

Then, instead of splashing into the water, we end up on top of it. The river is frozen now, and we're sliding as if we were on ice skates.

Up ahead there's a roadblock, although I guess it's more of a river block since we're on the Hudson.

A bunch of soldiers are there pointing guns at us. They start shooting and something in the engine of the bus catches fire. I look down at the meter on the dashboard and see that the gas tank is full. Right as I notice that, the bus explodes and

I wake up.

I'm on D'Argyle's couch.

I worry that I might have yelled or made some sort of noise in my sleep, but nobody has come out to check on me.

I look towards the door and all the locks are still bolted.

The clock on their cable box tells me it's 3:17 AM.

I try to go back to sleep, but my heart is racing.

CHAPTER 43

WE PACK OUR KNIVES AND GO

LITTLE NOISES KEEP DISTRACTING ME.

The city's always been full of sounds at night, but I've never been so scared by them.

There's cars driving around on the streets just outside D'Argyle's. That's normal, except now I wonder if those cars are full of crooked cops or mafia thugs with guns.

Then, farther away, I hear louder engines. Usually, that's just drag racers around Amsterdam Ave, but tonight I think it might be tanks or some other army trucks storming into Washington Heights to lay down the law.

Periodically I can hear a very low horn, either a train running up the Hudson, or maybe some sort of cargo ship? The big ones don't float up the river, but I've seen smaller ones heading up to deliver oil or machine parts or whatever's in those boats.

And that's just the vehicle sounds.

Within the building, there are other noises. People coming home late in the evening, their footsteps echoing in the halls, their keys in the locks, their doors opening and closing. On any other night, I'd hardly notice, since NYC is a 24/7 kind of town. Now, though, I can't sleep, and I wonder if the person I hear walking through the building might be coming to kill me. Or at least coming to threaten me so I'll tell them where Ms. Marrillion is.

The radiator makes noises too, even though it's summer. Maybe it's broken? It bangs and thuds just like the one in my building does in the middle of winter. I've grown up with it so it's never seemed like a big deal, although we've had some overnight guests from outside the city who seem freaked out because it does sort of sound like something is about to blow up. If you've never heard it, imagine somebody trapped inside a big metal box, hammering away at it, trying to get out. I guess it's the steam that makes that noise?

Like I said, it's always been part of my life, so I learned to just tune it out. But now every time I hear it, I panic. It could be somebody kicking in the door.

I keep picturing that guy who shot his way into Ms. Marrillion's, even though I didn't actually see it. I only heard it, but somehow there's a vivid image in my brain of how it went down, and that's what I picture every time the radiator rattles and thumps against itself.

Even the refrigerator is terrifying. Every 20 minutes or so, it whirs to life, and the sound startles me even though it's one of the most harmless sounds in the world.

Part of me wants to bury my head under the pillow to drown it all out. Except, if I do that, then I might not be able to hear if something actually does happen.

So I just lie here on the couch, trying to ignore the regular noises and listen for the irregular ones.

Other sounds that happen every night:

Fireworks.

Car doors slamming.

Bottles breaking.

Dogs barking.

Buses starting and stopping.

Subwoofers blasting from passing cars.

Police sirens chirping.

Ambulance horns blaring.

The only thing I realize I don't hear is birds. I guess they're all asleep, in their nests or on their tree branches, or on fire escapes maybe. I've never seen a bird go to sleep, so I don't know how they do it.

———

I guess I must fall asleep again at some point because after a while, I notice that I *do* hear the birds. And also there's light coming in through the windows. Not just the streetlamps and security lights on the outer walls of the building, but sunlight, or whatever they call the light just before the actual sun. The sky is illuminated, but there's no direct sunlight yet.

Still, it's getting brighter, and the animals are awake, and I guess that means it's time for me to get up and face the day.

I shower and then borrow some of D'Argyle's clothes.

None of them fit very well, but that makes them pretty useful as a disguise—I don't look at all like myself.

There's still no email from mom or Ms. Marrillion, which scares me, but I try to act brave.

We still haven't told D'Argyle's mom what's going on, but she leaves for work pretty early, and then we can talk freely once she's gone.

I don't have my cell phone or the knife, so I feel a little exposed.

D'Argyle has a plan for all that: First, he gets another knife from his kitchen.

"We're going to have to buy you a bunch of replacement knives when this is all over," I say.

"Nah, we mostly eat carry-out. Mom won't miss a few old knives."

He doesn't stop with the blades, though.

He gives me a stack of magazines and tells me to tape them around my body.

"I saw it in this movie about hackers," he says. "The guy from *Thor* did it so that the bad guys couldn't stab him on the street."

"It's hard to move," I say. I feel like I make a strange paper crinkling sound every time I turn my body.

"Once you put a jacket on, it won't be as noticeable," D'Argyle says.

"A jacket? Bruh, it's like 90 degrees outside."

"Do you want to be cool or do you want to be alive?"

"Alive, I guess."

"Then you gotta wear these magazines. I'll try to find a light jacket so you won't sweat too much."

"Yeah, I bet damp magazines don't offer very much protection."

Still, it's nice that D'Argyle's looking out for me.

We wrap some magazines around my legs too.

"You have a big artery in your thigh," he says. "This could save your life."

"What if I get a lot of paper cuts from the magazines and bleed to death that way?"

"It's not that bad."

"I don't see *you* covering yourself in Bed Bath & Beyond catalogs."

"That's because nobody's trying to kill me!"

He has a point.

Once I'm covered in paper, duct tape, and a jacket, we head towards the McDonald's, making a plan as we go.

"I think I can scope out the scene first," D'Argyle says. "I know what your mom and Ms. Millennium look like, and they would both recognize me. But hopefully none of the thugs know what I look like."

"Maybe they saw you dancing yesterday?"

"How will they know I was doing that to cause a distraction? If they see me, they'd probably ask for my autograph on account of I'm a great dancer."

I doubt this, but don't say anything.

"Nobody should know about our meeting point, though. I think it should be safe for me."

"Yeah, but you don't want to get trapped inside a fast-food restaurant. It's better for you to be out on the sidewalk, where you can run if you have to."

I can't argue with that.

We're walking south on Broadway.

The cocoon of old magazines around me has settled a bit, and isn't too uncomfortable yet.

Since it's early, the sun hasn't had a chance to heat up the morning air. I rarely get up this early when I don't have school, so it's weird to be outside at 7:30 AM.

There's more people than I would have expected out on the streets. I guess everybody has to go to work even when school's out for the summer.

I didn't sleep very well last night, but I still feel a lot better than I did last night when I was running around.

I try to stay alert and keep my eyes out for trouble.

CHAPTER 44
THE HOUR OF CHAOS

THEN I SEE Ms. Marrillion's face right in front of me.

Staring at me.

It's not actually her, though. It's a photograph of her, taped to a stop sign on the corner.

Missing Elderly Woman:

Willa Marrillion.

Please call if spotted

$1,000 Reward if it leads to her

There's a phone number on the page.

Somehow I doubt it reaches anybody good.

The sign is pretty convincing and touching. If I didn't know better, I'd call the number if I saw her. These guys have got their shiz together.

I look up the block and see them plastered all over the place: on street lamp posts, on those old red fire alarm call boxes, even tucked under windshield wipers of cars.

They must have been busy at the Staples last night, using the color copier. Or maybe they have their own machine in their offices. It doesn't look like an official police flyer, so I wonder if it's just something the mob or somebody else put together.

Up until now, they've been aggressive, but not very smart. This makes me think there's someone else behind all the guys who've been chasing us so far, somebody with brains.

D'Argyle is in the McDonald's, pretending to look at the menu. I know it's just an act. He knows that thing like the back of his hand. Doesn't everybody? Except maybe for a tourist from a country where they don't have Big Macs, but what would they be doing all the way up here in Washington Heights? They'd probably be at the Mickey D's in Times Square.

Still, D'Argyle is a ham, really nodding his head up and down like he's considering all the options at a fancy restaurant. But he's also looking around to see if somehow my mom or Ms. Marrillion slipped in wearing a disguise. And I hope he's also keeping an eye out for killers.

I'm starting to get itchy. It might be nerves, but it's probably just all the paper wrapped around my body.

On top of that, I'm getting hungry. Usually I'd eat breakfast before leaving the apartment, but this isn't a normal day.

For a second, I think about texting D'Argyle to get me an Egg McMuffin, until I remember that I don't have a cell phone. It's so strange to be without it.

If we weren't in the middle of this situation, my mom would probably be excited and tell me I'd learn a lot about surviving without it. Of course, she'd also be mad that I lost it. Like she said before, she can be mad and proud at the same time. She's funny like that.

I could run up to the falafel place that also sells breakfast bagels, but then I'd be ditching D'Argyle, and without a phone, something as simple as walking 100 feet could lead to us getting separated and not finding each other again.

Especially if I run into trouble.

So it's safer to stay here, on the sidewalk, keeping tabs on the corner of 181st and Broadway.

Luckily, there don't seem to be any flyers with my face on them. I hope that's because they don't know who I am yet. Whoever *they* are. It's possible they do know me, and are just concentrating on finding Ms. Marrillion. After all, they'd only need me because I could help find her.

I don't want to end up on a flyer anytime soon. Everyone from school would recognize me, and some idiot would call the number to turn me in and get a reward, if they offered one. I wonder if I could call the number myself and get the money in that case. I doubt it. These guys probably don't even really have money to pay the reward. They'll just take the information and run. And maybe torture me to find out what I know.

No reward is worth that.

A siren in the background suddenly grows louder and two police cruisers roll up on the block.

I panic and try to hide my fear.

Up the hill towards Fort Washington Avenue, I see two women duck inside a bodega.

I want to go and see if it's my mom and Ms. Marrillion, but a big black SUV races into the intersection and stops in the middle of traffic. I'm afraid if they spot me, they could follow me to the bodega and catch everybody at once.

So I have to leave.

D'Argyle comes out of the McDonald's, looking around like he heard all the noise.

I shake my head from side to side and back away.

CHAPTER 45
CUT AND RUN

IT GETS LOUDER and louder as I stumble from the intersection.

More cars pull up, and pretty soon a helicopter is hovering overhead.

I don't really have time to stop and think it through, but my brain is running through every scenario.

Did they somehow follow me and D'Argyle to the meet-up? I don't think so, because they probably would have swooped in and grabbed me if that was the case.

Did they get a line on mom and Ms. Marrillion? Maybe they used their phone and tracked them to 181st? Maybe mom was turning her phone on periodically to check if there was any word from me. I get mad at myself for losing my phone. Maybe I caused all this.

I realize it's suspicious the way I'm backing up Broadway, so I turn around and walk, head down, minding my own business. It's a thing you learn pretty early in the city. Sometimes it's a commotion, other times it's just one loud, rude person you want to avoid engaging with. Anyway, you just focus on something else and don't make eye contact.

You can't take it *too* far, though. If you're trying to avoid some-body or something too much, then it becomes noticeable. It doesn't work to actively turn your head away. What you have to do is just pretend you're engaged in something else. Music is great. Last night I pretended I was listening to music. In the daylight, it might be a little too obvious that there's nothing in my ear. And I don't have my phone to look at as if that's distracting me.

So I just try to force myself to look casual, like all the sirens and the helicopter aren't part of my world. I'm just a kid on my way somewhere who happened to pass through all the chaos on the block.

I'm not really sure where I'm going. I guess I'm vaguely headed back towards D'Argyle's place, but maybe that's not a good idea. The more I stay in any one location, the more likely they are to find me, I think.

Then I start wondering if there's a way I can help mom and Ms. Marrillion get out of that bodega.

Maybe I could cause a big distraction? Would that get the police and everyone else to leave that block and follow me?

Probably not.

There's so many of them swarming the block now that they'd have enough men to run me down and still keep a presence on 181 to find my mom and Ms. Marrillion.

Can they sneak out the back door? My mom can be a tough talker and pushy when she wants. And she knows a lot of people in the neighborhood, so that should give them a chance. It will be a bit harder with Ms. Marrillion, who can't move as quickly.

I keep thinking about the distraction idea.

Even if it wouldn't work right now, I wonder if I can get the police to move to another block.

I see more signs with Ms. Marrillion's face as I head north up Broadway, and then I get the idea to call the number. If I give a really credible report, that might get them to move their resources somewhere else. Especially if they didn't actually see my mom and Ms. Marrillion and were just, like, following a phone signal or something.

Now I just need to figure out how to call in a fake report when I don't even have a phone. There used to be phone booths everywhere on the sidewalk, something I know from old movies. That's how Superman used to change into his costume.

They're all gone now.

Sometimes the hardware is still there, old pay phones that aren't plugged in or with the loose ends of cords dangling in the air. But everything's been cut off.

I think about where I could find a telephone to call in a fake sighting of Ms. Marrillion. I don't have any quarters, so I couldn't use a pay phone even if I found one that worked. I'd have to get change first.

Maybe the library? I don't think they're open this early.

I remember those weird Wi-Fi poles the city installed where pay phones used to be. I think they have number pads on them, so maybe they can be used for outgoing calls? I've never looked that closely, though, because I never needed one when I had my cell phone. And usually they're blocked by unhoused people watching internet videos or something like that.

I could try to borrow somebody's phone by pretending I lost mine. People do that sometimes, but it would be suspicious when they heard the phone call I made.

"Hello, I'd like to report that I saw that woman you're looking for…" Only I'd name a location wildly far away from where we were and the person would know I was lying. What if the people at that number called back? Or tracked the phone's owner down and asked about me? Too risky.

I suppose I could buy a prepaid phone somewhere on Broadway, but would that be a waste of the remaining money I have?

Especially because I don't know if I could keep using the phone or if they'd track it somehow.

Could I use it to call my mom first? Just to tell her I'm ok? Before I call the number on the missing woman poster, they won't have any way to trace the number to me. Unless they're monitoring my mom's phone. Then they'd see my new number on the incoming call log and the new phone would be traceable.

It's tricky. There's almost no way to do anything anymore without the government or some big company being able to figure out who you are and what you're doing.

Then in my head, I remember a phone booth near D'Argyle's apartment at Broadway and 193rd. I've never used it, but for some reason it caught my eye once. I think because it's across the street from a deli with a really old sign, like from the 1970s or something.

It's probably what the place looked like in Times Square, where that lady from the cab ate clams.

Anyway, I pick up my pace a bit. I don't want to run, which might make people look at me closer, but the faster I can get there, the better.

I don't think I've ever actually used a pay phone before, now that I think about it. I can run into one of the bodegas and get change from them. Or probably buy something, if they're cranky and won't give me change without a purchase.

I've seen them behave both ways. Somebody will come in from the street and ask for change for some reason, and they'll give it to them, but when kids my age go in, they usually say no. I think they just don't like children and think we're all up to no good.

In that case, I'd have to make sure to buy something that would leave me with enough change for a phone call. Something that costs like $1.25 so I still have 75 cents leftover. If it costs $0.99, then I'd only get a penny back and I'm pretty sure I'd need a quarter.

I've heard people say "drop a dime" on someone to refer to calling the police about them, but there's no way it only costs ten cents to make a phone call. Maybe it did back in the old days, when Ms. Marrillion was a little girl.

I get to the corner and realize I was right.

There *was* a phone here.

I can see the patch in the sidewalk where it used to be.

But it's gone now.

CHAPTER 46

A BRIGHTER SUMMER DAY

I KEEP MOVING.

I *need* to keep moving.

Did they rip out *all* of the payphones that used to be in the city? Or will I find one if I keep looking?

I need to find one fast for my plan to work. I'm assuming mom and Ms. Marrillion are hiding out in the bodega and nobody's captured them yet. I hope I'm not too late.

What if somebody sees them and calls to get the reward from the flyer?

That gives me an idea.

I tear one of the flyers off the nearest poles and run into the bodega.

"Do you have a phone?" I ask. "I saw this old woman outside the Cloisters just now. I want to call and get the reward."

"What?" asks the man behind the counter.

I point at Ms. Marrillion's face.

"I saw her outside the Cloisters. If I call this number and report it, I can get $1,000! I just need to use your phone."

"What do we look like, a public phone shop?"

I leave that flyer on the counter and go outside.

I find another just down the block and do the same thing all over again:

"Hey, do you got a phone? I saw this woman on the flyer. She was right outside the Cloisters, and if I call this number, they'll give me a thousand dollars!"

"Get out of here, kid, unless you're going to buy something."

I leave the flyer behind again.

Hopefully, at least one of these shopkeepers will get greedy and decide to call the number themself.

I run up and down Broadway, tearing down flyers, running into businesses and emphasizing that I saw the woman right outside the Cloisters.

Luckily, nobody asks why I was outside the Cloisters so early in the morning, or why I can't just call on my cell phone. I leave the flyers behind so they have the phone number and can call in the tip themselves.

It's exhausting.

But on the bright side, I'm also getting rid of a bunch of the flyers, so that if somebody actually does see Ms. Marrillion later, they won't know who to call.

After about 20 minutes, I can sense a change. Up the hill from where I am on Broadway, a helicopter hovers low over the park, about where the Cloisters museum is. I hear police cars and big SUVs headed my way from 181st, sirens wailing and engines revving. A few vehicles stop near the entrances to the park down here, like they're watching for her to come out.

If my plan works, then this drew enough of them away from the bodega where Ms. Marrillion and my mom *actually* are.

I feel sorry for the museum staff at the Cloisters, who are probably dealing with a bunch of cops and thugs barging in. It was such a peaceful place yesterday, and now I've unleashed all this fury on them.

Still, I remember that Ms. Marrillion said her taxes and my mom's taxes help pay for the museum, so we shouldn't feel bad if they have to deal with this scary situation just like we do.

Now that the heat's headed in this direction, I make my way back towards the McDonald's and the meeting point. I doubt they're still there, but it's worth a shot, and maybe I can find D'Argyle again.

If he's not there, he'll probably have gone back to his apartment, and I can try to find him there later.

I keep my head down because I don't want the oncoming cop cars to notice me.

They don't.

They're probably all too busy trying to figure out if *they* can claim the reward when they find Ms. Marrillion, or if it will just be considered part of their job.

Not that they'll find her where they're going.

———

The day is really getting started now. All the early risers have been up for a while, but the slowpokes and sleep-in types have finally joined them.

If it was a normal day, of course, I'd still be in bed.

Well, I'd have gotten up when my mom was getting ready for work, but then gone back to bed for a nap after she left. Or maybe I'd be sleeping on the couch, or just kind of half awake flipping through TV channels.

It's strange to think that I miss that.

You expect people to miss big moments and huge life events. But wasting time on the couch? That's not usually what people talk about when they're on their deathbed, breathing oxygen through a tube:

"I wish I'd spent more time relaxing in front of the television instead of sharing quality time with the people I loved."

I mean, it's not that I would rate naps more highly than cool family experiences with mom. It's just that everything got so stressful yesterday afternoon, and I wasn't ready for it.

If I go away to college, I'll at least have time to plan for that, so it may be exciting and tense, but I'll know when it's coming.

This situation came out of nowhere. One minute I was at the grocery store, the next I'm running for my life, or at least for Ms. Marrillion's life.

Even she had a sense that her life was changing when they picked her up from the orphanage and drove her through the dark night. She didn't know *how* it was going to change, but she could tell it was a turning point.

I was just standing in the kitchen, and the phone rang, but that kind of thing happens all the time. There was no dramatic music, nothing like that. It's like those stories you sometimes hear of a stray bullet coming up from the street and hitting someone who was just sitting in their home minding their own business. Or a guy is mowing his lawn and a falling piece of airplane lands on him without warning.

I'm passing more people, and it's easier for me to blend in with the crowd. If we're lucky, it will be the same way for mom and Ms. Marrillion.

It works both ways, though.

It's easier for me to mix in with the crowd, but that means it's easier for hitmen and government agents to sneak up on me. When the streets were emptier this morning, I could get a pretty good look at anybody coming my way. Now there's a whole crowd for them to blend in with on the sidewalks. Somebody could get up close and grab me without me realizing it.

People who sell things on the street are setting up their stalls and tables, laying out their merchandise.

As I get close to 181st Street, I can overhear people talking about the excitement from before, speculating about all the cops swarming in suddenly. Some people think it was a drug deal. Others say it must have been an escaped prisoner hiding out nearby.

I wonder what they'd say if I told them all that fuss was for an old lady who didn't do anything wrong. In this part of town, they'd probably believe me. They know how hard it is for someone to catch a fair break. And they know that the government and police aren't always the good guys.

Pretty soon, I'm back outside the McDonald's. Only now I'm really, *really* hungry.

I wonder if I should risk going in and getting a sandwich. I look around for D'Argyle without any luck. I also keep an eye out for my mom or Ms. Marrillion.

I don't see any of them.

I head for the bodega they ducked into. I doubt I'll find them there, but I have to check.

CHAPTER 47
THE BODEGA

INSIDE THE BODEGA, it's quiet.

Way too quiet.

It takes me a little while to realize what's wrong.

There's no music playing. No TV. No talk radio. Nothing but the sound of the refrigerators humming.

It's what they call eerie, like in a horror movie when someone's about to be killed.

You could hear a pin drop … if for some reason you had a pin you didn't want, and you let it fall to the ground.

The silence is almost louder than regular noise would be.

I realize I've never been in a store when it's as quiet as this. There's so much sound in the city in general: cars, trains, shouting, Bluetooth speakers, trash trucks, and all that. Everything that kept me up in D'Argyle's apartment last night, but multiplied by a thousand during the daytime.

On top of that, a place like this, a bodega, has its own specific kind of sound.

Making your way through the city, through your neighborhood, you get to know what different shopkeepers are into—some have soccer games playing nonstop, while others listen to Spanish language broadcasts, or some kind of imported music and news from the Middle East like at that one place up the hill, the Fort Tryon Grill. Also known as the Fort Tryon Deli & Grill. And sometimes the Fort Tryon Grill & Juicebar. They're always updating their name to catch the latest fad. Pretty soon it will be called the Fort Tryon Grill & Vape Shop, I bet.

But this place I'm in now is just quiet, so I know something's wrong.

I look at the guy behind the counter and he barely makes eye contact with me.

That's also strange. Kids my age, we're always getting stared at by store managers worried we're going to steal something or start some kind of trouble.

This guy is just minding his own business, minding it harder than anyone I've ever seen.

I look closer and see he is holding a pen and looking intently at a crossword puzzle on the counter.

Except this puzzle is completely finished already. So he's only pretending to look at it.

The question is, can I trust him? Is he just the regular neighborhood grocer who maybe saw my mom and Ms. Marrillion come in earlier? Maybe he even saw where they went, and whether they got away?

Or is he some sort of cop, planted here to watch out for anyone who might be looking for the two women from before? Like maybe they already captured my mom and Ms. Marrillion and now they're just trying to catch all their known associates, and they left this guy here pretending to be a shopkeeper to grab anyone who asks about them.

I decide I have to figure it out—is he real or just a plant? I can't pass up the chance to find out what happened to mom and Ms. Marrillion if he knows.

Then I realize I can test him, figure out if he's really a bodega guy.

I grab a can of Arizona iced tea from one of the coolers, the kind that says $0.99 in big print on the side.

"Yo, how much is this?"

He finally looks up at me.

"Dollar twenty-five," he says, and then I know he really works here. A hitman or mafia dude would have probably guessed 99 cents, not knowing about the mark-up.

I put the cab back—I can't waste my money on a giant iced tea this early in the day.

"Hey," I say, approaching the counter. "Did you see a woman and an old woman come in here before? Like half an hour ago?"

He comes out from behind the counter and runs over to the door. Then he turns the *Open* sign around so it says *Closed*.

He locks the door.

He laughs, and it scares me.

"Yeah, I saw them," he says.

CHAPTER 48
LOST IN THE BACKYARDS

THIS GUY'S got me trapped in his bodega.

I look toward the back—maybe I can escape out there? Although he clearly knows the building better than I do.

"Relax, kid," he says. "I'm not gonna hurt you."

I must look like I don't believe him.

"Seriously. I just closed the shop so no one else could get in."

"What if I want to get out?"

"Be my guest. But I thought you were looking for those two women."

Can I trust him?

I figure I don't have much to lose. If he was after my mom and Ms. Marrillion, he probably already got them. And if he wanted to hurt me, well, I bet he's got a baseball bat or gun or some pepper spray behind the counter. He could have already knocked me out, or worse.

"I am looking for them," I say. "Are they here?"

"Nah," he answers. "I offered to let them hide in the bathroom, but they figured it was safer to keep moving."

"You got a bathroom?!" I ask. Every bodega I've ever been in claims they don't have a bathroom.

"Just for me," he sighs. "Not for the public."

I can tell he's upset he let his secret out.

"What, you think bodega owners pee in a jar behind the counter? Close the shop in the middle of the day so we can take a whizz? Of course we got a bathroom. We just don't want customers messing it up."

He is walking back as he says this.

Then he opens the door to what I assumed was a storeroom.

"It's back here."

There's a little hallway filled with broken-down cardboard boxes, and then a plain white door.

"It don't say bathroom on it, just in case some sneaky jerk goes back trying to find it."

He opens the door. It's, well, a normal bathroom.

I don't know what I expected.

"It would have been a tight fit for both those ladies, but I offered just the same. I could tell by the look on their face they were in a tight spot. Lotta heat coming down on them, huh?"

"You could say that," I answer.

"They went out the back," he says.

Then he kicks open a door out into the concrete space behind the building. It runs pretty far back, then connects with the lots behind all the buildings on 180th Street and 181st from Fort Washington down to Broadway.

"They could be in any of those buildings," he says, gesturing with this hand at all the rear windows and fire escapes of the apartments. "Or maybe they went back out onto the street. For a while, it seemed like they were trapped in here, with cops and g-men swarming all over. But then, real quick like, they all vanished. It sounded like they went north. Good luck for those old broads."

I want to say, "My mom's not an old broad," but he doesn't seem to mean it as an insult, so I let it slide. Besides, it sounds like he helped them.

"If you catch up with them," he says, "don't startle them or nothing. I gave them the stun gun I keep behind the counter. It seemed like they could use it."

"Thanks for looking out for them," I say.

"Hey, it's what we do. A place like this? We can't let 'em ride all over us, with their badges or gang signs or whatever they bring. If I got a problem in here, I don't call the cops, they take too long. It's the people who live here that come help me and look out for my shop. So I get a chance? I look out for them in return."

I want to give him something in exchange for the help he gave my mom and Ms. Marrillion.

"Don't worry," I say as I leave. "I won't tell nobody about your bathroom."

It's the least I can do.

———

I walk out into the maze of back alleys and concrete patios.

You can tell a lot about a building by the way its outdoor space is maintained.

Some are decorated with lights, others have well-kept gardens or potted plants.

Others are full of children's toys: Big Wheels or cheap knock-offs of Big Wheels, old rusty bikes, little fountains and pool play sets. All kinds of brightly colored plastic, beat up over the years.

Then there are buildings where the super is less reliable. The weeds are growing out of cracks in the pavement, choking off the fences and overcrowding the usable space.

Old newspapers and empty bottles and cans and plastic bags have gotten caught in these areas and never removed.

You can go five feet from a welcoming backyard to the kind of place you'd expect to find a dead body.

Except I don't want to find one today.

I'm trying to figure out which way my mom and Ms. Marrillion would go when they were here before me.

I think they'd want to get inside quickly, because I feel

exposed. There isn't a clear line of sight to the street from where I am, but all it would take is one person climbing over a fence to see me, and when things were as chaotic with cops as they were this morning, it wouldn't feel safe here.

My mom might have been able to climb up one of the fire escapes, but I can't imagine Ms. Marrillion doing the same.

So that narrows things down a bit.

Think, Lee. *What would they do?*

I guess they'd try all the doors and see if any of them are open?

On the one hand, I'd hope all the doors lock, for the safety of the people inside.

I know our building's back door locks, and I need a key to get in.

Some days, though, I find it propped open. Maybe a delivery man was bringing in furniture or a new refrigerator or something, and used the metal hook to latch the door open. Then it stays open until they're finished and go back to their truck. Or even longer if they forget to close the door after they're done. Maybe they go out the front door once they've made their deliver.

I look around and see if any of the doors here are open.

It's tricky, because I'm not just looking for ones that are all-the-way open. Sometimes they *look* closed, but there's a brick or wooden wedge that keeps them open just a crack.

Then it strikes me that mom probably would have closed a door behind her if she went inside, so that people chasing them wouldn't know where to look.

It seems pretty hopeless.

Still, what other options do I have?

I hop a fence and try the first door I come to.

It's locked.

I keep doing the same, hoping that nobody calls the cops on me.

I'm not dressed like a prowler and it's not the middle of the night, so maybe there's a chance I can just pass for some weird kid and not somebody who you'd have to call the police to come arrest.

Honestly, the real trouble is dudes who come in through the front door, after pressing all the buzzers, and then grab a bunch of packages from near the mailboxes, and leave.

I've seen them on the neighborhood Facebook group, and on flyers around the block.

Sometimes they'll have a razor or knife and just cut open all the packages while they're in the building, taking out the smaller things inside. I guess it's easier to get away with a few small stolen items in your pocket than to walk out the door of a building with several Amazon boxes.

One time, on the subway, I saw a guy open his backpack and sort through a bunch of stuff that he'd pretty clearly taken out of a building nearby. Then he caught me watching him and cursed at me and pulled out a knife.

I switched cars at the next stop.

Anyway, that was a while ago.

Now I probably look like him, creeping up to people's apartments and trying the back door.

On my fifth try, a door just swings open.

I figure this building is as likely as any to lead me to my mom and Ms. Marrillion as any other, so I go in, pulling the door shut behind me.

And suddenly it's pitch black.

Maybe this was a bad choice.

CHAPTER 49

THE MAN WHO SAW THEM

I IMMEDIATELY BANG my shin against something hard and metal and probably rusty. Luckily, the catalogs wrapped around my legs protect me.

I reach out for the wall to find the light switch, but my hand doesn't feel anything. Just something kind of damp, which is nasty, so I pull my hand back.

Under normal circumstances, I'd use the light on my phone to see what's going on, but I can't do that now, of course.

Instead, I use my foot to push open the door I just came through, letting in a little bit of light.

Then I can see a lightbulb hanging down a few feet away, and a cord below it, the kind you yank down to turn on old-fashioned lights.

I let the door close behind me again, and I'm in the dark, but I'm walking to the lightbulb, avoiding the shelf I banged my leg against earlier.

Reaching out into the darkness, I find the piece of string and pull down on it.

Nothing.

It makes a little clicking noise, but no light.

Not even a flicker.

Now what?

It's completely black in here.

There isn't even like a little light sneaking in through windows or anything like that. I guess they've covered them over with wood or painted them. I'm not sure I've ever been to a place so dark. Even the planetarium at the Museum of Natural History, where we went on a field trip, didn't get this dark. I remember because everyone was talking about what kind of stuff they were going to do in the dark, but there were emergency exit lights and then the glow of the projections, so we could always see each other.

I guess it makes sense that nothing works here. There's no lock on the door, and the bulb is burnt out. They must have a lazy super who doesn't take care of the building.

Knowing it's a bad building doesn't help me very much.

Then I remember I don't need to keep the door shut. My mom and Ms. Marrillion needed to, if they came this way, and people were following them, but I don't. The police and everyone else have moved uptown.

So I move back towards the door again and kick it open.

This time, I'm looking around on the ground for something I can use to prop it open.

There are a few crushed old beer cans on the ground near the door, and it hits me that they're there for a reason. I pick one up and squeeze it into the space near the door hinge. It fits perfectly, like it's been there before, and it keeps the door from swinging shut.

In the dim light from outside, I can see the door at the other end of the storage room, and I head in that direction. Along the way, I'm looking for clues that my mom or Ms. Marrillion came this way.

The floor is dirty and sticky, too nasty to be able to tell if there are any footprints. If this was a movie, I'd find some sign of them, a handkerchief or something, but I don't really expect that. Unless you're Hansel and Gretel leaving a trail of breadcrumbs, most people aren't constantly dropping things that people following them can find.

Still, I don't have any other leads, so I keep going, through the next door, which takes me into a basement hallway.

I'm kind of hoping I'll simply find them, huddled together, waiting for me.

But nobody's there.

Just an empty hallway.

I walk down it to the elevator and push the button.

The car rattles its way down to me. I hope it's not as busted as the room I came from.

I get in and hit the button for the ground floor.

It brings me up slowly, shakily, and the door opens onto an ugly, rundown lobby with a door onto the street.

Then it strikes me that, if they came this way, they might have wanted to avoid the sidewalks for a while, since the heat was coming down hard.

So I press the button for the sixth floor and ride it all the way up, then get out on the top floor of the building.

I'm not really sure what I'm looking for, though. Hopefully some sort of sign that they passed this way. But what would that be? It's not like my mom would have written on the wall with a pen. So there's not going to be a note that says, "Hey Lee, if you're looking for us, here's where we are."

I don't know. Maybe I'll recognize a name on a door plate and if it's one of my mom's friends, I can ask if they've seen her. Although I don't think she's ever mentioned knowing someone in this building, and I've never come here with her before.

Still, I have to start somewhere.

So I walk from one end of the hall to the other, looking for some clue.

And I don't find anything.

Then I walk down a flight of stairs and repeat the same thing on the fifth floor.

No luck there, either.

I do get a sense of how each floor has its own personality, sort of like in my own building.

Somebody's cooking a kind of stew on 5, but on 4, it smells like ammonia. Maybe there's a cat lady who doesn't clean her apartment enough?

On the third floor, I can feel the rumbling bass of a video game.

The second floor is quiet and doesn't smell like anything. Maybe everyone who lives here is at work.

Then I'm back on the ground floor, in the lobby, without knowing anything I didn't know before.

That's when I hear a voice:

"Hey, you! Yeah, you, kid!"

Part of me wants to run, but another part tells me to stay calm. The voice doesn't sound angry. At least, it doesn't sound angry like the guys who were chasing me yesterday. It's a little more confused.

So I turn around.

"Hey, kid, what're you doing here?"

It's an older man in a green jumpsuit with a rag in his hand.

"Oh," I say. "I was just visiting my friend. You know Guzman?"

I figure there's a good chance someone with the last name Guzman lives here.

"Oh, uh, maybe."

My super would know the answer right away, but this guy isn't on top of things, as I could tell from the situation in the basement. The kind of guy who doesn't change burned out light bulbs is probably the same kind of guy who doesn't know the names of the tenants in his building.

Then he asks, "Did you see two old ladies?"

That's the same question *I* was going to ask *him*!

"Two old women? One much older than the other?"

"Yeah. Do you know them? You're not with them, are you?"

I'm about to say yes, but something tells me not to.

"Uh, I seen them, you know, out on the street."

"Those old bags stole my shovel! Tell me—when you saw 'em, did they have a shovel?"

I don't know what he's talking about. Especially since I haven't actually seen them since last night.

"Like a snow shovel?"

"What? No! A snow shovel in the middle of summer? That would be crazy. Maybe you saw different women, then."

He points up to the corner of the lobby.

"We only got one camera here. I'm always watching! Can you believe I saw two old women come through this lobby with my good shovel? My *good* shovel, too! Not my snow shovel!"

"That's wild," I say.

Was it my mom and Ms. Marrillion? Maybe they took a shovel from the basement for self defense? They had the pepper spray from the bodega, but maybe they wanted something heavier. Not that I can picture either of them swinging a big heavy shovel.

"*Wild?* It's not wild. It's illegal, I tell you. Shovel thievery! That's what it is. It's why I called the cops just now. They're on their way. They were *real* interested when they heard about the ladies. I'm gonna get my shovel back for sure."

Now I hear sirens again.

The police are coming.

I need to leave.

CHAPTER 50
UNDERGROUND

I WALK AS QUICKLY as I can.

If I run, the super might get suspicious and try to stop me.

Once I get to where he can't see me, I start jogging.

I try to make it a casual run, though.

If the police roll up and see me sprinting down the street, they'll stop me just to figure out why I'm running. It's always dangerous to run too fast in this neighborhood. I mean, half of the time, cops ignore what's clearly a crime being committed. But then the other half of the time, they stop kids who are just running because they're late, and then it can escalate from there.

East on 180th Street, I hit Broadway, and turn left, hoping to get lost in the crowd around the McDonald's.

Usually there's a mix of people getting food, people waiting for buses, people selling CDs and gloves on tables on the sidewalk.

It's these people I blend in with, somewhat safe, knowing that the people chasing after Ms. Marrillion don't really know this neighborhood and would have a hard time picking me out of a crowd.

And then I think.

Think hard, Lee.

What would my mom and Ms. Marrillion need a shovel for?

The obvious answer is: to dig a hole.

But I can't jump to any conclusions.

Doing that could lead me off in the wrong direction and waste a lot of time. Time I could use to find them and see my mom again.

So: Why would you need a shovel besides to dig a hole?

As a weapon?

Maybe, but the super made it sound like a big, heavy shovel, and I can't imagine my mom swinging it like a bat. Certainly, Ms. Marrillion wouldn't be able to wield it like a sword. And it's conspicuous, big and noticeable, so it would draw more attention than it would be worth, if you were just looking for something you could hit people with. A broom or a baseball bat would be better.

What else could you use a shovel for?

To lift something? Like, as a lever with a solid metal piece at the end?

In physics class, we learned how levers can increase your strength. That dude Archimedes said, "Give me a lever big enough, and I can move the whole world." I guess he also asked for something to place the lever against. Anyway, we spent a whole class figuring out how long the lever would need to be to move the world one inch, and it was way too long. Like you wouldn't be able to see that you'd moved the world for several years, because of how long the light would take to reach you.

Which is a long way of saying: they probably weren't using the shovel as a lever.

Did they want to smash a window with it?

Again, that seems unlikely. Maybe they would have used it to smash a window in the basement, but there'd be no need to take it with them, as the city is filled with things that can be used to break windows. I once saw Spike Lee throw a garbage can through the window of a pizza place. Of course, most garbage cans are made of plastic these days, so it would be a little harder to accomplish. Still, you wouldn't need a big shovel to do it.

I think a little more and can't come up with anything else.

Which leads me to the conclusion that they must be planning to dig a hole or dig something up.

Now the only question is what they're digging. Because if I figure that out, then I'll know *where* they're digging.

It has to be something that Ms. Marrillion buried, or knows is buried somewhere.

Because my mom doesn't even own a shovel, so how could she have buried something? And why would she need to dig it up now? For instance, if she somehow knew there was a gun buried somewhere that she could use to protect herself and Ms. Marrillion, then she would have dug it up last night, or at least mentioned it.

If it's not something Ms. Marrillion buried, what are the other options?

They both suddenly got into gardening and landscaping? Nah.

They want to pose as construction workers, digging up pavement? Unlikely.

They're doing a scavenger hunt and need a shovel to win? No way. They're busy being hunted down by the government and the mob. They don't have time for fun and games.

Which leaves me with the question of what Ms. Marrillion would have buried that she'd want to dig up.

She lives by herself, so it's not like she would need to hide something from roommates or anyone who lives with her.

Maybe she's got a jar of pennies somewhere?

I laugh at the idea, but then wonder if there might be something to it.

A lot of old people keep money under the mattress, they say.

She's not old enough to have lived through the Depression, but I've heard people call into radio shows saying their grandparents didn't trust banks and kept money stashed around their homes. They'd be doing renovations, tearing down a wall, and then find big stacks of cash behind it. Or after an old relative died, they would clean out the basement and find a suitcase full of dusty cash. I guess it's more of a suburban thing, where people have houses.

Still, you could go into your old granny's apartment and discover a drawer full of rubber bands and old folded up plastic bags, and then, suddenly, thousands of dollars stacked up in the back. Or in the cookie jar.

I remember that once, when an older lady in our building died, her family told us they made sure to open up all the food containers in the freezer to make sure none of them were just hiding places for cash.

"All we found was old frozen blocks of soup," they said.

It must have smelled pretty bad and been a big disappointment.

The only problem is: Ms. Marrillion was an orphan. So she doesn't have any old family treasure to dig up anywhere. Because she doesn't have any old family. And if she and my mom need money, my mom could probably get it. So it's probably not a treasure chest or anything like that.

This is like trying to solve some sort of word puzzle.

My logic tells me that they must be digging up something that Ms. Marrillion herself owned and buried.

I realize that I never heard the end of her story, of what happened that night when she was dragged away from the orphanage to witness the conspiracy. Maybe she stole something from the room that can help her out now? I can't imagine what it would be.

Still, that might be enough.

Assuming it's something she snuck out, then it must be pretty small. Not like a rifle or any kind of big weapon.

So it wouldn't necessarily be in a big field. I don't have to go down to Central Park.

Maybe up near the Cloisters?

Except that I think the ground around there is all rocky. That's why it's so hilly, because the ground rises up. Bennett Park, where I walked with Ms. Marrillion just yesterday afternoon, has a little plaque saying it's the highest natural point in Manhattan. It's too solid to dig.

Plus, an old lady digging a hole with a shovel would look pretty suspicious, so wherever it is, it's probably a place with enough trees to offer privacy.

That probably rules out the area around the Cloisters, too.

Then it comes to me.

They're probably taking that shovel to Inwood Hill Park.

It's full of caves and stuff.

You could hide anything in there.

Or anybody.

CHAPTER 51
I COVER THE WATERFRONT

EVEN IF I'M WRONG, if they're not up near Inwood Hill Park, there's another reason for me to head north that way.

Our second pre-arranged meeting place is the Starbucks at the corner of Dyckman and Broadway, at the end of the day.

Since I'm pretty sure they tried to meet up with me at the McDonald's this morning, it's a safe bet that they'll also try to make the rendezvous near Inwood tonight.

The fastest way would probably be to walk along Broadway, but that might be a little dangerous and I'm feeling cautious now.

On top of that, if I go closer to the river, near where the park is, I have a little chance of spotting them if they are there instead of at Inwood Hill Park.

I know: it's not like I'm going to just see the two of them digging a big hole near the sidewalk. But there's a chance I'll hear something, maybe some people passing by talking about that old lady they saw with the shovel, or maybe I'll hear the sound of digging?

It can't hurt to try.

And I *know* I won't see them walking along Broadway with the shovel, so why not take the route by the park and Hudson River?

It will get me to Inwood Hill Park, just a little slower than taking Broadway. But I'm not in any rush.

So I walk west on 181st Street, which leads to the strip of green land between the city and the Hudson. It's a park where people bike and jog and picnic and take selfies along the water.

One thing that surprises me is seeing a couple of police boats out in the water.

It can't be a coincidence, can it?

It's not like I come out here to the water all the time, but I *have* been here a bunch of times because I live so close, and I've never seen police boats out in the water. I remember hearing once that somebody saw them out here looking for a body a few years ago. And when I was just a little baby, that airplane landed on the Hudson, and there were probably a bunch of police boats out on the water that day, although further downstream.

Anyway, the boats seem to be speeding up and down the river, full of men with binoculars and telescopes. What are they looking for? Hopefully not me! Probably Ms. Marrillion, and my mom, since she's with her.

Could they also know about the shovel? Are they trying to find out where they're digging?

I decide I don't want to spend so much time out where they can see me, so I head back inland, to Fort Washington Avenue, then up to the entrance to Fort Tryon Park. It'd be pretty hard for them to dig up anything here without getting yelled at by some of the flower lovers who wander the gardens, but I don't know what else to do.

If Ms. Marrillion had buried something important along the route we walked yesterday afternoon, she probably would have mentioned it, right?

So I try to take an alternate path, down past the dog run.

I pass a lot of joggers, and walk through a few clouds of weed smell.

I keep my ears open, but I don't hear anything about two ladies digging a hole.

That's okay, because I didn't really expect to. The trail leads along the hill to the Anne Loftus playground. I don't know who Anne Loftus is, but I bet Ms. Marrillion does. Maybe she was even friends with her?

There's still a lot of police and suspicious SUVs in this neighborhood.

That could be my fault, since I called in that fake sighting a little while ago.

I hope that didn't make it harder for my mom and Ms. Marrillion to get wherever they were going.

A man is posting new flyers with Ms. Marrillion's picture on them. They look like the ones from this morning, but now it says there's a $20,000 reward. I doubt they're going to pay it, so why not raise the rate?

The man looks over at me and stops what he's doing.

Then he yells:

"Hey, kid, come here!"

I pretend not to hear.

"I'm talking to you!"

He stops posting signs and starts walking towards me.

"You see these signs?"

The guy is practically in my face, yelling.

"Yeah," I say. "I seen 'em."

"You see how I put them all up and down Broadway?"

"Uh huh," I nod, trying to avoid eye contact.

"Well, I'm sick of it. I been doing it all morning. How about I give you five bucks, and you post the rest of them?"

He didn't recognize me. I breathe a sigh of relief but try not to show it.

He doesn't know I'm involved in this whole thing.

He just thinks I'm a kid wandering around the streets, looking for something to do and maybe out to make a quick buck.

"Sure, I could do that," I say.

I *could* use the money, after all.

"Don't get no funny ideas, though," he says. "Don't take my

money and then go buy yourself some ice cream or a vape pen or bubble gum. You understand?"

"You… you want me to save the money? Like for college?"

He snorts.

"I don't give a rat's pink tail what you spend it on, kid."

"Oh, I thought you were worried."

"Nah. I meant, don't spend the money first. You gotta put all these flyers up, and then you can spend the money. If I find out you didn't post all these signs? I'll come find you."

"Sure. Sure. I'm responsible. I'll put up all your posters before I do anything else."

I'm lying to him, of course.

First of all, with all the cops and mobsters coming after me already, am I really going to be scared by a guy armed with a roll of tape and a stack of flyers? He can't do anything worse than what I've already faced since yesterday.

And besides, I don't want to help these people find Ms. Marrillion.

So as soon as he hands me the money and tape and walks away, I get ready to dump the flyers in the trash. I spend a few minutes slowly putting up one in case he's watching, then run down into the Dyckman Street subway station.

I know, I know. There are trash cans up at street level. But somebody might find the flyers in there. Maybe that guy would realize I stiffed him. Or somebody might just see one while they're throwing something away and recognize Ms. Marrillion. Then they might call the number to report it, and that could lead to trouble.

Down near the subway, though, they've got different kinds of garbage cans, ones with smaller openings on top, so if I throw this stack of flyers inside, there's no chance anyone will see it, except maybe the MTA garbage man. Even that seems unlikely, though. He'll probably just bundle up the trash bag and tie it shut. Examining the garbage is probably the last thing he wants to do.

If I weren't in the middle of an emergency, I would try to

recycle all the paper, because that's better for the environment. I feel a little bad just dumping it in the trash, but it's safer that way.

By this point, I've sweated through the catalogs and paper wrapped around my body, so I tear them off and stuff them down on top of the flyers, to hide them even more. Nobody will reach their hand past wet magazine pages, I hope.

Then I head back up to street level, $5 richer than I was a few moments ago. The roll of tape is too big to fit into my pockets, so I stick my hand through it and wear it like a big, ugly cardboard and plastic bracelet.

After that, I walk west on Dyckman towards the base of Inwood Hill Park.

It's the scariest of the local parks—I think they've found a few bodies there.

And D'Argyle says there's a movie where Samuel L. Jackson plays a serial killer who lives in one of its caves, and that it's based on a true story.

I don't doubt it.

If I was a serial killer, I'd probably live there, deep in the woods, where nobody could find me.

CHAPTER 52

WHERE TO GET AWAY WITH MURDER

YOU MIGHT THINK that a park in the city is scariest at night, but you'd be wrong.

At least, I *think* you'd be wrong.

I haven't spent many entire nights in the middle of the woods, except for one time on a sort of camping trip when I was a little kid.

I have gone into parks after dark, though. A lot of them are supposed to close at sundown, but it's not like you can build a fence around an entire park, right? At least, not a big one. Some of those little playgrounds and pocket parks for rich people have gates, but the big ones are open 24/7.

So me and my friends hang out there at night. It doesn't feel dangerous. There's usually late-night joggers and other normal citizens who make it feel safe, at least near the entrances and exits. Maybe it's different if you go deep into the woods.

Earlier in the day, like today, seems worse to me.

Maybe it's because there aren't as many signs of life. The trash cans have all been emptied recently, and there's not as much litter and junk as you would find on the ground in the afternoon and evening.

Don't get me wrong—I think trash on the ground is bad. All

the same, it tells you that people have been nearby recently, which is comforting somehow. When there's no sign of human life, that's when it gets scary to me. Maybe it's because I'm a city kid.

Probably, there's all kinds of people who grew up on a farm or in the middle of a forest, who enjoy the quiet there and the fact that there are no signs of mankind, no cars or tire tracks, no old plastic bags stuck in the tree branches, no orange soda bottles on the ground filled with a liquid that is obviously not orange soda.

To me, as I leave the sidewalk on Payson Avenue and start up the trail into the park, it gets creepy and weird. After 20 feet or so, it's hard to remember I'm in the middle of the city because the trees around me have swallowed up all the light and sound.

If someone grabbed me and I screamed, nobody would know.

This is the kind of forest they talk about where a tree can fall and nobody is there to hear it. That's supposed to make you think about whether it makes a sound. But it obviously does! The squirrels or birds can hear it. Maybe I just don't understand what they mean by that.

But I'm not a tree. If someone hit me with an axe and I fell down, you can bet I'd scream and make a sound, even if there was nobody around to hear it and help me.

I realize I should have looked at the map on my way in, so I don't get lost in the trails or keep walking around the same spot. This is another one of those times when having a phone would be clutch. Then I could just download a map.

Instead, I have to do it the old-fashioned way. Either memorize the routes of all the trails, or make a drawing on a piece of paper. Except that would require me to have a pen and some paper, and I have neither. I'm certainly not going to dig old paper out of the trash.

I guess I shouldn't have thrown away *all* those flyers a few minutes ago. I could have used one to make a map.

OK, so I'll just have to use my mind.

After walking back to the park entrance, I study the trails drawn in brown on the green map.

How will I be able to remember where I've checked for my mom and Ms. Marrillion so that I don't keep walking the same ground over and over again?

Then I think of a plan: I'll just keep turning left every time I come to a place where the trail splits off in two or three directions.

We read a poem in school about a guy in New England who came to a place where the road split in two and didn't know which way to go. He tried to figure out which path had been used the least and went on that one.

I guess that makes sense. If I hope to find my mom and Ms. Marrillion digging a hole somewhere, they'll probably be off the beaten path, in an obscure part of the park where no one will find them.

But I can't tell which path is the least used one.

I guess they didn't have a Parks department and paved trails when that dude wrote his poem, otherwise he'd have had to flip a coin or something.

Pretty soon, I feel like I'm deep in the woods.

The logical part of my brain tells me that it would actually be harder for someone to kidnap me here than on the street. Where there's a bunch of cars, it's easy to pull up next to someone in a van and shove them inside.

In the forest, someone could jump out from the trees and grab me, but then what? They'd have to carry me through the woods, and I could be yelling the whole time.

Of course, that only helps if they're trying to kidnap me.

If they just want to kill me, this is a better place to do it.

The streets are filled with witnesses and security cameras. Every store has one now, and a lot of cars have dashboard cams. Plus, everybody on the street has a phone with a camera.

Well, everyone but me.

Seriously, I've seen unhoused dudes with iPhones.

There's this one guy in my neighborhood who even posts on Facebook. My mom sees his posts sometimes, where he says he needs money for a place to stay or some food and is asking people to Venmo him. Apparently there are a bunch of arguments in the local community group about whether to allow him to panhandle on Facebook, and even about whether he actually needs the money.

So if even that guy has a smartphone, then pretty much everyone does.

In the woods, though, there are no security cameras. The chances of someone passing by and witnessing a murder are pretty low. I think that's also why people dump bodies out around here. At least, I've heard they do. My mom says it's mostly urban legend, and gangs aren't dumping corpses in Inwood Hill Park.

There was a murder here a few years before I was born. Apparently, it was a college student, and the case was never solved. Which just goes to show that it can be dangerous here.

Maybe it's just statistics, though.

Even if there are killers hiding in the trees, what are the odds that they'll see me? The forest is huge.

I tell myself that as I go deeper into the park: What are the chances one of the men hunting Ms. Marrillion will find me? It's really unlikely.

But if that's true, then it means I *also* don't have a good chance of finding my mom and Ms. Marrillion. Nobody can find anybody in the woods.

Assuming that they're even here in the first place.

I can't think of anything else to try, though, so I might as well look around until it's time for the rendezvous at the Starbucks on Dyckman.

I had planned to keep going left at every path, but now I'm starting to doubt that. If they are trying to dig something up, it would probably be where there's patches of grass or other soft ground of some sort. I don't think you can bury something right under a tree, because the roots are too thick there.

So when I come to the next map inside the park, I try to look at it and figure out where someone would be likely to find a patch of ground where they could bury something they didn't want anybody to find.

There's a place called Inwood Hill Park Lookout. That seems like it must be a hill, which probably means it's rocky and too hard to dig.

Same thing with Fort Cockhill. It's got a funny name, and it would be funny to see Ms. Marrillion in the Deez sweatshirt, digging at Fort Cockhill. But if it's a fort, there's probably a bunch of rocks and stones.

There's a spot called Indian Caves. Well, on the map, it's called "Rock Formations." But somebody has written "Indian Caves" next to it in pen. That's probably the old, racist name for it. You could probably hide something there pretty easily, but you'd run the risk of some kids finding it. I bet people are climbing in and out of the caves all the time.

There's also a place called Shorakkopoch Rock. I think that's supposed to be where that old Dutch dude bought Manhattan from the Lenape back before the United States was a country. Of course, we learned in school that a lot of that story is nonsense. Anyway, if it's an important historical site, even one based on a lie, it's probably not a good place to hide something under ground.

Then I find what I'm looking for.

I mean, I *hope* it's what I'm looking for.

It's an area called The Clove.

If they're digging up something important, that's probably where they'll be.

CHAPTER 53
THE FOUR HORSEMEN

I START RUNNING NOW.

For some reason, you're allowed to race through a park, but it's dangerous to do that on the street if you're not dressed in the right sort of clothes.

White people in jogging outfits with fancy heart monitors run all through our neighborhood. If you're not wearing that uniform, though, you look suspicious. Which is weird, because some people might want to exercise but not be able to afford the right kind of gear.

I suppose it's because on the street, you might look like you just robbed a bank or a Starbucks or mugged somebody and you're trying to get away. In a park, everyone assumes you're there for leisure. Still, you could rob somebody who was having a picnic and then run away from them *in* the park. Or maybe you were on the street and you held up an armored car at gunpoint, then ran into the park to get away.

What I'm saying is: people running in the park could be just as dangerous as people running out on the street.

Still, it works out for me now, so I'm just going to go with it.

I run along the paths, only stopping to check maps posted along the trail every once in a while to make sure I'm headed in the right direction. In here, there's no direct path from one place to another, and nothing's organized like the city blocks.

I guess not every city's like New York that way. Most places have roads that wind around rivers and landscape features, but some guy a long time ago decided to put all of Manhattan on a grid, which makes it easy to find everything.

Normally if I run this much, I get tired, but I guess I've got a lot of pent up energy. Maybe it's nervousness.

Pretty soon I find myself at the place called The Clove.

At least, I think that's where I am.

I don't see any big sign or anything.

Still, I guess landmarks inside a park aren't always the same as landmarks in the rest of the world. They might put something on a map that's just an empty field, or a specific kind of tree.

I'm not sure I know for certain what a clove actually is, but this seems like what I pictured in my head. It's some sort of clearing surrounded by trees. I guess "clove" is a fancy way to say "clearing."

It *does* seem like the kind of place somebody could dig for something because there aren't too many boulders and there is soft dirt on the ground in a lot of spots.

Now the trick is for me to figure out where around here they might be digging.

I wonder if I should climb on a bench or fence to get a better view from up high.

But maybe that would draw too much attention.

I think to myself that I haven't seen anyone suspicious in the park yet today, so maybe it's safe.

Looking around to see if anyone's paying attention, I creep towards the edge of the trail. I want to hop off the path.

Except that I spoke too soon about it being safe.

Because just at that moment, a bunch of cops ride up on horses.

I didn't even know they had police horses up here! I thought that was just around Times Square and the bottom of Central Park.

Maybe they brought them up for the special occasion.

They're intimidating, which I think is why they have horses in the first place. Motorcycles and bikes are faster, but you can threaten to stomp somebody when you're riding a bicycle.

They don't seem to pay attention to me, but they're scanning all the woods around The Clove.

They stop and turn their horses around in a circle, looking for something.

Probably the same thing I'm looking for:

My mom and Ms. Marrillion.

CHAPTER 54
THE OLD MAN AND ME

THIS ISN'T the time to find out whether I can beat up a horse in a fight. Because I'm pretty sure I can't. And even if I could, I wouldn't want to. I *like* animals. Especially if they're not doing anything to me. A horse would only be my enemy because the cop riding it was making it behave that way. Not to mention the fact that, if I *could* beat up a horse, I'd still have to get through four cops and three more horses.

Instead, I slink away.

In case they're watching, I try to pretend like I was a normal teenager in the park who doesn't hang around cops, but just on general principle, not because I'm up to the specific trouble they're looking to prevent.

The best I can do is slouch over like I'm looking to drink or smoke somewhere, and not like I'm searching for two fugitive women, one of whom is my mom.

I'm not a great actor, so I can't say for sure how good a job I do, but they don't chase after me.

A little ways down the path, I come to an old man on a bench.

"Now I seen everything, kid! You saw it too, didn't ya?"

"The cops on horses?"

"Yeah. Yeah. It's how they used to terrorize us back in the day.

Swingin' their billy clubs, cracking skulls open and breaking bones. I remember the riot years. They used to shoot down every leader we had, and when we got upset and tried to protest, they'd show up with their horses, ready to stomp the spirit right out of us!"

I think about what Ms. Marrillion saw as a child, the men who were planning to kill Kennedy. If I remember my history right, he was the first one that got shot, then MLK and Malcolm X and the other Kennedy. Plus the Black Panther guy, Fred Hampton. They just made a movie about him recently. He was only a few years older than me when he was killed, and he had already been a successful social activist. People must have grown up faster in the 1960s, because of Vietnam and all the other social troubles.

This guy seems old enough to remember some of that. Maybe all of it. He'd probably have a good conversation with Ms. Marrillion if he got the chance.

Then I wonder if he did.

"Hey, did you happen to see two women come by here? One older than the other. Probably carrying a shovel?"

I wish I could remember what they had been wearing, to help describe them. Although if they still have the shovel, that's probably an easier way to identify them than the color of my mom's shoes or something like that.

"Two old ladies, you say?"

"Nah, man. One old lady, and then a younger lady. Like my mom's age."

"How I know how old your mom is, young 'un?"

"Take a guess," I reply. He sure seems cranky.

"What you want with them even if I have seen 'em? Maybe you're with the cops, gonna snitch on them."

"Do I look like a cop? I haven't even finished high school yet!"

"The way some of those clowns in blue behave, I reckon most of them ain't never finished high school, neither."

"I'm just trying to find them to help them. They're probably looking for me."

"Oh," he laughs too loudly, slapping the bench beneath him. "Those old ladies are looking for you, huh?"

He stops laughing and grabs my arm.

His grip tightens as he looks me in the eye.

"Then I guess that would make you Lee, wouldn't it?"

His grip is tight, tighter than I'd expect from an old man.

"You tryin' to go somewhere, kid?"

He doesn't let up at all.

"Now, later in the day, when I been drinking, you might slip away from me. 'Cept it's still early yet. I got my wits about me."

I think about kicking him. Maybe then he'd let me go.

"Calm down, no need to get violent," he says with a smile. "I'm just holdin' you here so I can have a chat with you."

"What?" I ask.

"I saw those two old ladies you're lookin' for."

"It was just one old lady and a younger one with her."

"Both a bit older than you, I think."

"Just tell me if you saw them."

"I did, at that. I seen 'em come this way and dig a big hole out yonder in the woods. I'm not supposed to say which direction, you understand?"

This guy was really enjoying his role and the fact that he knew something I didn't.

"Now, you understand, I say live and let live. They left me alone, so I like to leave them alone. Only, they kept looking my way the whole time. Maybe they were suspicious of me? It wouldn't be the first time. Everyone's suspicious of ol' Jerome. Let them be suspicious."

I started to wonder if this was the guy they based that Samuel L. Jackson movie on, the crazy old man who lives in the caves of the park.

"So then. These old women. Sorry. This old woman and this not-so-old woman, they finish digging their hole and they pull out some sort of old box. Maybe it's like a suitcase. It was wrapped in a garbage bag, and they take it out and look around like they're up to no good, then start walking my way.

"*Jerome*, I think to myself, *these women are trouble with a capital T*. What they want with me? Then they say, 'Hey, sir.'" He laughs.

Thinking he's distracted, I try to pull my arm away.

"Not so fast! We ain't done with our conversationalizing, kid."

He pulls me closer.

"I was just getting to the good part, you know. They called me 'sir.' Nobody calls me that anymore, so I figured, these two old ladies... Sorry! There I go again. This old lady and this *much younger* lady who's old enough to be your mother, I figure they must be trustworthy, on account of they called me *sir*.

"And this is the part you been waitin' for, I suppose. They said to me, 'Sir, if a kid comes by here, curious and asking about us, you can tell him where we went. But don't, on no account, tell anybody else!' They was very certain of that. 'Don't tell nobody else where we gone, not the cops, or the mob, or the FBI.' That scared Jerome quite a bit, I tell you. I had cops bother me more times than I can count, but never the FBI. That's some serious stuff. They want me to pay taxes and all that kind of nonsense."

I relax a bit. He may be a drunk, but it sounds like he's on our side now.

"This kid, they say, goes by the name of Lee. And so then, here you come, just after the cops rode by on their horses like the darn cavalry at Little Big Horn. You start asking about them, so I figure you must be Lee."

"Yes," I say. "That's me."

"Then I'm supposed to tell you where they went. Just remember, you can't tell no one else."

"I won't," I say. "I promise."

He closes his eyes and sighs.

"They gone where nobody could ever find them."

CHAPTER 55
BALL OF CONFUSION

THEY WENT *where nobody could ever find them?*

I have no idea what that means.

I'm starting to suspect this man is drunk, even though he claims he's sober.

He starts laughing, and now I'm really questioning why I'm listening to him, other than the fact that he's got a tight grip on my arm.

"You look confused, kid."

"I don't know what that means."

"Confusion! It's the state of the world. When a man can't tell up from down, nor late from right, nor early from easy. How can you not know what confusion is?"

"I understand 'confusion.' I meant I don't know what it means that 'they went where nobody could ever find them.'"

"Confusion is everywhere…" He didn't seem to have heard me. "Confusion, consternation, combustion, ka-boom! Minds are blown every day. It's a great big ball of confusion. You get me?"

"No."

"Ahhh, that's okay. You just a young 'un, ain't you? Listen. They said for me to tell you, *Tell Lee we're going where…* Let's see, how did she phrase it exactly? She said, *Tell Lee we're going where nobody could find a spot.* Yeah, that's it. *Where nobody could find the spot."*

He lets go of my arm.

I take off running, not sure where I'm going, but eager to get away from him and from the four policemen on horseback.

I *think* I'm headed out of the park, but I've gotten so turned around and twisted on the maze of paths that I can't really be sure.

They went *where nobody could find the spot?*

I don't know what that means.

I mean, assuming that's even what they said. It seems likely that the man on the bench got it wrong or misremembered it.

Why would they even have trusted that man to give me the message?

Then my mind is racing, just like my feet.

What did they dig out of the hole?

He said it was some sort of briefcase. Or suitcase.

If this was the sort of movie D'Argyle watches, there would probably be a sniper rifle inside, buried by a secret hitman in the past. Except that D'Argyle watches a lot of unrealistic movies, and Ms. Marrillion is *way* too old to be a secret hitman.

I find myself at the big set of tennis courts near Isham Street.

I slow down so that I don't look suspicious running outside of the park.

Then the sidewalks take me down Isham towards Broadway. I try to look nonchalant the whole time.

Where can I go?

I need somewhere I can sit and think and try to decipher what the old man said.

The Church of the Good Shepherd is right on the corner, a big stone building where the doors are always open. Then I remember that Ms. Marrillion was suspicious of churches because of what happened to her when she lived in the orphanage. She thinks they're involved with this whole thing, so that's not an option.

Partway down the block, past the church, is another Buunni

Coffee location. It comes back to me how they helped us yesterday afternoon, when that guy was looking for Ms. Marillion, and they pretended she was somebody else to confuse him, then gave him fake directions to send him in the wrong direction.

If they were helpful then, at the Pinehurst branch, maybe they'll be cool here at the Inwood location too.

If they don't hassle me, I can sit in the air conditioning and try to figure out where my mom and Ms. Marrillion went after they dug up whatever it was from Inwood Hill Park.

I've been moving nonstop since this morning.

I need a break.

I walk into the cafe.

The way my luck has been going, I halfway expect to find a bunch of cops inside, or gangsters, or government agents in black suits.

Instead, it's mostly empty. There's a few people set up at tables with laptops or books. I guess people who don't have day jobs. Maybe they're college students or maybe they work nights. Perhaps they're college students *and* they work nights. Sometimes it's tough to make ends meet.

Along one wall, I spot an empty table that's just been vacated recently. I can tell, because there's still an empty coffee cup on it, plus a rolled up napkin. The staff seems pretty on top of things, so I know they wouldn't have let that sit out for too long.

Before someone can come clean it up, I sit there and try to pretend it's my table.

Even though it's gross, I even raise the cup up close to my lips as if I'm drinking from it.

That should buy me some time.

If I look like a customer, they can't kick me out, can they?

Not unless one of the employees has a good eye for details and remembers that someone was just sitting here, and it wasn't me, or notices that I never bought anything at the counter.

Still, how worried can they be about a teenager sitting at a table for a little bit? It's not like I'm causing any trouble.

The situation would be different if it was a bar, and it looked like I was trying to sneak a few sips of some other patron's alcoholic drinks that I'm not old enough to buy. Coffee, though? There's no law against kids drinking coffee.

Now I have some time and space where I can think.

Jerome, the guy on the bench, said they told him they were going *where nobody could find a spot.*

What does that mean?

The first thing that comes to mind is a parking spot. Maybe it's some part of the neighborhood where it's hard to find parking? But we don't really know, since we don't own a car. From what I hear, though, it's hard to find parking all over this part of town. So *the place where nobody could find a spot* wouldn't really narrow things down.

What else could it mean?

I picture something covered in polka dots. That doesn't help, though.

There's also a phrase: X marks the spot. Which might have been important before they found that thing and dug it up, but they told Jerome the thing about *where nobody could find a spot* after they'd already located the place where the suitcase was buried.

Next I wonder if it could be the name of a club or something like that: The Spot. It doesn't sound like a very good club, at least not a modern one. Maybe they'd call a nightclub The Spot in one of those old black-and-white movies that Ms. Marrillion likes. I can't remember ever hearing about such a place in Washington Heights, though.

I get so caught up concentrating on trying to figure it out that I absent-mindedly drink from the old coffee that was on the table.

Eww! It's somebody else's leftovers. There could be spit in it!

The idea of that makes me gag and start coughing.

Now I'm worried because a lot of people turn to look at me.

I'm stuck, because my throat is sort of dry, and normally the way I'd stop coughing is to drink some water or other liquid, but I don't have any water, all I have is the empty cup.

I get up and walk over to the table where they keep creamer and napkins and a pitcher of water, and I pour myself a small cup. After a couple sips of it, I finally stop coughing.

"You okay, kid?" asks the barista behind the counter.

"Yeah, I'm good, thanks," I say.

I must have made a bit of a commotion, because someone even sticks their head out from the kitchen and yells, "Is somebody choking?"

"No, sorry, it was just me. Some coffee went down the wrong pipe."

"Gotta be careful of that," the cook says. "I thought I'd have to find that poster that says how to do the Heimlich maneuver."

Then it comes to me.

I know the message my mom had Jerome give me.

I know where they went.

CHAPTER 56

NEW AMERICA

A FEW YEARS AGO, a new restaurant opened just up the hill from our building.

It's always weirdly exciting when something like that happens, especially when it's different from the options we normally have. There's a few Chinese places nearby, and a bunch of pizza places, so it doesn't really do much for us when another one of those opens.

But when it's a new restaurant with a new menu, then it can really change our life.

My mom would be upset with me saying that, because it implies we eat out a lot, or get carryout too often. I don't think that's the case. She's a good mom, and she cooks a lot. Still, on weekends, or special occasions, like when somebody is visiting, we'll go to one of the restaurants nearby.

Obviously, there's a whole lot of restaurants in New York, so we could technically eat anywhere we want.

It's nicer, though, to be able to eat and then walk and be home soon without having to get on the subway or take a cab.

Maybe it's different if you live some place where you have to drive to get to *any* restaurant. Because once you get in the car, it doesn't really matter if you're going one mile or 20 miles. When walking is an option, though, it just makes everything a little cooler and easier.

So when this new place opened, we were really excited.

To be honest, we were excited even before it opened, because we saw it coming. First the old place, a Mexican restaurant, closed down. That was sad, and then there was just an empty storefront for several months.

We walked by it all the time, wondering what would go in there next

Before they started doing construction, we saw signs in the window. Well, not *signs* exactly. It wasn't like they were advertising anything. These were permits required by the city. Some simply listed the contractor and said who was doing the actual work, and what number to call if you saw unsafe working conditions.

At the same time, though, there was another notice, which said that the people taking over the space had applied for a liquor license.

"That's good," my mom said. "Although I liked when you could bring your own to the Mexican place."

Since they hadn't had a liquor license, they didn't mind if you brought your own beer and wine and drank it with your meal. If the new place was allowed to serve alcohol, you wouldn't have to stop at the bodega before dinner and buy your own beer or wine, like my mom did. On the other hand, she said, restaurants charged more for alcoholic drinks than stores, so it would cost a little more.

"It feels more classy, though, if they pour you a glass of wine, instead of you opening your own small can in a brown paper bag." I wouldn't know, since I'm not old enough to drink.

On the notice about the liquor license application, we could also see the name of the restaurant: New American Industries d/b/a High on the Hog.

What did that mean?

"It could be barbecue," I said to my mom.

"Maybe," she replied. "Except that place is a little small to have a smoker."

She knows more about that sort of thing than I do.

"And if they're not actually making their own barbecue," she said, "then it probably wouldn't be very good."

"What does d/b/a mean?" I asked.

"That stands for 'doing business as.' That means there's one company, in this case, New American Industries, which is going to operate the restaurant. But that's not the name of the place."

"Why didn't they just all their company 'High on the Hog'?"

"There could be a few reasons. Maybe there are other companies called 'High on the Hog.' Or it's a restaurant company that operates multiple places with different names."

When we got home, I looked up New American Industries online and couldn't find their website. But I discovered that New American is also a kind of cuisine.

"Maybe that's what they'll be serving," I suggested to my mom.

"Could be, kid."

After that, we'd sneak a look at the construction going on inside while we walked by. They had the windows covered with newspaper, but there were little holes and tears, and if the lights inside were on, you could sometimes get a peek.

We saw where the bar was going, and then they installed booths.

By the time High on the Hog finally opened, we already knew exactly what it looked like inside.

They did what they called a soft launch, which I guess just means they weren't really ready to open.

At least, that's what it felt like.

One day, on the way home from school, I saw a sign in the window saying they were open that night to "limited guests." I told my mom, and she said, "Let's give it a try!"

New American means a bunch of different stuff.

I ordered a fancy sandwich, while my mom ordered pasta.

My sandwich came first.

"Go ahead and eat," my mom said. "Don't wait for it to get cold. My pasta should be here soon."

Except it wasn't.

I finished my sandwich, and she was still waiting for her pasta.

We flagged down the waitress, who said it should be out soon.

"We're still figuring things out," she said, apologizing. "Do you want a sandwich? I think that might be faster."

"I'd still like the pasta, if that's an option," my mom said.

"Um, we have all the ingredients for it," the waitress said. "But, well, nobody can find a pot. You know, to boil the noodles. In the kitchen."

"Oh," my mom said. "In that case, I guess I'll have a sandwich."

It was a rough start, but we ate there again a few weeks later, and it was much better. We still go there on special occasions. When we do, if the food takes a while to come out, we'll joke to each other that they may not be able to find a pot to cook it in.

We'll even say it at home sometimes.

"Sorry dinner is late, but nobody could find a pot," mom will tell me, even if it's not a meal that requires a pot.

That must be what my mom told that guy Jerome on the bench.

She and Ms. Marrillion were going *where nobody could find a pot*. He just misheard or forgot or tried to make sense of it in his head, and told me they were going where nobody could find a *spot*.

I stand up, throw away the empty coffee cup, and leave the cafe, heading for High on the Hog.

CHAPTER 57

THE LONGEST DAY

I WALK AS QUICKLY as I can down Broadway, away from the café.

Now that I know where they are, I'm almost more cautious than I was before. So many things could go wrong now. Before, it seemed as if the worst-case scenario was that I wouldn't find them. Knowing where they are, though, puts everyone at more risk. Someone could grab me and take me to a dark room somewhere, torture me until I tell them where my mom and Ms. Marrillion are.

I like to think I wouldn't give them up too quickly, but I don't know. Based on what I've seen so far, these guys don't mess around. If they really wanted to hurt me, they'd find a way.

That's why it's all the more important to get to the restaurant without drawing any attention. I don't want them to be caught at all, but if they do get caught, I don't want it to be my fault.

When we finally went back to try eating at High on the Hog a second time, they let us sit in the courtyard behind the restaurant. It was cozy and cute. We noticed that we could easily open a gate and walk into the apartment building on the other side of the courtyard.

"If we lived in that building, we could eat here without going outside," my mom said.

"Yeah, that'd be good if it was raining," I said.

The restaurant's part of the courtyard had a little tent-like roof over it, so we'd just have to make it five feet from the other building to the safety of the tarp.

Now I realize why mom thought of that place to go. The covering in the courtyard means nobody in any of the nearby buildings would be able to see her and Ms. Marrillion out there. But at the same time, they wouldn't be trapped, because if the police or the mafia show up, they can slip into that apartment building. And they can get food while they look through the brief-case or assemble whatever's inside it.

On top of all those factors, it must have appealed to my mom that she could have Jerome give me a message that would be meaningful to me, but not to anyone else. If the cops grabbed him and asked him where my mom and Ms. Marrillion went, he could honestly tell them he didn't know. In his mind, it was just *the place where nobody could find a spot.*

I see and feel danger around every corner. I get the sense that things are going to change, now that they found the briefcase. Instead of just running, we'll be able to fight back, to offer some-thing in challenge.

It's getting pretty close to the time I showed up at Ms. Marril-lion's door yesterday, almost 24 hours ago. It feels like a whole lifetime. I was a different person then, and the world was a different place.

I cross Dyckman and head into Fort Tryon park. Not deep into it, just staying along the path that skirts the edge of the grass near the sidewalk. Somehow I feel less noticeable in here.

This time of day, there are more people out walking their dogs. There are construction workers, taking a break and eating sand-wiches. There are college kids sitting on the lawn, reading books.

Is that what will happen to me if I go to college? It always seemed like a boring thing to do, but after everything I've been through, it would be nice to lie down on a blanket and not have anything to worry about except a made-up story in a book.

I'm paying too much attention to the people in the park, and I don't notice the vans pulling up on the sidewalk. The men swarm out of them and come running for me.

They grab me and put my hands in cuffs before I have a chance to get away.

I try to scream, but they put a bag over my head.

One of them takes the knife out of my pocket, then I hear it clatter to the ground.

I can't see, but it feels like they carry me to the vans and toss me in. I hear the door slam.

Then the engine revs and we start moving.

Where are they taking me?

CHAPTER 58

KIDNAPPED

I'VE NEVER BEEN KIDNAPPED before.

I guess most people haven't.

With handcuffs on, I can't really do much. Not that I know what I could do. Jump out of a moving van? Karate kick a bunch of FBI agents? Or are they CIA agents?

I don't think they're the mob—they seem too organized and precise for that. If it was the mafia, I'd have been roughed up a whole bunch already, especially if they knew how many of their guys I'm responsible for getting beat up, or hit by cars, or falling down shafts into basements. They owe me a pretty good beatdown, by my accounting. Although I don't mind if they never pay me back. That's a debt I'm happy to keep holding for them.

I don't notice us stopping for any traffic lights or stop signs, which is another reason I think it must be the government that grabbed me.

I'm trying to think my way through this, because if I stop concentrating on little details like that, I know I'll get scared and panic will set in.

There's a radio up in the front of the vehicle. I think it's a police scanner. D'Argyle would know for sure.

Maybe there will be something on the radio that lets me know if my mom and Ms. Marrillion are still out there, on the loose. I try to listen for mention of *the two women* or *the female suspects*. Nothing.

It must be a good sign that I'm not dead already.

If they just wanted me out of the picture, they could have slit my throat and tossed me out by the side of the road. Maybe not here, in the city, but I imagine they could have driven into New Jersey and found a dump pretty easily. I haven't been there very much, but some people say most of Jersey *is* a dump.

Eventually, the van, or maybe it's a truck, comes to a stop.

I think about jumping out.

I mean, what's the worst that could happen?

If they're planning to kill me, it won't matter either way.

If they were going to beat me up, I think they'd have done so already.

I guess I could be charged with resisting arrest, except that I don't think I'm under arrest. They never identified themselves as cops, and I'm pretty sure they have to do that when they arrest somebody.

So I don't really see what the risk is of trying to get away. It'd be different if I thought they were the good guys and were trying to protect me. But good guys don't put hoods over people's heads and drive them to undisclosed locations.

I can see only one real danger in making a break for it. I can't see, so if I jump out of the van, I could end up in the middle of the street, and get hit by a car.

That could hurt. Or kill.

So I listen as hard as I can, trying to figure out if I'm on a busy street or highway. The door is on the passenger side, so that should be pretty safe.

Maybe, since I'm a kid, they won't be guarding me too much or holding on too tightly. I'm already in handcuffs. If I act pretty docile and subdued, they may forget I have feet and can run. I'm probably a little quicker than they are, since I'm young. If I use a basketball move on them, fake one way, and then run the other, I may be able to get out of their grasp. Then I just have to hope I'm right that they won't try to shoot me. Or tase me. And if I can get my hands up to my head, I can take off the hood, even while my wrists are still handcuffed together.

It's weird, but I think these handcuffs aren't tight enough. They're probably meant for adults, and my wrists are too small. Plus, they locked one side over the old tape roll I was wearing. If I can slide the cuff off the tape roll, it will be even loser, and then it might slip off if I pull hard enough.

I hear the side door slide open.

The hot outside air comes in and I feel a hand on my shoulder.

"Alright kid," the guy says. "It's time to go."

I don't say anything, but I agree.

It's time for me to go.

The first thing I have to do is make them think I've given up, that I'm defeated. If they believe I'm not a threat, then I have a better chance. I need them to underestimate me.

So I try to move sadly, with my shoulders hunched over.

My mom always says I shouldn't slouch so much, because bad posture is bad for my back and suggests that I'm lazy.

I can't wait to tell my mom that slouching paid off when I see her again.

If I see her again.

"I'm going to take the blindfold off," the man says. "No funny stuff."

"Alright," I mumble in my most sullen voice.

Just like my bad posture, my ability to mumble might finally be paying off.

He pulls the bag off my head, but I don't look up at first, as if I don't care.

Then he grabs me by the arm. "Come on, just a step onto the sidewalk."

I get out, as slowly as possible, and then just stand there.

Until I feel him let go of me for a second to close the van door.

It's all the time I need.

I kick his kneecap as hard as I can.

He bends over to grab at it, and I take off, finally looking up as I book down the sidewalk.

I have no idea where I am, but that doesn't matter.

I just need to get away for now.

Behind me, the guy yells, "Hey, grab that kid!"

Of course, nobody listens to him.

Why would anybody want to get involved?

Plus, he didn't say he's a cop, and he's not wearing a uniform, so he might just be a kidnapper, for all anyone knows.

I hear him running, and the doors of the van slamming, as I assume some other guys have gotten out to run after me.

Maybe if I run across the street, they'll get hit by a car like the guy with the gun yesterday.

It's worth a shot, and I figure I'm quicker than them, can turn and move faster.

So I bolt out into traffic, hear the screeching of brakes and violent shriek of car horns as vehicles try to avoid me. It's a little harder than I expected, because the handcuffs prevent me from using my arms for balance when I turn quickly.

It doesn't sound like anyone behind me gets hit, but their footsteps sound a little further away, so I might have gained some speed.

They haven't yelled anything else, no "Stop or I'll shoot" or "You're under arrest" so I keep running.

Once across the street, I get back on the sidewalk and take a quick look around to see where I am.

I don't recognize anything right away, but I'm somehow still in the heart of the city, with tall office buildings on both sides of the road. Maybe they drove me down to Harlem?

The sidewalk is almost more dangerous than the street, because it's full of people looking at their phones, people with strollers, people selling junk on blankets and tables.

I dart between them all, moving as fast as I can.

I cut left when I get to a big intersection.

Based on the traffic patterns, I think I've been running south on Broadway or some other avenue.

Now I can't hear the people chasing me, just the curses and swears of people who I almost ran into.

I decide to risk looking back to see if they're still on my back.

When I turn my head, I can see them right away, three guys in black suits running down the sidewalk, shoving people out of the way. They're less worried about bumping into people than I am, so they're starting to gain on me.

I turn my head back and slam right into a guy standing on the sidewalk.

He's much bigger than me, so he doesn't move, and I bounce off of him and crash into a giant rat.

CHAPTER 59

STRIKE

IT'S NOT A REAL RAT—IT'S one of those big inflatable ones with pointy teeth and beady red eyes that they put up on the street when there's a strike and picket line.

"Whoa, kid, watch where you're going!"

"Sorry," I say to the man I bumped into. "Those guys in suits are chasing me!"

I point towards the men running down the sidewalk towards us.

"Suits? They're probably management, then. We *hate* management, don't we?"

A bunch of the other big, burly men around us agree and create a wall of bodies. They're all holding picket signs, which they lower and start to wield as weapons.

It turns into a full-on brawl, and the union guys come out on top.

"Technically," the guy says to me, "that's why we're only allowed to use cardboard tubes to hold up our signs. Back when we used two-by-fours, things could get a little bloody."

The guys in suits are getting hit pretty hard with the pro-union signs, and it looks like it hurts.

"Between you and me," the guy whispers, "some of our gang

may have snuck metal pipes *inside* their cardboard tubes. But that's why you shouldn't mess with the Teamsters, you know?"

"Thanks! I should get out of here."

"Sure, we've got your back. As long as you don't cross that picket line."

"I'm too young to work," I tell him.

"Uh, actually, now that I think about it. If you're on the run, maybe you should go inside. Most people will be too afraid to follow you, and then you can sneak out a back door."

"You're a lifesaver," I say. "I promise I'm not a scab!"

"Scabby the Rat will hunt you down if you are," he laughs, pointing at the mascot. Then he tells the gang to let me through, and they let me slip into the office building they're picketing.

Before today, I didn't know the giant inflatable rat had a name.

Inside the lobby, I see that there's nobody at the reception desk. That's good, because normally they would stop me from opening the door behind the elevator, which probably leads to the back of the building. Maybe they called in sick because they didn't want to cross the picket line?

This isn't the time to figure out where they went, though.

It *is* the time to look over the edge of their desk and see if there's anything I can use as a weapon to protect myself.

There's a pair of scissors in a coffee mug along with some pens and Sharpies.

But first I have to free my hands. The cuff on the old tape roll slides off pretty easily, and then I remove the old tape roll, too. Now I'm just cuffed on one wrist. Between the looseness of the lock setting and how sweaty my wrist is, I'm able to hold the other cuff against the desk and pull my hand out. It only hurts a little. I guess that's one benefit of being a kid and having small wrists.

I take the scissors, and a Sharpie, just in case. Maybe I'll need to leave a note for my mom and Ms. Marrillion somewhere.

No need to linger too long, though. So I head back through the brown metal door that says:

BUILDING "STAFF" ONLY

My English teacher would be upset about the unnecessary quotation marks around the word "staff." I'm amazed that sign-making companies don't fix those kinds of typos. Unless they're paid by the character, in which case the extra punctuation marks mean more profit for them, even if they're grammatically incorrect.

I tell myself it's legal for me to go through the door, since "staff" is in quotes. That probably wouldn't hold up in court, but I doubt I'd get sued for sneaking out the back door of a building, anyway.

The back hall, with its old linoleum floor and concrete walls, is empty too. I guess none of the building staff wanted to cross the picket line. Usually, this type of place has a guy working the freight elevator, but there's a sign on it that says "Closed Temporarily."

I look around for anything else that might be helpful later.

Near a stack of broken-down cardboard bundles, I see a box cutter hanging from a nail in the wall. Our apartment building has one just like it, for tenants to slice the tape on cardboard boxes in order to flatten them.

I already have the scissors, but figure it doesn't hurt to have backup, so I use the scissors to cut the thick cord connecting the box cutter to the wall, slip both blades into my pockets, and now I'm ready for action again.

Looking around, I try to get my bearings and figure out where I am.

I can't take too long, though, because I need to get away from here quickly, before those guys in the suits realize I slipped into the building and then out the back door. If they find me again, then I can't meet up with my mom and Ms. Marillion at High on the Hog.

It's just half a block to the corner, where a street sign tells me

I'm still in Washington Heights, at the corner of 168th and Broadway.

This isn't my usual part of town, but I've been here a few times. And I'm only 20 blocks south of the restaurant where my mom should be.

If it wouldn't draw too much attention, I'd run so that I could get there quickly. But that might bring the heat down on me. Even if the cops weren't out to get me, I don't think they'd look too kindly on a kid my age with scissors and a box cutter in my pocket.

So, instead, I walk as fast as I can.

Would it be safer down along the Hudson? There's a water-front park that runs all the way up the western part of Manhattan.

On the one hand, there's probably fewer places to hide down there. Or, at least, fewer places where I'd feel comfortable hiding, like the alleys and bodegas up here in the city. Down along the water, I could run into the woods, but I don't know anything about what it's like there. What if I grab some poison ivy? Or just get into some thick bushes that slow me down until the feds can catch up with me?

That would be bad.

On the other hand, if I go to the waterfront park, I'd be able to run without anyone paying me much attention, since the path through the park is full of joggers and bicyclists.

Since they last saw me on the city streets, I figure it will be better to change things up, and I head west towards the river.

This is where my phone would come in handy, because I could look up on a map where there's a good place to cross from the streets to the waterfront.

There's an elevated highway I have to get under, but also a set of train tracks I have to get over. They're set down lower than the rest of the ground, almost like they have cliffs on either side, so it's not just a question of running across the tracks between trains. I have to find the nearest footbridge across the tracks, but those aren't located in any sort of obvious spot. It's not like there's a bridge every 10 blocks, or anything like that.

So I walk north and cut west again whenever I have the chance.

It gets a little scary, since there's nobody else around down near these roads. Nobody to hear me shout or help me out if things get rough. Any sounds I make would be drowned out by all the traffic on the highway above us. I just have to hope nobody sees me down here.

Pretty soon, I'm under a bunch of big overpasses, which I think are ramps leading on and off the George Washington Bridge. There are no signs for pedestrians, but eventually I spot a worn down trail through the grass. That must lead somewhere, I think.

My mom told me those are called desire lines—they represent where people *want* to go, even if the guys who built the park didn't expect people to walk that way. Sometimes you'll see a big green field of grass with a few paved pathways, but then all kinds of worn down, dirt strips showing the shortcuts people take to get from one area to another.

Hopefully, all the people who wore down this trail I'm following were trying to get to the river, and not some abandoned dead-end alley where they could do drugs or something like that.

It leads around a bend, and through some thick trees, until a little while later I find myself on a trail maintained by the parks department, and then a bridge across the train tracks.

At this point, I start running, because this is the kind of trail people use to jog for exercise, and nobody will think it's weird.

It's kind of uncomfortable to run with scissors and the box cutter in my pocket, but I don't dare leave them behind.

CHAPTER 60
ANOTHER BLOCK

NOW I'M RUNNING NORTH towards the George Washington Bridge, in the hot sun, surrounded by joggers and bikers and families having fun. For all of them, it's just a beautiful summer day. They're not worried about someone trying to kill them.

When I run past the tennis courts, I think about all the back and forth of their games. Some players look like they're always on the defense, running ragged over the court while their opponent stays in one place, casually swatting the ball in one direction, then the other. Once you start running, it's hard to stop, because you're just reacting to the other person's attacks.

That's how it's felt since yesterday.

I hope we can go on the offensive somehow. Maybe whatever they dug up will help stop the conspiracy of men trying to kill Ms. Marrillion.

I sure don't want to spend the rest of my life running, always looking behind me, listening for footsteps or searching for a too-familiar face in the crowd.

It reminds me of a scene from some movie I heard once:

"When did you start being so paranoid?"

"It was when they started plotting against me!"

Up until now, whenever I saw some guy muttering to himself about how *they're* out to get him or shouting on the subway about the secret government plot to destroy him, I didn't take them seriously. *They need help*, I always thought.

Now, though, I wonder if maybe some of them were being honest. It isn't hard to imagine them being the victim of an actual conspiracy, or maybe just the target of one group. There seem to be so many different people coming after Ms. Marrillion. But it wouldn't take all that to drive a person beyond their breaking point. Just the mob, by itself, could probably put the screws to somebody and either get them to do what they want or make them lose their mind.

So maybe I was right, just not in the way that I thought.

They need help, I told myself. And maybe they did, but it wasn't the help of a psychiatrist they needed. It was the assistance of somebody who could get the FBI or CIA or mafia or church or Russia off of their back. Somebody to stand up for them.

Here I am, now, in the same position.

I need help.

We need help.

No matter what Ms. Marrillion has up her sleeve, no matter what she's kept buried underground in case of emergency, I can't imagine she can stop all of the forces bearing down on her.

She has me and my mother, sure, and even D'Argyle.

But will that be enough?

I come up to the base of the bridge, and the small lighthouse there, the one that's just for show.

People are standing there, taking selfies with it in the background.

It makes me miss my phone.

I think of how much trouble it's caused not to have it.

I really hope when I meet up with my mom, she can figure out a way to get me something else to use. We could buy a burner phone, except it wouldn't be a smartphone with access to the internet and maps. Still, at least I'd be able to call her or text D'Argyle, who could use his laptop to look something up for me from his apartment if I needed.

The path diverges from the river here, up a hill through some trees, then doubling back on itself, first across a bridge over the train tracks, then under an archway that holds up the highway above. After that, it winds its way to a jogging trail that eventually takes me to a pedestrian walkway across another highway.

And, finally, after that, I'm back in the city.

I would walk all the way back up to Fort Washington Avenue, except that there's a set of stairs that makes a shortcut up towards Pinehurst, which is where High on the Hog is.

It's not quite as many flights as the stairs over near my apartment, but it's a couple stories at least.

Once I get to the top, there's a little dead end area, because the road stops. I sometimes see people trying to turn their cars around here, but it's difficult because there's no circle, just the end of the road, and people are usually parked on both sides of the street.

Pinehurst leads me up a hill that isn't quite as steep, and then I'm at the park again, the one with the plaque saying it's the highest natural point in Manhattan.

It's hard to believe that just yesterday I was hustling past here with Ms. Marrillion after that guy shot up our building trying to kill her.

All that running, and I'm right back where I started.

I stay on the edge of the park, near Hudson View Gardens, a big set of apartments that look like old English buildings from back in history when they had the Plague. It's the kind of place I want to ask Ms. Marrillion about when all this is over. I'm sure she knows all about it, but we'll probably have more important things to think about for now.

It's just one more block to the restaurant.

A light flashes in my eye and I get scared for a second.

Is someone shooting at me?

Then I see it's just the flashbulb of a photographer.

He's actually using an old-fashioned camera, with a flash and a big silver reflector of some kind. It's strange, because it's pretty sunny out. If I hadn't lost my phone, I'm sure I could have taken a decent photo with it without any of the fancy equipment this guy is using.

I guess he wants a really good photo. Somebody seems to be modeling for him, a guy who's trying to look serious.

"Point your chin at me," the photographer says to him.

He does, and he looks really weird. It reminds me of the photos they take at school, where they make you hold your head at an awkward angle, and all the time you're thinking, "I'm pretty sure I look like an idiot."

But the photographer assures you everything is fine. Then he sends you a link to the photos online, and sure enough, you look like a robot pretending to be human or something. It's almost like they don't trust that the truth will show up in a photo, so they have to go over the top with poses and lighting.

"Keep your chin pointed at me, but move your eyes toward that brown car."

I don't have time to figure out what they're doing or why the guy is posing for such a strange photograph, so I don't hear any more of their conversation.

Then I'm outside the restaurant.

It's a fancy place. I wonder if they'll ask me if I'm alone when I go in, because it's not the sort of place a kid my age would normally eat at by themselves.

There's no time to lose, though, so I just push the door open, nod at the woman at the bar, and walk out towards the back patio as if somebody out there is expecting me. And I hope with all I have that it's true.

CHAPTER 61
NOTES ON A CRIMINAL CONSPIRACY

AND THERE THEY ARE, sitting around a table, looking at the suitcase they dug out of the ground.

Ms. Marrillion is sitting, but my mom is standing, bent over.

Then she looks up and sees me, comes running over to hug me.

"You're safe, you're okay?"

"Yeah, mom, I'm fine," I say.

Her hands run through my hair and she turns my head one way, then the other, looking for wounds or something like that. Almost as if I could have been shot in the head, then still found my way over here? Although I guess maybe it's an instinctual thing, because I think I've seen animal moms do it to their kids on nature documentaries.

Ms. Marrillion asks, "How'd you find us?"

"I talked to the guy on the bench at Inwood Hill Park," I reply. "How else could I have found you?"

"We left messages with a lot of people," my mom says.

I guess she was worried.

"Did you lose your phone? Or was it stolen?"

"It fell out of my pocket in the car I took away from the hotel."

"And you're fine? Really?"

"I had a close call with some guys in a van a little while ago, but we can talk about it later. Tell me what's going on now."

"Ah, you mean this?" My mom points to the old suitcase. "This is Ms. Marrillion's evidence."

I walk over to see what they're talking about.

It's a bunch of pieces of paper and some little black squares.

"You stole that? Or did they let you keep it?"

"They didn't just let me keep it, Lee," she says. "They forced us to take it. Both Carol and I had to take one of these packets with us."

She holds up some of the papers.

"It's what they're looking for, probably the reason they killed Carol."

"I don't understand," I say.

"Ms. Marrillion explained it to me on the way over here. Do you mind telling the story again?"

"No," Ms. Marrillion says. "I've kept it bottled up all these years. It actually feels good to tell somebody."

She shuffles all the papers into a neat pile.

"Let's see, then, where did we leave off?"

"With you and Carol? It was the middle of the night, and you were with the people who were planning to kill the President."

"Indeed. We were, of course, already scared, just from being dragged from the orphanage in the pitch black night and thrown into this building with these strange men. But when we realized what they were talking about, what their mission was, we were petrified. Anybody would be."

She picks up one of the documents from the suitcase.

"When they finished, when they had agreed on the time and the place, they had an older woman, a senior secretary of some sort, type up a summary of everything they'd decided. Then the leader of each group signed it and affixed some sort of seal. The man from the church had an actual seal, the kind you press in hot wax. Have you seen one of those?"

"Only in movies," I say. "Old guys in wigs sent secret messages that way."

"It had fallen out of fashion by the 1960s, so he was the only one who had one. The others had to mark their signatures in some other way."

She points to various signatures and symbols by them on the piece of paper.

"The men from the CIA and FBI stapled their business cards. Nowadays, you could make a fake one at any Staples or Office Depot. But back then, a business card meant something."

Then she points to a religious image.

"This is a saint," she says. "The man from the mob pricked his finger and bled on this, then they attached it to the contract. I looked it up, much later in life, and it seems to be a variant of a Cosa Nostra ritual. Since the mafia doesn't keep written records, they must have just used something they knew from the past. In the mob ritual, they would have burnt the saint card afterward, so they wouldn't leave any evidence."

Next, she points to seven drawings around the edges of the paper.

"The Cuban made these marks. There was some argument about that, as it did not seem as binding as what the others had done. At least that's what I thought they said. Apparently, the Cubans had wanted to attach a packet of gunpowder to the contract, but everyone else thought that was too dangerous and unstable for long-term storage."

"I don't get it," I say. "Wasn't this a secret conspiracy? Why would they want a record at all?"

"That is something I've thought about for most of my life," she says.

CHAPTER 62
AMONG THIEVES AND KILLERS

WHY WOULD the members of a secret assassination plot want to keep records?

"I think it was a sort of insurance against anyone going public," Ms. Marrillion says.

"How could they go public? They'd be admitting that they killed the President."

"Yes, they would. And all this documentation would prove it. I think that was the point," she says. "They didn't trust each other. They were forced to work together, because they had the same violent purpose, but they were paranoid. Everyone thought that someone else would go to the authorities and point the finger at them."

"Throw them under the bus," my mom says.

"Yes, although we didn't use that expression back then," Ms. Marrillion says.

"Because they hadn't invented buses yet?"

Ms. Marrillion and my mom both laugh at me.

"We had buses. I'm not so old that I rode around in a horse and carriage," Ms. Marrillion says. "It just wasn't a phrase we used. I'm not even sure it was a concept back then, although I'm sure people did it. But perhaps not as frequently."

"So you think they were all afraid of each other?" my mom asks.

Ms. Marrillion nods.

"The CIA, for example. They obviously didn't want to be connected to Kennedy's assassination. If they exposed the mob and provided evidence that the mafia killed him, it would not only get them off the hook for murder, it would make them look like heroes for catching the bad guy. But if the mob had evidence that the CIA was involved too, that would provide insurance. Because then the CIA couldn't go after the mafia without their own dirty laundry getting exposed."

"So everyone had some skin in the game," my mom says.

"That's another new expression, but it fits." Ms. Marrillion puts the documents into a new plastic bag, one she got from the restaurant's takeout and delivery supplies. Then she sighs. "It was like a suicide pact, I guess. If one of the conspirators went down, they'd take the rest with them. In that way, they all kept each other from blowing the whistle."

"Honor among thieves," my mom says.

"Thieves?" I ask. "I thought we were talking about killers."

"In a way, they were thieves," Ms. Marrillion says. "They stole our future. Or, at least, that's what it felt like at the time. Although it's hard, looking back, to imagine that JFK could have gotten us out of Vietnam easily, or prevented the tumult and revolution of the 1960s."

"It's possible that his assassination inspired all the others," my mom says. "If he had lived, maybe Martin Luther King and Malcolm X would have survived as well. And RFK, too. Once people saw how easy it was, there was a whole decade of political killings in America."

I don't say anything because I don't know as much about history as they do.

"And despite all that," my mom says, "they couldn't really keep it a secret. There have always been rumors and hints about a conspiracy."

"Ahh, yes," Ms. Marrillion says. "I paid close attention to all the whispers and investigations. The Warren Commission gave an official report. But later, outsiders like Jim Garrison and Oliver Stone had some new version of the story. Everyone claimed to know the truth… at the very least, to know some small part of the truth."

"I guess the conspiracy theorists were right," my mom says. "People thought they were a bunch of cranks, but they knew who it really was that killed Kennedy."

Ms. Marrillion smiles.

"Actually, they were wrong. That's the grand irony of it all. That's what made such a confusing mess of history. There *was* a conspiracy to kill Kennedy, but it never came to fruition. The back-room players didn't get to go through with their killing."

She laughs a little to herself.

"They had their deadly plans, but Lee Harvey Oswald beat them to the punch."

My mom is shocked.

"If they didn't kill Kennedy, then why are they trying to kill you? And what happened in Dallas?"

Ms. Marrillion shrugs.

"I can only guess in both cases. The men we saw in that midnight room, they planned to shoot the President at the Dallas Trade Mart. Although his schedule hadn't been finalized, they seemed to know he would give a speech there."

"Is that some sort of mall?" I ask.

"It sounds like one, doesn't it?" she says. "I guess, in a way, it was, but not for the general public. It was a big wholesale center. Back before the internet, stores had to get their merchandise from distributors, and this was one of the places they went."

"Was the President gonna go shopping there?"

"He was supposed to give a speech to a large group of businessmen in the Grand Courtyard. That's where he was going when Oswald shot him. Over the years, I did a little research about it because it was a name that got stuck in my head, the Dallas Trade Mart, and I wondered what had happened."

"I'd be curious too," my mom says.

"It wasn't easy, back then, to do research on something like that. This was before the internet, you know." She says this directly to me. I guess my mom remembers what that time was like to some extent, and I'm the only one who doesn't. "And after the assassination, I thought it might be suspicious to ask too many questions about Dallas. I wanted to put the whole thing behind me. Later, though, when it seemed safe, I made some inquiries. The Trade Mart was one building in the Dallas Market Center. If you wrote to them claiming to be a businessman planning a conference, they would send you a brochure with photos."

She hands my mom an old pamphlet that had been in the suitcase.

"I told them I was George Evans, and I represented the Middlemarch Development Corporation. I guess nobody there studied English literature."

Mom hands the pamphlet to me. There's not much to it.

"It wasn't until very recently that I was able to find something really interesting," Ms. Marrillion says. "On YouTube, somebody uploaded news footage from that day. Of course, I thought I'd seen everything, in so many documentaries over the years. The Zapruder film, and Walter Cronkite's broadcast. But something I hadn't seen was the raw footage captured by the news team at the Trade Mart to cover Kennedy's speech. They were all set up to record his address to the business leaders of Texas after they ate their fancy lunch in the Grand Courtyard. Little do they know that everything's about to change."

"They didn't cancel the lunch?"

"Nobody knew about the killing when they served the food. Remember, Lee, this was before cell phones as well. The only way to get up-to-the minute news was from the radio or television. But you couldn't carry those things around in your pocket like you can today. Somebody might have a portable radio, but they wouldn't be listening to it at a formal event where the President was supposed to show up. News traveled more slowly back then."

She rubs her face with her hands, as if she's tired.

"It was like having a time machine, watching that video. I was back there with them, in those last moments, before everything started to fall apart. Even though I'd been there in that planning room, part of me hadn't taken it seriously. I didn't want to believe what I'd witnessed. But when I heard the news that day, I knew it was real. And it wasn't just that the President had been killed. For me, it was knowing that I'd seen them planning it. It took a few months before Carol and I were able to figure out what had happened, that Oswald hadn't done it on behalf of the shadowy men we'd seen in the dark room." Her voice trails off a bit as she seems to remember the past. And then she snaps back into the present, looking at my mom. "What was your other question?"

"If they didn't actually do it, if they didn't get a chance to follow through on their plan, then why are they trying to kill you after all these years?"

CHAPTER 63
FOUNDATION OF LIES

IT'S quiet in the back patio part of the restaurant for a few moments. A certain kind of quiet you only get way uptown where we live.

"Knowledge is power, as the old saying goes." Ms. Marrillion smiles at us. "Somebody is probably cleaning house somewhere. As everyone involved gets older, there's perhaps a fear that someone will spill their secrets on the way to the grave. But there's too much at stake now. Even if the players themselves are dead, imagine what would happen if somebody had definitive proof that the CIA teamed with the Russians to kill our President? World wars have started for less. I think somebody has decided to eliminate the possibility of that ever happening. It's probably not the survivors, who are too old to be very active. But some of them must have passed their secrets on to their successors. And rather than risk being exposed, they're targeting us."

"How could they have found you?"

"I believe the way it was set up, only the church knew who Carol and I were, and where we ended up. That was their way of holding a piece of the puzzle for themselves. In a way, it was clever. The CIA could access all kinds of government records, but adoptions ran only through the church back then. They controlled all the records, not Uncle Sam."

"And you think they're trying to kill you?"

"Not directly. My guess is that they traded me for something. I doubt this was the only trouble the church got into in the past hundred years. Maybe the government had evidence of some sort of massive abuse. They could have offered to make it disappear in exchange for finding out where Carol and I were."

"You're just a pawn to them."

"They've never cared much about me when they didn't have to, except to take advantage of the fact that I had no parents. In any case, Carol and I were a danger to everyone involved. Once the conspirators started dying off, the mutual assured destruction of exposing the secrets lost its efficiency. It became safer just to kill everyone who knew. I bet the hitmen were lied to about why they were being asked to shoot old men and old women. Over time, more and more players were being knocked off the board by other players who didn't know why. I guess that's an old story too, like the Hatfields and the McCoys. People start killing each other, and pretty soon it becomes a vicious circle, where each murder leads to another and nobody can remember what even started it in the first place. Except that I still remember."

She reaches into her pocket and pulls out a small envelope. From inside it, she pulls out a photo of a young girl, and a picture, probably cut from a magazine, of John F. Kennedy.

"Is that you when you were little?" I ask, pointing at the girl.

"No, this is Carol. Now she's gone, just like him." She taps the picture of Kennedy. "And I'm the only one left. I hate to think of myself as a loose end, but that's really all I am to them. As a child, I was a pawn on their chessboard, disposable. Now I'm a mess that needs cleaning."

"Don't let them define you," my mother says.

"Oh, I don't intend to," Ms. Marrillion replies. "I've lived a good life, and they're not going to take it from me, not without a fight. And if they do kill me, I want to make sure the world knows what they did, how they plotted, even if it kills our faith in the institutions that once kept us safe. We can't build a future on a foundation of lies."

"We've tried," my mom says, "for hundreds of years."

"And what has that gotten us? If we can't have peace, we should at least have the truth." She laughs. "Listen to me! I sound like one of those young people occupying the town square. Well, they messed with the wrong old lady, I guess."

"Mom said you shouldn't call people your age *old*," I say.

"Ah, I suppose you're right. I should have just said, 'They messed with the wrong woman.' Now then," she says, patting the suitcase with her hands. "We've got the evidence. What do we do with it?"

This was something I had been thinking about. And while I didn't have the answer, I knew who did.

"We should call D'Argyle," I say.

My mom is a little wary. She's never seen him in action, being smart like he can be—she generally just thinks of him as a doofus.

"He knows about the internet, more than I do," I say. "And he's seen enough movies to know all the tricks. He'll figure out some way to take advantage of this."

Mom sighs, but she doesn't have any better ideas.

"As long as it won't get him in trouble. You're already in this mess, but I can't put someone else's kid in the line of fire."

"We'll just use him for behind-the-scenes tech support."

Mom pulls out her phone.

"I guess we can call him."

"No," I say. I've finally learned my lesson. "We need to keep everything clear of connections to him. That will keep him safe, but also keep us safe, because he can do things without the government tracking him. Do you know anyone else in his building? We could call them and ask if they can go to his apartment to give him a message. Maybe a phone number he can call that isn't connected to us."

"I bet the restaurant would let us use their phone if I ask nicely," Ms. Marrillion says. "I'll pretend I'm too old to have a cell phone."

She walks towards the front of the restaurant while my mom scrolls through her contacts list.

"Remember Mrs. Rejouis? She used to live on the third floor."

"Kind of," I say. I don't really remember her, but it seems rude to say so.

"Anyway, when her husband died, she downsized from that two bedroom in our building to a one-bedroom in D'Argyle's building. She wanted to stay in the neighborhood."

"Wouldn't she be at work?"

"No, she made enough by selling her old apartment to retire a few years early. Hopefully, she'll be at home."

She punches in the number and I hear it ringing.

After a few seconds, Mrs. Rejouis must answer, because mom turns away to talk quietly. I don't know if she's saying something secret, or it's just a habit. She thinks it's rude to talk on the phone in front of someone else, I think because she's old. Not as old as Ms. Marrillion, but still.

Soon, she covers the bottom of her phone and asks me what D'Argyle's unit is. I have to think for a moment, because, as always, while I know how to find it in the building, I rarely think of what his apartment number is. But then I picture his door, see the number, and tell my mom.

Luckily, Ms. Marrillion returns at this point, with a High on the Hog menu. She hands it to my mother and says, softly, "Tell them to ask for Angelica." Then she winks at me. "I didn't want the restaurant to know my name," she laughs.

Mom says "Thank you" a bunch of times and disconnects.

"She's going to check. It will be a while because she said she wasn't dressed to go out."

We sit back down.

All we can do now is wait.

CHAPTER 64
THE DEAD MAN'S SWITCH

WE SIT SILENTLY for a few minutes, waiting for Mrs. Rejouis to call back. I guess we're all talked out, after everything Ms. Marrillion just explained to us.

Honestly, none of it is too shocking to me, but it must be pretty strange for my mom to find out how much of what she thought knew about history was wrong. Learning there was a secret world of murderers in the background of the past half century is a lot to take in.

The world I've known has always been filled with conspiracies and dark web chatter. Even if most of it is nonsense, it's not surprising to discover one or two pieces of their paranoid puzzle are true.

Mom's phone rings and she answers it.

"Hello?"

There's a brief pause.

"He is? That's great. Can you ask him to call this number and ask for Angelica?"

She gives her the restaurant's phone number slowly and I can hear Mrs. Rejouis on the other end repeating it to her.

"Thank you, Rachelle."

Mom disconnects the phone.

"D'Argyle should be calling us soon. What are we going to ask him to do?"

"I bet he can figure out some way to use this stuff, this evidence, against them," I say.

"You think we should expose the whole thing?" Ms. Marrillion asks.

"Maybe. Or we just let them know we have it and if they kill you, we'll go public."

"It could work," my mom says. "Or they could try to kill all of us."

"That's what D'Argyle has to figure out. How we make it clear that there's a copy of all of this stuff. And if something happens to us, it will automatically get released on the internet."

"A dead man's switch," Ms. Marrillion says.

I don't know what that is, and she can tell from my face.

"It's an old railroad term, or at least I think it is," she says. "To keep trains from going out of control, they require somebody to actively hold a lever in place or press a button. That way, if the driver has a heart attack, the train doesn't keep going, running into another train or crashing at the train yard. If he died, he would release the switch, and then it would stop moving."

"So we have to hold down a button to keep this information secret, and if we all die or go to jail, nobody's pressing the button, and everything goes public?"

"Something like that," she says. "Some bombs are set up that way. When the person in charge dies, they release the trigger, and it detonates. Bank robbers and terrorists sometimes do that to make sure the police don't shoot them."

"Well, this does seem like a bomb waiting to go off," I say. "It's too bad you don't have any pictures. That would be a lot more scary to them than some signatures."

"The ravages of time got the better of us there."

She opens the suitcase up and pulls out the bag. Then she removes the black squares I saw earlier.

"These were Polaroids. Do you know about them?"

"Instant photos, right?"

"Yes. Back before we all had cameras on our phones, we used to have to take pictures on a camera and hope that they turned out. We'd take the film to a Fotomat and they would develop it and make us prints. It took a long time. It was kind of nice, though, because you'd go on vacation, and then a few weeks later you could relive the magic when you got your photos back."

"I'd get bored of waiting," I say.

"That's because you get everything you want all the time now," my mom says, rubbing my head.

"But then they invented Polaroid instant cameras," Ms. Marrillion continues. "You pressed a button, and right away, the picture came out. Although you couldn't see it at first. Then, after a minute or two, the image showed up. Maybe faster, if you shook it."

"Like in that Outkast song," my mom says. "Remember when I explained that line about 'shaking it' to you?"

"Oh yeah," I say. I don't actually remember, but I don't want my mom to think I don't listen to her.

"So they brought in this camera, which was new at the time, and took photos of us standing together in a group, in front of the chalkboard where they'd been making notes. It took forever, because they had to take so many different pictures to get copies for everyone to take with them. If it hadn't been so scary, it might have been funny, like they were making souvenirs. Carol and I each got a bundle of Polaroids. All the witnesses did. Everyone else seemed happy to take them, but we were wary. We wanted to destroy them, but we also knew, somehow, that keeping those photos might be the only way for us to stay alive."

CHAPTER 65
BURIED

THERE'S A BIG PROBLEM, though.

The photos don't prove anything anymore, since they've decomposed or broken down or whatever happens to old Polaroids that were buried underground for decades.

"It's too bad we can't see anything in those pictures," I say.

"Yes," Ms. Marrillion says. "But I've been thinking. *They* don't know the photos didn't last. If they were well preserved, the images might still be visible today."

"What do you think happened to them?"

"Probably moisture or something like that," she says. "When they drove Carol and I back to the orphanage, we kept all the evidence under our mattresses, but only for a few days. In a place like that, nobody had any private possessions. It was too easy for one of the other girls or one of the nuns to dig through your belongings while you weren't there. I guess it didn't really matter, for the most part. We were orphans. It's not like we had anything valuable. Or, I should say, nothing that would be valuable to anybody else—cash, jewelry, rare stamps. Some of the girls might have keepsakes of their former lives, if they hadn't been dropped off as children of unwed mothers."

"Like if their parents died?"

"Yes. It was less frequent, but it happened. Usually, in those days, if your parents died, some other relative took you in … a grandparent, an aunt or uncle. But if you are all alone, with nobody living near enough to claim you, you could end up there. And then you might have a photo of your parents or that sort of thing."

"Couldn't those girls have something valuable? Like jewelry they inherited?"

She shakes her head.

"No, it didn't work out that way. If you came from a family with enough money for you to have nice things, you wouldn't end up in the orphanage. *Somebody* would claim you, or a lawyer would find someplace decent for you to live, with a caretaker. It was only the poor girls who fell through society's cracks."

"That's sad," I say.

"I wish I could say things are better," Ms. Marrillion answers, "but I'm not really sure. In any case, a few nights later, Carol and I snuck out and buried all the evidence in the woods. We didn't have a suitcase or a plastic bag, so we just stuffed all the papers and photos into an old pillowcase we stole from the laundry wing of the orphanage. Did I tell you about that? We had machines to do our own laundry, but also to wash clothes for other families and businesses in town. It was a way for the orphanage to make money. Although none of us girls got any of it."

She sighs.

I keep forgetting how old she is.

Living on the run and revisiting the past must be making her tired.

"When I eventually moved away, I tried not to think about it for a while. But every so often, something would remind me. I'd see a story in the newspaper about an investigation into Kennedy's assassination. Or a tabloid would run a photo of a mafia killing in the city. Every time, I'd think, what if someone comes for me? So, after a few years, I drove out to the orphanage in the middle of the night. It was scary, since I was alone this time. I found where we had buried the pillowcase full of evidence and dug it back up. Then I drove back to my apartment. I kept it hidden in my closet for a few years, until I got back in touch with Carol, who had been adopted and left the orphanage before I did.

"We decided we should both know where the cache was and be able to get at it in case of some sort of emergency. It wasn't as though we thought we'd release it to the press or the government. Honestly, I think we expected someone to show up after midnight with a gun and ask for all the evidence."

"Wouldn't they have killed you after you gave it to them?"

She frowns.

"Probably. So that's why we split it up and each kept a portion. I buried mine in a field outside of town, and then dug it up a second time when I moved to New York. I didn't feel safe keeping it in my apartment, and I didn't really have the room, you know, for a suitcase I never used. So that's when I buried it in Inwood Hill Park. I figured there was a good chance I'd go to my grave without ever digging it up, and the past would stay buried…

"And, so, here we are," Ms. Marrillion says, clapping her hands together. "I guess it's up to us to put an end to all this, somehow."

One of the servers from High on the Hog walks back from the kitchen toward us, carrying a cordless phone.

"There's a call for you, Angelica?"

She hands the phone to Ms. Marrillion, who takes it, even though the call is for my mom. No sense confusing the restaurant staff.

"Hello, is this D'Argyle?"

He must say yes, because Ms. Marrillion smiles.

"Hold on a minute, dear," she says, then passes the phone to my mom.

Except that she doesn't keep it very long, either.

"Hi D'Argyle, it's Lee's mom. I'm glad Mrs. Rejouis got you the message. I'll let you talk to Lee now."

Then I get on the phone and explain everything as quickly as I can.

"Let me think for a minute," D'Argyle says. "Should I stay on the line or do they need their phone back?"

"They probably need it to take reservations and things," I answer.

"What? People ought to be using OpenTable or some other app like that. I guess old people like to talk on their phones for some reason. Alright, I'll call you back."

He disconnects.

"I'll take it back inside," Ms. Marrillion says.

Maybe she drank a Red Bull when I wasn't looking, because she seems to have more energy than she did a few minutes ago.

I tell my mom that D'Argyle is trying to figure out a solution to our problem.

"We'll do our best," she says, patting me on the shoulder.

She must be trying to comfort me, or maybe comfort herself.

Just in case D'Argyle doesn't think of anything, I try to map out our options. We need to take a picture of the evidence and put it on the internet. But we probably want to do it anonymously, and keep it somewhat hidden. That way, it can be a sort of insurance policy to keep Ms. Marrillion safe. We want the people coming after her to know that she has evidence and that it will be released if anything bad happens to her.

Or maybe we could just release everything right away?

No, that would be dangerous. I think they'd probably try to kill her as soon as possible to try to shut her up.

I mean, I realize they are trying to kill her already, but it seems like they're not trying their hardest. Maybe it's only one smaller group of all the people involved? That starts to make sense to me. Like if the mob wants her dead, but the government only wants to put her in jail or something less deadly like that. Except that if everyone decides the only solution is to kill her, things would go downhill much faster.

The government has access to missiles and tanks and snipers.

So the best option is to let them know there's evidence that implicates everyone and convince them to back off. From what she said, the conspirators were afraid one element might try to throw everyone else under the bus—that might be what's happening. In which case, getting all of them back on the same page of trying to keep the secret as a group would do the trick.

Then it would be in their interest, once more, to keep Ms. Marrillion alive and her secrets safe.

We need to make them think that if she dies, then the whole thing will blow up in their faces.

I'm hoping D'Argyle knows enough apps and websites to figure out how we can do what we need to do, to shut down the conspiracy again, and send them back into the shadows.

CHAPTER 66
VERY SHARP THINGS

CAN we pull this off without getting murdered?

So many people involved just want us dead, because it would be much easier for them that way. The only way to guarantee our safety is to make it impossible for them to kill us.

It's like how the police used to get away with all kinds of bad things before everyone had cell phone cameras and they were forced to wear body cams. Of course, they still get away with it most of the time, but at least more people know what they're doing now. It's hard to deny video evidence.

"We need someone filming the whole thing," I say, "whenever we meet with them. That way, they can't try anything sneaky."

"Back in the Sixties," Ms. Marrillion says, "protestors yelled, 'The whole world is watching,' when they wanted to keep the police from getting unnecessarily violent."

How can we get the whole world to watch us?

"I thought about going to the press," Ms. Marrillion says. "We might be able to get a reporter out here, but maybe not. They might think I'm just a kooky old lady. And in any case, they wouldn't put us on the air live—they'd have to record it and then a producer would decide whether it was worthy of going on TV. Anywhere in that process, the government could clamp down, or the mob could kill a reporter. They'd make it look like a traffic accident or random violence, so it didn't seem suspicious."

"That doesn't seem like a good solution, then," I say.

"You know, even back in the sixties, when they yelled, 'The whole world is watching,' it wasn't actually true. It would be, eventually, but they recorded the news on film back then, and then had to develop it and edit it in time for the nightly program with Walter Cronkite. They didn't have live footage. The networks still had to choose what went on the air in those days. They might decide not to show something if it got too bloody, even if it demonstrated that the authorities had instigated the violence."

Then it occurs to me how we can get on the air live, without tipping our hand, without letting the conspiracy figure out what we're up to.

"I know a way we might be able to pull this off," I say.

They both look at me.

"We just need to go to the hardware store before they close."

"We better hurry, then," my mom says. "They close early."

"I might slow you down," Ms. Marrillion says. "So maybe I should stay here and wait for D'Argyle to call again."

"That makes sense," my mom says.

For some reason, as we're leaving, I hug Ms. Marillion like she's my grandmother or something.

"We'll be back soon," I say.

"The only time we go to the hardware store is to buy plungers and roach traps," my mom says. "Please tell me your plan doesn't involve either of those things."

I laugh.

"It doesn't. But we are going to set a kind of trap. We just need to buy some screws and nails and things like that. Sharp objects."

"You're not going to make weapons, are you? I probably shouldn't have let you watch those zombie movies where they use baseball bats with nails in them as weapons."

"Don't worry, mom," I say. "I'm not trying to get into a fight with these guys. They have guns, remember?"

Then we head out into the streets and take the big staircase down towards Broadway. The hardware store is pretty close to the police station, but that's a risk we'll have to take.

I can tell the employees at the hardware store are a little annoyed when we show up. They are getting ready to close, and our shopping just slows them down a bit. Still, the store is supposed to be open until 5:00. If they want to close at 4:30, they should change their hours.

On top of them wanting to go home, my mom and I don't really know what we want.

I mean, I *know* the things I want, I just don't know what they're called.

This isn't like a big Home Depot where all the merchandise is out in the aisles and you can search for it. This kind of place only has a few shelves, and most of the stuff is in the back, so you need to ask for it.

I try first.

"We need a lot of long screws."

"How long?" asks the grumpy clerk.

I hold my fingers a couple of inches apart. "About this long?"

He lets out a huge sigh, like this is the worst thing that's ever happened to him in his entire life—a kid who doesn't know the exact size of screws to buy.

"What's this for? You shouldn't be drilling into your walls if you don't know what you're doing. You could hit a pipe, or worse."

My mom steps up to the counter.

"It's for a school project. Lee has to make a sculpture for art class," she says. "So we don't need to worry about the exact size, or whether they're wood screws or something else. I think mostly two-inch screws will work. We need 40 of those. And then about 10 more in different sizes. Let's say five that are one-inch, and five that are one-and-a-half inch."

"We're not an art supply store, lady."

An older guy behind him who was listening in says, "Just sell them the stuff, Doug. We're a store, that's what we do, we sell things."

The first guy clearly resents being told what to do by his boss, but what choice does he have? He makes a note on a piece of paper.

"So you want 40 two-inch wood screws, and then five ones and five one-and-a-halfs. Anything else?"

"A box of nails?"

He sighs again. "How long?"

"Two inches? Just whatever's cheapest."

He shakes his head like we're crazy and walks into the store area in the back, muttering, "Don't blame me if you make a mess of your apartment."

My mom whispers, "I know you could have figured it out, but I thought we should do it as quickly as possible and try not to be too memorable, in case anyone asks later."

When the man returns, he puts everything in a bag and my mom pays in cash.

She hands me the bag as we leave the store and says, "Don't touch anything. We don't want to leave fingerprints."

"I don't think you can leave a fingerprint on a screw," I say.

"You might be able to, on the head. Or DNA. Just don't touch them yet. We'll see if we can borrow some gloves from the restaurant."

I hadn't really thought about it from this perspective. We're already in a lot of trouble, so I hadn't been worried about the potential extra trouble we could get into as a result of my plan. Even if we can make the conspiracy go away and leave Ms. Marrillion alone, I could still end up getting arrested for what I'm about to do. Luckily, my mom thought about all that for me.

Sometimes it's good that she worries about me so much.

We hurry back to the restaurant.

CHAPTER 67

CAR JAMMING

WHILE WE WERE GONE, Ms. Marrillion charmed the restaurant staff, and it's quite easy for us to borrow a few rubber gloves from their kitchen. Then it's just a matter of redoing our disguises, in case anyone from around the neighborhood has reported seeing us recently. We're still wanted people, after all.

I'm not old enough to be a food delivery person, but you'd have to look very closely to see that. And everybody generally ignores the people on bikes dropping off food, unless they're the ones who placed an order.

So all it takes is a High on the Hog baseball cap (my mom pays for it) and a few plastic bags full of takeout food with receipts stapled to them, and I look like I work for Seamless or Uber Eats or something like that. It'd be more convincing if I had a bicycle, but I doubt even Ms. Marrillion can sweet-talk someone into giving me their bike.

Anyway, I think I look as disguised as I'm going to get, and I head out onto the street, heading down Pinehurst towards 181st Street. My route would be suspicious if anybody was following me, because it's not the quickest way to get from the restaurant to where I'm going, but hopefully no one is on my tail.

I cut left towards Fort Washington Avenue and get ready.

Inside my bags, along with the food, are the nails and screws we picked up at the hardware store.

I sprinkle them into the street from the crosswalk as unnoticeably as possible. I'm sure somebody sees me doing it—how could they not? But I'm counting on the fact that it's New York City and people do crazy stuff all the time. Generally, it's best to let the weirdos be rather than get involved.

My spikes go down on the road at the intersections. 183rd Street, 181st Street, 180th Street, and 179th Street. Should I be worried about the trouble I'm causing? Mom said modern cars will just get flat tires over time—they won't blow out like in action movies, where the cars flip over and explode.

And Ms. Marrillion even smiled slightly, the way she sometimes does, and said, "That's the cost of driving a car in New York City."

There's no guarantee these will cause a car to get a flat tire. So many things need to line up for that to happen: the car needs to hit one of the nails or screws at just the right angle, it needs to puncture the rubber, all that sort of stuff. But I'm laying down a *ton* of sharp metal. Surely one or two will pay off?

Because of the way the roads are set up, it's much easier to reach the lanes of traffic that head out towards New Jersey than the ones coming back across the river to New York. Luckily, that's what we want, since most of the rush hour traffic will be workers headed back across the Hudson to the Garden State.

Most of what I'm dropping ends up on the feeder lanes that dump traffic onto the George Washington Bridge from the Heights. I try to toss a few handfuls at the lanes that have already merged into the roadway running on the bridge's lower level. This is harder to do without looking suspicious because of the fences blocking the road and because I need to throw the nails and screws a lot further to get them where I want them.

Finally, I run out of ammo, and it's time to regroup with mom and Ms. Marrillion.

If this actually works, it's time for some traffic problems in

Fort Lee, Teaneck, Leonia, and the rest of the New Jersey towns just across the bridge.

Back at the restaurant, I find out how mom and Ms. Marillion have progressed with plans while I was gone.

D'Argyle has gone to the subway station at 190th Street. It's close to his apartment, in case he needs to run home, but meanwhile he can tap into the MTA wireless network to monitor traffic. He can look at Google maps and even find footage from live traffic cams online.

It doesn't take long for him to report success: he tells us that an SUV has pulled over to the side of the road somewhere near New Jersey. He looked up the rules and said that, technically, people are supposed to keep driving slowly if that happens, and then try to fix the tire once they're off the bridge. Lucky for us, nobody seems to know that.

Ms. Marillion and mom head out, since Ms. Marillion walks slowly, and I stay behind to keep in touch with D'Argyle. I can run fast enough that I think I'll be able to catch up with them out on the bridge, even though mom would be happier if I stayed here.

The plan is pretty simple. If there's a big traffic jam on the George Washington Bridge, all the local news stations will send their helicopters to cover it. This means that Ms. Marillion can talk to the people hunting her while remaining in relative safety. They can't just kill her in cold blood on live TV in front of everyone. At the same time, she won't have revealed what she knows of the conspiracy to any news networks.

If all goes well, this means they will have to let her live, at least while the cameras are on.

If she went public, they'd probably do whatever it took to kill her as fast as they could, assuming that would help them keep things quiet. But as long as everything stays secret, she may be able to convince them to let sleeping dogs lie, as she put it.

Ten minutes later, D'Argyle calls the restaurant's phone again to let me know there's another flat tire. This time, it's in Manhattan, a few blocks past where two lanes of bridge traffic let out into Washington Heights. This won't cause an immediate backup, but in about a half hour, it should lead to more delays, this time on the inbound traffic from New Jersey. D'Argyle even spotted mom and Ms. Marrillion on a camera at Fort Washington and 179th Street.

Things seem to be shaping up pretty well, and I wouldn't be surprised if there are one or two more flats in the next hour or so.

D'Argyle says he's packing up his gear and heading to meet me at High on the Hog. It's not too far for him—he just has to take the elevator up from Bennett Avenue to the top of the hill, then run down Fort Washington or Cabrini. I tell him instead to meet me at Bennett Park, near the old cannon. It seems like a fitting place since we're practically at war.

That means I can burn this location's phone, so I call 9-1-1.

"What's your emergency?"

"Uh, that old lady everyone's looking for? The one I saw on the news? I just saw her! It was crazy, she was in disguise, but I could tell it was her! She was walking out onto the George Washington Bridge. I hope it's her because I want that reward money!"

I hang up before the operator can ask for my information.

Just to be sure the message gets through, I call 3-1-1, the city hotline.

"I can transfer you to the police, if it's an emergency," the operator there tells me.

"Nah, nah," I say, trying to disguise my voice in case they compare phone calls. "I just wanted to report to y'all that I saw that old broad, the one from the news, walking out onto the GWB. I hope she ain't senile or lost, you know what I mean? You should send somebody to help her! She out on the George Washington Bridge all by herself."

I hang up again before they can ask me who I am.

Then it's time to pack up the suitcase and go. I thank the restaurant for all their help.

I can hear helicopters hovering nearby as I head to the park to meet up with D'Argyle.

CHAPTER 68
TAKE IT TO THE BRIDGE

IT HELPS to have lots of people on their way home from work out on the streets, so I don't stand out in the crowd so much. I'm hoping that means mom and Ms. Marillion won't get too much attention either, at least not until they want it.

I'm at the cannon for just a minute or two before D'Argyle shows up, out of breath from running all the way here.

"Take this somewhere safe," I say, handing him the suitcase.

"I know just the place—"

"Don't tell me where," I say. "I think it's safer if I don't know where it is. That way, they can't make me tell."

He laughs a little.

"So if they torture you, all you can give them is *my* name? That's brutal, dawg. Then they'd just come after me!"

"You'd take it like a pro, though."

"Bet."

D'Argyle hands me a small bag in exchange for the suitcase.

"Stay safe, Lee," he says.

"I'll try!"

I take off running for the bridge.

Well, at first, I try to do that thing where I walk really fast, but I soon realize that looks even more suspicious than flat out running as fast as I can. There are always so many people jogging that it's not very weird. But somebody speed-walking after the workday is done? That would draw eyes for sure.

I almost get hit by cars a few times, not because they're aiming for me, but because I run across intersections without really looking. I'm worried about letting two old women face off against everyone alone on the bridge. Although my mom would hate that I called her old.

The helicopters are really loud, especially as I get closer to the Bridge. On top of that, there's a steady amount of car horns honking. I believe it's because of the enormous traffic jam we've caused.

Once I'm past 181st Street, I don't even have to worry about getting run over, because all the vehicles are at a standstill, brake lights giving everything a red tint as they inch forward as much as possible.

The angriest sounds are the delivery trucks blaring their horns, which are so loud they seem like the foghorns of big oil tankers in the ocean.

I guess I feel a little bad about causing all this chaos, but somebody else started the madness yesterday, shooting up our building, then going crazy all over town trying to kill Ms. Marillion. We're only doing what we had to do to stay alive.

At last, I make it to the Northwalk entrance, the long, curving ramp for bicycles and pedestrians to access the George Washington Bridge. Soon, this path will be for bicycles only, while people on foot use the south side of the bridge. But since that's still under construction, cyclists and walkers have to share this one path for now. I sprint through the gate and run around the loop, past the observation area. It's even louder when I get up to the roadway of the G.W.B. as the cars up here have no escape route. They can't turn onto a side street like the people back in the Heights. They're just stuck on the bridge, trying to get back to New Jersey.

There are more cyclists than walkers as I make my way out

over the water, suddenly realizing how high up I am. A few moments ago, I was at street level, but then the cliffs gave way beneath me and now I'm 200 feet in the air, looking down at barges floating in the Hudson.

If I fall or get thrown over the edge, there's no way I'd survive.

I better make sure that doesn't happen.

Then I can see mom and Ms. Marrillion up ahead, standing almost halfway between New York and New Jersey, waving at me. They're alone, so I finally slow down for a moment, feeling how tired I am having run the whole way from the park.

I wave back, and then, behind them, see three men in black business suits walking towards them from the other side.

The men seem to be in their 40s. I assume they have guns somewhere under their jackets, or maybe on their belts, but I can't see anything at the moment.

I reach my mom and Ms. Marrillion a few moments before they do.

We stand on the walkway, surrounded by cars and the heavy metal of the bridge. It's quieter than it was earlier. I guess people near the heart of the jam have started turning off their engines and realized that honking won't help at this point.

So it's almost too quiet as the men approach.

"You're too young to have been in that room with me, back in 1963," Ms. Marrillion says to them when they stop a few feet away from us. "Do you even know what this is about?"

"We know. And we'll do whatever needs to be done to keep it under wraps."

The one who says this seems to be the leader. He has short black hair and is wearing aviator sunglasses. Behind him are a blond man and a bald man.

"Don't try anything stupid," my mom says. At first, I'm not sure whether she's talking to me or the men. Then she points to the helicopters. "People are watching. And filming."

"Yeah, you pulled a heck of a stunt," he says with a sigh. "Do you know how expensive a traffic jam like this is?"

"Do you think we're worried about money?" Ms. Marrillion asks. "You shot up my building and ran roughshod through the city. *You destroyed my neighborhood.* Who's going to pay for that?"

He turns to the men behind him, who merely shrug.

"Look," he says. "Things have gotten out of control. Everyone will admit to that."

Then he seems to notice me for the first time.

"The kid probably shouldn't be here, huh?" He reaches into his pocket, and I worry that he's pulling out a gun, but it's just a cell phone. After scrolling through it for a moment, he looks back up at me. "Your phone's in Bay Ridge. We figured you were safe hiding out there. What are you doing here?"

"You tracked Lee's phone?!" my mom yells.

"Just to keep an eye on the kid," the man says. "To make sure Lee was safe. But your kid outsmarted us, I guess."

"No," I say. "I just left the phone in a car by accident."

The man laughs.

"Well, I guess we've been keeping a security detail outside a taxi driver's house for no reason, then." He looks at Ms. Marril-lion. "You don't have a smartphone, do you?"

"I still have a landline," she says, shaking her head.

"Then I just need to see your phone," he says to my mom. "So that we can talk and I know you're not recording anything."

"What if you throw my phone in the river, and we need to call for help?"

"I won't do that. But I can see why you might not be in the trusting mood." He turns to the bald man behind him. "Give me the pouch."

The bald man hands him a small black bag. I guess it's the same kind of thing they use at stand-up shows or concerts. The talkative guy hands the bag to my mom.

"Put your phone in there, and then you can keep it."

My mom is hesitant.

"Go ahead," Ms. Marrillion says. "There are enough people around that they won't try anything, I don't suspect." She gestures at the cars stopped on the bridge beside us. None of them are filming us, but most are scrolling through their phones or talking on them while they wait for the traffic to start moving again.

My mother puts her phone in the pouch, then slips the pouch into her pocket.

"Okay," the man says. "Let's talk."

CHAPTER 69
CLEANING UP

"LET me begin by saying that I didn't start this, and I'm trying to stop it," the man says. "But I need assurances that it won't all blow up in my face."

"Assurances?" Ms. Marrillion says, as angry as I've ever seen her. "It doesn't even sound like you're in control. What good is making a deal with you if you can't control the mob, the Russians, everyone else in this conspiracy?"

"I understand your frustration. Let me reiterate that I only found out about this recently, and I am the one trying to clean it up."

"Clean it up?" my mom asks. "I don't like the way the government has cleaned things up in the past."

"Ladies, I'm not here to argue about the past. What's done is done. I didn't do it, I wasn't part of it, and I can't change it. All I can do is try to make things better in the future. Let you live your life without looking over your shoulder every minute."

"And just how do you propose to do that?" my mom asks. She's using the same voice she uses on me when I've gotten into trouble.

"We have ways to make the other parties play nice. Part of the reason everything blew up is that some of the groups involved have lost their power and status over time. When we were all equal players at the table, we worked as checks and balances over each other. But the mob is a shadow of what it used to be. The church is losing ground, at least in America. Russia … hasn't been involved as far as we can tell. If they wanted you dead, you'd be dead, and we wouldn't be able to stop them. It's possible Cuba never told them about the conspiracy. And Cuba is a mess, no longer a player outside of its own borders. At the CIA, though, we've been increasing our power over time. Especially after 9/11. We're the big dogs now."

"You're from the CIA, then?" Ms. Marrillion asks.

"Yes." He reaches into his pocket, and I'm less worried about him pulling out a gun than I was a minute ago, but still not totally at ease. Thankfully, he pulls out a wallet with identification in it. It looks like a real CIA badge, but I'm sure you could buy something like that off of eBay or even print it yourself at Staples.

Ms. Marrillion reads his name out loud.

"Are they also with the CIA?" my mom asks, pointing at the other two men.

"Yes."

"Because you know who we are, but we don't know who they are."

The man rolls his eyes so hard I can see it even through the sunglasses, but he turns to his colleagues and says, "Go ahead."

His men both hand their identification to Ms. Marrillion, who reads their names out loud as well, like a suspicious school teacher, before handing all the wallets back to their owners.

"As I was saying," the lead agent restarts his little speech. "The CIA is in a different league than those other groups now, at least in this country. We know what we're doing. They're a mess, and they're losing their grips on power. They've all been making deals with each other to try to pool their resources. Then they started stabbing each other in the back."

My mom asks, "What kind of deals were they making?"

"We don't have complete evidence, but it seems like someone

at the church tried to get the mob to take care of some outspoken victims of abuse, as if they could make the problem go away by taking their accusers off the table."

"They tried to kill their own victims?"

"It would seem that way. We're not sure if it was just one rogue priest or an organizational decision. In any case, all they had to offer the mob as payment was the identities of the church witnesses to the 1963 assassination planning agreement." He pulled a piece of paper from his pocket and looked at it for a moment. "That would be one Carol Waymer, who was killed early yesterday, and Wilhelmina Marrillion. You."

"So they killed Carol?"

"The FBI has picked up a few mob suspects and is holding them in Chicago. It sounds like they don't know why they were asked to do the hit. But we suspect they were trying to get at the evidence you and she were holding."

"Don't they have their own copies? The mob was in the room with us that night."

"No. They made the mistake of stashing theirs in a warehouse that was seized by the FBI in 2003. The capos who ran the mob didn't really know what they were sitting on at that point, since most of the original guys involved had died. By the time one of the Dons realized, it was too late. After some wrangling with the FBI, we've now got it all at Langley."

"The men from the mob could still come forward, then?"

"Without any physical evidence, it would just be an old gangster who looks like he's making up stories to get out of a prison sentence. That's why they were so desperate to get what you and Carol had. To be honest, you'll always have a price on your head while you're holding onto those documents. If you hand them over to us, we can keep them—and you—safe."

I think this is supposed to be comforting, but it definitely sounds like a threat.

CHAPTER 70
NO GUARANTEE

"WHAT IF I decide to hold on to the evidence?"

The man frowns at Ms. Marrillion's question.

"In that case, I cannot guarantee your safety."

"That doesn't make sense," my mom says.

"What I'm saying is: Give us the evidence, and you'll be safe. If you don't give us the evidence, you'll be in danger. You might not even make it off this bridge."

Now I'm sure it's a threat.

"We don't have it with us, of course," Ms. Marrillion says. "We're smarter than that. But I think we can point you in the right direction. Do you have a way we can contact you? Just you, nobody else listening in. Then we can call you and give you the location once we're safe."

"If that's how it has to be," he says. "Although … how do I know you actually have it?"

I reach into the bag D'Argyle gave me and pull out a piece of paper. Hopefully, D'Argyle followed our instructions to disguise his handwriting and be sure not to leave any fingerprints on the paper.

"What's this?"

"It's a URL," I say. "You're familiar with the internet, right?"

He gets angry. He probably doesn't like losing control of the situation.

"Yes, I *know* what the internet is."

"Sometimes, old people don't understand it," I say. I figure the angrier he gets, the more likely he is to make a mistake or a bad decision. "You just gotta type that into your browser. You know, Chrome, Safari. Maybe Internet Explorer at your age. Or AOL."

He looks at his phone and types in the address with one hand, holding the slip of paper in the other.

"Give me the paper when you're done," I say. No sense letting him keep the evidence. It could have DNA on it or something like that.

He clearly doesn't want to, but if he refuses, it will be clear he's trying to walk us into some sort of trap, and we still have the evidence he wants. He hands me the slip.

"That's just a sample," I say. I can't see his phone, but if D'Argyle set it up right, the man is looking at a photo on some hosting site. It's probably on a porn site, because D'Argyle said they made it easiest to post anonymously, for obvious reasons.

"We didn't have time to put the whole cache online," Ms. Marrillion says. "Nor do we want to. This is just proof that it exists, and we have it."

I can see him try to zoom in with his fingers, but it's not going to show him what he wants. D'Argyle knew to put the Polaroid photos just at the edge of the image, enough so that the man could see the distinctive border of the pictures, but not the fact that they have degraded over the years.

"Do you have a business card?" my mom asks.

"I do, but the number on it isn't secure and private," he says.

"That's fine," she says. "Write the number we should call you at on the back of your business card. Once we're away from here safely, and confident that we're not being followed or targeted, we'll call you and let you know where to find the evidence."

"If something happens to us," I say, "our associates will

publish the whole thing to the internet. You don't want that, do you?"

"No, obviously not."

He takes out a business card, but doesn't have a pen.

He has to ask his bald henchman for one. The bald guy searches his pockets and pulls out a big green pen, which I can tell is from TD Bank.

"The government can't even afford its own pens?"

"We have pens," he whines. "We just don't usually bring them into the field with us."

He finishes writing the phone number on his card and hands it to Ms. Marillion. It might be useful to have as evidence if we need it, since his fingerprints are on it.

"We'll be in touch," my mom says. "Start walking back in the direction you came from. And if you have any men waiting for us, this is when you'd want to call them off." She's once again using the voice she uses when I'm in trouble, and it has the same effect on the CIA agent.

He turns to the blond man and says, "Tell them all to stand down."

The blond man speaks into a radio and communicates the order.

We turn towards Manhattan and see a bunch of out-of-place pedestrians turn towards us. One of them shrugs.

"They want to know where to go," the blond man says to the boss.

"Tell them to jump," I say.

"They wouldn't survive the fall," the boss says.

I was just kidding, but I think he actually considered it.

"Tell them to walk this way, and then they can go back to Fort Lee with you."

The boss nods, and the blond man conveys the message.

Now we have to wait here while the CIA agents clear that half of the bridge, walking in our direction.

"Wait a minute," my mom says. "They're probably wearing bulletproof vests, right?"

"Just to be safe," the CIA boss says. "We didn't plan to shoot anyone."

"We'll take five of those vests," my mom says. "Just to keep *us* safe."

We'd really only need three, maybe one extra for D'Argyle. But my mom probably figures this will confuse the man about how many of us there are.

"I can't just hand over government property like that."

"Pardon me," Ms. Marrillion says, "but this card says you're the Deputy Director of Operations. That seems like a powerful job with lots of authority. Surely you can authorize the release of a few pieces of equipment."

"We could probably buy them on eBay anyway," I add.

"Fine," he says, turning to the blond man. "Tell someone on the tactical team to gather up five vests and stack them on the walkway." He looks at us. "That way, the news cameras won't see me hand them over to you, which might look suspicious."

"Sure, you don't want to get your hands messy," my mom says.

"Are we done here?"

"For now. Wait for our call, and don't do anything stupid," my mom says.

We stand and try to enjoy the view as the CIA agents walk past us and amass on the other side of the three agents.

"You know, they considered naming this bridge after Charles Lindbergh," Ms. Marrillion says. I can't tell if she's talking to me or the CIA agents. "We're lucky they didn't. Sometimes the hero of one generation turns out to be the villain of the next. You never want to be on the wrong side of history," she says.

The men have all disappeared, and the walkway back to New York is mostly clear, except for what we hope are actual pedestrians.

"Alright," my mom says. "Let's go home."